REMEMBER WHAT YOU READ

USE THIS SPACE FOR YOUR

MARK OR INITIALS

ALSO BY JULIETTE SOBANET

Sleeping with Paris

Kissed in Paris

Dancing with Paris

MIDNIGHT
TRAIN TO PARIS

JULIETTE SOBANET

Montlake
Romance

Text copyright © 2013 Juliette Sobanet
Originally released as a Kindle Serial, April 2013

Published by Montlake Romance
P.O. Box 400818
Las Vegas, NV 89140

ISBN-13: 9781477808757
ISBN-10: 1477808752

LCCN: 2013939491

DEDICATION

For you, my loyal readers.

You are the reason I get to do what I love every day.

Thank you.

EPISODE 1

PROLOGUE

December 24, 1937

Lausanne, Switzerland

Rosie Delaney stood on the empty platform, gripping the handle of her cherry-red suitcase with ice-cold fingers. She desperately wished that she'd remembered her gloves.

Thick, heavy snowflakes poured from the black winter sky, dusting the tracks in an eerie white glow. Save for the giant clock ticking overhead, the silence in the Swiss train station that night was deafening to Rosie's ears, which had never been so alert.

Despite her nerves, Rosie was certain she'd covered her tracks well. She'd put on quite the show with Alexandre before slipping out of the annual Morel Holiday Gala unnoticed. She'd even resisted the overwhelming urge to say good-bye to the one person she would miss.

Her mother.

Swallowing the lump in her throat, Rosie thought of the lovely sights of Paris and the even lovelier man who would be waiting for her there, in her favorite city, in only a few short hours.

Jacques Chambord.

She'd made the right choice.

Of course she had.

She'd left behind a closet full of shimmering evening gowns, fur coats, jewels, and high heels. Her meager suitcase contained only a few changes of her most practical, modest clothes and a box of letters.

Those letters meant more to her than any jewel-studded closet ever could.

Running her thumb over the newly bare skin on her ring finger, Rosie remembered how suffocating Alexandre's elaborate diamond ring had felt on her left hand. And it wasn't only the ring that had been suffocating.

The memory of him made her forget how to breathe.

If only the train would get here.

A nervous glance at the clock revealed that it was 11:37 P.M.

They would surely be wondering where she had gone by now. She could almost see Alexandre's dark furrowed eyebrows, his beady brown eyes combing the party, searching for his fiancée, his *trésor,* his *poupée.*

Rosie was finished being Alexandre's treasure, his doll.

She was finished keeping him and his elitist, power-hungry family happy.

A train whistle thundered through the night, and adrenaline shot through Rosie's veins as she glimpsed the steam locomotive barreling down the snow-covered tracks.

Only one word soared through Rosie's mind at the sight of the Orient Express on that snowy winter night in the Swiss Alps.

Freedom.

CHAPTER 1

Washington, D.C.

Blinding white snow surrounds my sister's silky chestnut locks, her violet eyes screaming out to me.

"Jillian...Jilly. Come! Please come." Isla's delicate red lips form another sentence, but the blustering winds are unforgiving as they swallow up her quivering voice. Iridescent flakes stick to her long lashes, blanketing the tips of her ears, her pink nose, and finally resting atop her high cheekbones, until that beautiful face—the face that I love more than any other—vanishes.

I see only white as I reach for my twin, shouting her name until my throat hurts. "Isla, come back! I'm here, Isla. I'm here!"

Combing through the mountains of snow gathering at my feet, I curse the flakes, which fall in huge, thick clusters, making it nearly impossible to see even a foot in front of me. My feet are as heavy as bricks, stuck to the bitter, wet ground, the snow swallowing them whole.

"Isla!" I scream once more into the white blasts. But a tornado of wind and snow whip around my head until the cold turns my fingertips blue, my tongue freezing inside my mouth. I cannot scream for Isla any longer.

The freeze travels up to my eyelids, transforming my tears into ice.

I've been crying these frozen tears for Isla our whole lives.

Isla's face appears one last time, a single drop of scarlet blood rolling down her pale cheek.

She doesn't speak this time. Her violet eyes say it all.

"You're too late, Jilly. You're too late."

My eyes pop open, two fresh tears leaking from the corners. Dread coats my stomach as I spot Natalie, my editor, hovering nearby. Disapproval is written all over that scrunched-up forehead of hers as she crosses her bony arms and takes one purposeful step closer.

"Jillian Chambord. In my office. *Now.*"

I lift my head from its resting place between three lipstick-stained coffee mugs, a scattered assortment of pens, and stacks of newspaper clippings. I clear my throat to speak, but my feisty boss is already jetting across the newsroom in her tall black boots.

I tie my wavy brown hair back into a messy bun as I chase her through the bustling offices of *The Washington Daily*, my place of employment and second home for the past six years. The sounds of fingers tapping furiously on keyboards, the ringing of phones, and the exchanging of story ideas comfort me as I ignore the fatigue that threatens to swallow me into a black hole of endless sleep.

What I wouldn't give for just one full night's rest.

But this would be worth the past two weeks of insanity. *It has to be.*

Inside Natalie's upstairs office, which overlooks the madness of the newsroom, she nods for me to sit, but I ignore her, instead pacing in front of her desk. A flurry of snow gathers on the windowsill; her view of the snow-dusted grass on the National Mall leaves an uneasy feeling in the pit of my stomach...but I'm not quite sure why. Maybe it has to do with the fact that I've already had two cups of coffee this morning on an empty stomach. Or the fact that I can count on one hand the number of hours I've slept over the past two weeks.

"Jillian, what is going on with you?" Natalie starts in, tapping a sharp black pen against a stack of rival newspapers on her cluttered desk. "You're running yourself into the ground, and I have yet to receive a page of decent copy from you this week. This isn't like you."

I open my mouth to respond, but a vision of my twin sister's deep violet eyes—exact replicas of my own—forces its way into my consciousness. Sparkling white snowflakes fall around her troubled face, making her blink as red tears pour from her eyes. I stop pacing, gripping the edge of Natalie's desk while I try to erase the scary image from my mind...but I can't shake the notion that I've already seen Isla's face drowning in the snow once today.

"You have five minutes, Chambord. Spill." Patience has never been Natalie's strong suit, but that's what makes her such a damn good editor.

I clear my throat, forcing the eerie image of my sister's snow-covered face and blood-red tears out of my mind. It must've been a nightmare I'd had earlier.

I'm always having nightmares about Isla.

"I'm one step away from breaking the Senator Williams story," I say, feeling the adrenaline pumping through my veins, drowning out that nagging voice in the back of my head, telling me to call my sister back. "You have no idea how huge this is."

Natalie's razor-straight, shiny black hair swishes atop her crisp white blouse as she shakes her head at me. "I told you two weeks ago to leave that story alone. You already covered the murder of those two teenage girls, and you don't have any evidence to link Senator Williams to their death. That anonymous tip you received isn't going to cut it. So unless you have something else for me, cut the bullshit and get back to work." Natalie dismisses me with a flick of her wrist, then turns up the volume on the flat-screen television mounted on her back wall, the constant stream of news blaring through her chilly office.

"I have a source who's willing to go on the record that Senator Williams, *with* the aid of his chief of staff, is funneling money from a child prostitution ring directly into his campaign."

Natalie stops her violent pen tapping, turns the volume back down, then raises a perfectly lined brow at me. "Go on."

"The two teenage girls who were murdered two weeks ago, as you already know from my coverage of their story, were a pair of sisters from Anacostia. They'd been sold into an underground prostitution ring by their mentally deranged mother. What we didn't know at the time was that there's a *third sister*. She was present when the girls were killed that night, and she claims that Senator Williams is not only behind the murders but is also heading up the prostitution ring with the help of his chief of staff."

"*If* this is even true, why has this alleged Sister Number Three waited until now to come forward with her story?"

"Apparently, Senator Williams has his own private room at *Haven*, the high-end gentleman's club where the sisters were murdered, and the three girls had been taken there often, against their will. This particular night, they had a plan to drug the senator and escape, but things got messy. One of them was killed by the senator's security detail, and the other was strangled by a masked Williams. The third managed to get away, but not before stealing a glimpse of Williams without the mask on."

Natalie's stone black eyes show more than a flicker of interest.

"The senator fled the scene immediately, of course," I continue. "Sister Number Three has been hiding out ever since. She's terrified of coming clean because she believes Williams will have her murdered. And based on conversations she overheard at the nightclub between Williams and some of the other men, she's certain he's in cahoots with local law enforcement to keep his record clean at all costs."

"So how in the hell did you find her?" Natalie asks.

"I've been out every night for the past two weeks doing exactly what you've trained me to do—find a story."

"Which means what, *specifically*?"

I don't have the energy to recount the past several evenings I've spent in the slums of Anacostia looking for the third sister or the shady things I've done only to have one face-to-face meeting with her. Nor do I possess the desire to tell Natalie about the late nights I've spent undercover at that vile gentleman's club since it reopened last weekend, meeting equally vile men and trying to dig up dirt on what goes down in those private, expensive rooms…or more specifically, *who* visits them.

"You know I've never played by the rules, Natalie. That's what makes me such a damn good reporter. Who else would've drudged up this insane story for you?"

"One of these days, Chambord, your inability to follow rules is going to bite you in the ass."

Ignoring my boss's ridiculous prediction, I drive my point home. "What matters is that I've reached the third sister, and she's agreed to give us an exclusive with her statement."

"You *do* realize that Senator Williams and his staff have the power to ruin you, me, *and* this entire paper if we go to press with this and even one tiny detail in this girl's outrageous story doesn't check out. You're playing with fire here."

A tired smile graces my lips. "He *and* his chief of staff can throw all the fire they want when they're spending the rest of their lives behind bars, the sick bastards."

"Let's hope that's the outcome," Natalie quips. "Otherwise you've missed three deadlines this week, all for some trashy girl who wants to cash in on a few murders."

I smack the palm of my hand on her desk, startling the smug expression off her face. "She isn't lying!"

"How can you be so sure? Claiming the senator is running a child prostitution ring, funneling money from said prostitution ring into his campaign, and having sex with and *murdering* teenage girls is a monumental accusation. This isn't just another story to advance your career, Jillian. This is the type of story that will end that man's life. Do you understand?"

"I understand perfectly, and I could give a damn about advancing my career. I became a reporter to expose the truth. To expose despicable human beings like Williams."

A heavy silence settles between us, and I wonder if Natalie can smell the hatred that boils in my bones every time I say Williams's name. I wonder if she can see the desperation in my eyes...the desperation I feel to see him and everything he stands for go up in flames.

I don't care if I'm putting my career in jeopardy. For what that perverted man did to Isla, and now to another innocent set of sisters, I would stop at nothing to put him in prison.

I lean over Natalie's desk, narrowing my eyes at her. "In all the years I've worked for you, name one time when I've reported a story that was less than one hundred percent truth."

Natalie doesn't speak. She doesn't speak because she knows I'm right. And she knows she'd be a fool not to allow this innocent girl to come forward with her story so that we can be the paper that brings down such a nasty, demented politician.

"I know I don't have as many years in this business as you do," I say. "But I know one thing for sure: if we don't break the story first, someone else will."

"Desperate girls looking for money are capable of coming up with the best lies, Chambord. Breaking a story full of meaningless accusations—"

"The girl *isn't* lying," I say once more, feeling a fierce need to protect her. It's a need I can't explain to Natalie. A need I can't and *won't* explain to anyone.

Only Isla will ever know the truth.

"She's coming in today at 3:00 p.m. to go on the record with her statement," I continue. "And she's requested that we notify law enforcement as well. She'll need protection once this story breaks. We'll need someone clean, someone she'll trust. I'm thinking Officer Reynolds. This is the real deal, Natalie. I wouldn't have taken it this far if I weren't absolutely certain."

Natalie stands from her desk. "I assume you've been working alone on this story these past two weeks?"

"Seeing as how you explicitly told me not to follow this lead, yes; I didn't want to drag anyone else in."

"Well, now's not the time to hog all the glory, Chambord. Get Cooper, Martinez, and Mitchell to dig up everything they can on Senator Williams, his chief of staff, and this mysterious third sister. Does she have a name by the way?"

I'd promised the girl I wouldn't tell anyone her real name. Not until she knew she was fully protected and Senator Williams was in custody. She trusted me, and as someone who understood her pain, I would never betray her confidence.

"Well?" Natalie asks, resuming her obsessive pen tapping.

A harsh rapping on the door stops me from having to explain to my editor why even *she* can't be in the know this time.

"Can it wait?" Natalie calls, but Dave, one of our new interns, peeks his head in anyway.

"I'm sorry to bother you, but there's a detective here to see Jillian. He says it's urgent."

Natalie shoots me a questioning glance. "About the Williams story, I suppose?"

A nervous tingle shoots down my spine. Only one of my other colleagues knows that I'm onto this creep. I hadn't even used my usual police contacts to get to the bottom of this story. I knew I'd never get a word out of the third sister if I didn't gain her trust on my own. Plus, her allegation that Williams had someone covering for him in D.C. law enforcement probably wasn't too far off. Powerful, sleazy men like him usually had equally corrupt cohorts working for them all over the place.

So why in the hell is there a detective here to see me?

"Send him in," Natalie says.

As soon as the intern reveals the mystery detective, I feel my stomach tying up in a fit of knots.

Samuel Kelly crosses the room before I can let a word slide past my lips, his cool green eyes and sharp black suit bringing back memories I'd long ago chosen to bury.

He doesn't bother shaking my hand or introducing himself. Instead, the man I'd sworn off forever stops just inches from me, and by the lack of a smile on his rugged face, I'm certain he's not here to reminisce.

"Jillian." Samuel nods at me, his expression all business. "I need to speak with you privately."

The sight of his tall, firm body, his broad shoulders, and those full lips steals my focus *and* my breath in one fell swoop.

I don't trust myself alone with Samuel.

Not today. Not ever.

"Whatever you need to talk to me about, you can say it right here." I cross my arms and glare at him underneath a mask of lust, anger, pain, and love. I *will not* show him the power he still has over me.

Samuel shoots a reluctant glance toward Natalie, then levels his determined gaze at me. "Three women have been reported missing after taking a luxury train traveling through the Swiss Alps, en route to Paris. I'm sorry to be the one to tell you this, but your sister, Isla, is one of those three women."

CHAPTER 2

"That's impossible," I say, ignoring the memory of Isla's snow-covered, blood-streaked face from my terrifying dream.

"Of course that's impossible," Natalie echoes, stalking around her desk, one hand on her hip. "That's impossible because Jillian doesn't *have* a sister."

Samuel raises a questioning brow at me, but I can't respond. All of the breath has been sucked out of my lungs. Could Isla really be missing? In the *Swiss Alps*? And why on earth is *Samuel* the one delivering this news?

"Jillian, is there a room where I can speak with you alone?" Impatience lines Samuel's deep voice as he eyes me suspiciously. He remembers my secrets, my lies. After all, in the end, those secrets were our undoing.

He takes another step toward me, then leans into my ear. "We don't have a lot of time to waste," he whispers.

The familiar scent of his cologne makes it hard for me not to brush my hands over his sexy five o'clock shadow and down the front of his chest, the way I always used to every time I kissed him. It's been six years since I touched Samuel, but the muscle memory is still overwhelming...and maddening.

"Is it true then? You have a sister?" Natalie asks, an incredulous look shooting from her stone black eyes. *Finally*, some emotion.

I nod at my editor, the woman who trusts me to bring her the truth, and only the truth. Except this time, I'd lied about something as basic as having a sister.

And from all of my years reporting for Natalie, I know that she hates liars *almost* as I much as I do.

"Yes, Natalie," I say quietly, feeling suffocated under years of lies. Lies I can't take back now. "I have a sister."

I avert my eyes away from Samuel, furious that he brought this mess into my office, but even more furious at myself for asking him to talk in front of Natalie. He knows nothing about who I've become in the years since we split, yet I'm certain he'll see the same Jillian he knew before—the Jillian who wouldn't tell him the truth about her past.

If only he'd known *why* I couldn't tell him.

"You'll have time to explain later," Samuel says to me. "But right now, I need to ask you a few questions."

I turn back to Natalie, and for the first time since she hired me as an eager college graduate, I can barely look her in the eye.

"Please get the others on the story," I say to her. "I'll join them in the conference room as soon as I'm finished with this. I'm sure it's just a misunderstanding."

I lead Samuel out of Natalie's office without giving her a chance to respond. But as soon as we take a few steps down the hallway, he places a hand on my arm, the mere sensation of his touch sending a shock wave through my core.

"This isn't a misunderstanding," he says firmly. "You know I wouldn't be here otherwise."

The sting in his tone makes me flinch.

My legs feel wobbly as I continue down the hallway in silence, and even though Samuel's crisp black suit is swishing along beside me, I feel totally alone, wishing I had someone to hold me up.

But I don't. I've always only had myself to count on. And today would be no different.

Inside our small conference room at the end of the hallway, I close the door and round the table to reach the window. I need to get as far away from him as I can. I need air.

Outside, the snow is swirling in circles as a harsh wind plows through D.C., rattling the windowpanes, whistling past the building. Is Isla lost somewhere in the snow, crying out for me?

I turn to face Samuel, clutching the windowsill behind me. "What's going on with Isla? And why in the hell is the CIA involved?"

Samuel holds my gaze as he walks around the table, stopping only a few inches from me. I can't help but notice that the sharp white shirt he's wearing underneath his suit *isn't* adorned with a tie. He always hated wearing ties…or rather, he hated anyone *telling* him he had to wear a tie.

That was one of the only things Samuel and I had in common when we'd dated back in college—we never took orders from anyone. I *still* didn't.

"I'm not with the CIA anymore." Reaching into his breast pocket, Samuel produces a business card. "I'm a private investigator for an international agency that specializes in finding missing persons, and I've been assigned as one of the lead investigators on your sister's case."

"Isla isn't missing and she doesn't need a fancy investigator to find her. This is just another one of her disappearing acts." I release my death grip on the windowsill and take a step closer to Samuel. This has to be a mistake. Isla can't really be missing.

"When was the last time you spoke with your sister, Jillian?" Samuel refuses to show any emotion on that chiseled face of his, but I remember a different time. A time when his eyes were full of lust for me, filled with a hot, fiery passion. A time when his strong hands owned my body, his lips devouring me until I lost all control.

Samuel was like a drug to me…a dangerous drug that made me lose all my defenses. A drug that made me want to tell the truth about my past.

A past that could never be unraveled.

I shake away the memories. I'd already told Samuel too much. I couldn't have him fishing around about my sister.

"Isla called me yesterday evening," I snap. "She's clearly fine, so you can take that white horse you swooped in on and march it right back out into the snow."

"Did you speak with her?"

I don't tell Samuel that I was inside a drug-infested shack in Anacostia, tracking down the source for my latest story, when Isla's call came through. I don't tell him that it had been the third time this week Isla had tried to get in touch and the third time I'd chosen to put my job first and ignore her call.

Instead, I swallow my guilt and simply say, "No, I missed her."

"Did she leave a voicemail?" Samuel asks.

"I think she might have, but I haven't had a chance to listen to it yet. I'm about to break a huge story, and—"

"Where's your phone?"

"It's downstairs on my desk."

"On my way out, I'll need you to check your voicemail. Any indication Isla may have left you as to what went on yesterday could help us find her. So when was the last time you spoke with her?"

"It was about three weeks ago," I answer, not even sure if my timeline is correct. "She was in Paris, where she's been living off and on for the past two years, and she sounded...good. We didn't talk long—just a few minutes—but she didn't say anything to indicate that something was wrong. I'm sure she just decided to take off and travel without telling anyone. She's been doing that for years." But even as the words exit my mouth, visions of Isla's pale, distressed face cloud my head, those eerie, sparkling white flakes swallowing her up.

Closing my eyes, I wish away the nightmare. The harsh blizzard swirling around her violet eyes. And that teardrop of sizzling red blood.

I know what Isla's blood looks like. I've seen it once before.

As her voice echoes in my mind, her cries pleading for me to come find her, I realize that Isla has never sounded so weak, so terrified.

Not even when death stared her in the face.

Something isn't right.

"Jillian," Samuel says, placing a hand on my shoulder. "I think you need to sit down."

I want to argue, to scream at him that he's wrong, but the image of Isla's petrified eyes won't leave me. Numbness settles into my bones as I slide into the cold black chair.

Something has happened to my sister, and I wasn't there to protect her.

Once again, I'm too late.

"Where is she? Tell me what happened," I demand, my own voice trembling now, terrified to hear the truth.

"Isla was last seen taking the late night Venice Simplon-Orient-Express train through the Swiss Alps," Samuel says, taking a seat next to me. "In the morning, when the train arrived in Paris, Isla wasn't in her sleeping compartment, but her purse and suitcase were left on the train. There were two other girls on the same train last night who didn't deboard in Paris this morning either. And just like Isla, their belongings were left on the train."

"But how is that possible?" I ask. "Were they...were they taken?" Bile coats my throat as I try to keep from getting dizzy.

"After the train left Lausanne, Switzerland, which is the station Isla boarded from, it stopped briefly at the French–Swiss border because of a mechanical difficulty. Most of the passengers had already retired to their sleeping compartments by that point. We believe Isla and the other two girls were abducted from their sleeping compartments during that stop."

Once again, my breathing fails me as I attempt to wrap my head around the word that flowed so effortlessly from Samuel's lips... *abducted.*

This can't be happening.

"What was Isla doing on that train?" I whisper, wishing desperately that I knew the answer to that question. Wishing that I didn't have to gaze into Samuel's sea-green eyes, the eyes that had always shot straight to the heart of me, past all the bullshit, past all the lies.

"That's what we're trying to figure out," he says. "My team of investigators is already there, working with local law enforcement to interview the other passengers on the train, and a search and rescue team has been called in to comb the area. I'll be meeting them there first thing tomorrow morning."

"Why were you hired to find Isla and the other girls if you're living in D.C.?"

"I don't live in D.C. anymore. Ever since…" Samuel trails off, looking past me and out the window. His eyes glaze over briefly before he clears his throat. "Ever since I took this job, I go wherever they need me to be."

"I'm sorry about Karine," I blurt, knowing full well that it's too late for an apology. That I should've called Samuel when his wife went missing four years ago. I should've called him when my own newspaper covered her abduction…and her murder.

"It's in the past," he says, standing abruptly from the table.

"I'm sorry," I say again, registering the pain flashing through his eyes.

His jaw tightens as he grips the edge of the chair. "I'll do everything I can to find your sister, Jillian. You have my word."

I stand up, remembering all the ways I'd imagined running into Samuel again. Not once did I envision it like this.

"Who hired you?" I ask.

"Frédéric Morel, Isla's fiancé."

This time, it's my turn to grasp onto the chair. "Isla doesn't have a fiancé," I say through gritted teeth.

"And according to her fiancé, Isla doesn't have a twin sister," Samuel says. "Apparently, you haven't been the only one keeping secrets."

A shaky sigh escapes my lips. How could she not have told me she was *engaged*?

"The secrets are going to have to come out now, Jill. I know you've never liked to open up about what happened to you and Isla in the past, but this isn't the time to hold anything back. Not if you want to find your sister alive."

Downstairs, the ringing telephones and tapping computer keys have transformed into nails down a chalkboard. All I can think about is Isla drowning in an avalanche of snow. The business of the newspaper is irrelevant. I have to find my sister.

I lead Samuel to my desk, where I ransack my mess of notebooks and newspaper clippings, searching frantically for my cell phone. With shaky hands, I pull it out from underneath the list of contacts that led me to Sister Number Three in the Williams story.

The thought of Parker Williams's dirty face, of his big, rough hands makes me want to vomit. Isla would want him behind bars too. I would deal with that scumbag later…he could count on it.

One new voicemail.

"I can't listen to this in here," I tell Samuel. "It's too loud. Follow me."

I sling my purse over my shoulder, then lead him out of the suffocating newsroom, through the fancy lobby and out into the blinding white snow. It must be freezing outside, but I don't register the cold as I dial my voicemail. I turn away from Samuel and focus on the peak of the Washington Monument, which is barely visible against the dull white sky and the flakes that swirl all around it.

The streets of D.C. are eerily quiet. Not a single car passes as I wait to hear my sister's voice. The nation's capital has shut down due to the twelve inches of snow that's predicted to dump on the city over the next twenty-four hours, only two days before Christmas.

"Is it her?" Samuel asks, but I hold my finger up to shush him.

"Jillian…oh, Jilly," Isla's voice comes over the line, clear, excited. "You're not going to believe what I've done this time!" She pauses, letting out a devious giggle. "I know we haven't talked in a while...I mean really talked, and I miss you, Jilly. I..." Isla pauses as static rings into the phone, then a loud whistle.

A train whistle.

I brace myself against the cool bricks of the building as Isla's voice returns, softer now. "I have something important to tell you, Jillian. Please call me back. I—I'm..." Isla stops speaking, but the phone doesn't cut off. I can hear Isla's heavy breathing. Then a loud rustling noise followed by a grunt—a *man's* grunt.

And finally the sound of a little girl whimpering.

It's the same whimper I heard when we were only thirteen. The day the gunshots stole any last shred of innocence we had left.

Except this time Isla is twenty-eight-years old. A grown woman. Whimpering like a child because someone has taken her.

The line goes dead, but I've already died inside.

I drop the phone into the inch of snow that has collected at our feet and barely feel Samuel's hands as they reach for me.

You're too late, Jilly. You're too late.

CHAPTER 3

"Where's your car?" I ask Samuel, the urgency of Isla's situation suddenly making it clear what I have to do.

He nods toward a black Escalade parked illegally in front of the building. The windshield is already covered in snow.

I break free of his tight grip on my shoulders, scoop my phone up off the wet ground, and jog toward his car.

"Jillian, I need to listen to that message right now, and then I have to catch my flight to France," Samuel calls after me. "This is no time to mess around."

I turn to face him just as I reach the sleek SUV. "I'm not messing around. I'm coming with you to find my sister."

Samuel shakes his head as snowflakes dust the shoulders of his jet-black suit. "I don't think that's a good idea." He reaches out an open hand, the stern look in his eyes making me want to smack him.

"Give me the phone," he orders.

"Listen, if you don't want me to be involved in this case because of our history together, that's bullshit. This is my sister, Samuel. You know she's the only family I have."

"What about your mother?"

I back up against the door of the SUV, narrowing my eyes at him. How in the *hell* does he know about her? "We don't *have* a mother."

"Really? Because last I checked she was still serving her life sentence in a Virginia prison. Remember, Jill, I'm an investigator. It's my job to find out everything I can about the people I'm searching for. You can either help me with that, or you can obstruct my search for your sister and two other innocent women. Now give me the damn phone."

I look Samuel square in the eye, then unbutton the top of my white blouse and slide the phone into my bra. "I'm not letting you hear Isla's message until you unlock this car and take me to the airport with you. And then I want you to tell me everything you know about Isla's supposed fiancé and anything else you know about her life in France."

"Oh, so *you're* the investigator now?" he quips, eyeing the opening in my shirt.

"Open the damn car!" I growl.

"Listen, I understand why you want to come. But I know you, Jill. I know how you operate. If I take you over there with me, you're going to storm in and try to run this investigation, when you don't have a fucking clue what you're doing. You didn't know your sister was engaged for Christ's sake. And the high-profile family who hired me…well, I don't think it would be wise for me to show up with the sister they didn't even know existed until a few hours ago."

"Screw that family. *I'm* Isla's family. I clearly know more about my sister and how *she* operates than anyone else does. I'm the one who will be able to lead you to her. I know I can. Just open the car, Samuel."

"In case you're forgetting, someone has abducted your sister and two other young women from a train. Whoever is behind this is dangerous, and I can't have you running around, taking matters into your own hands," Samuel says. "It's not safe, and I refuse to waste valuable time making sure you don't get yourself into trouble. This isn't a story you're breaking for *The Daily*, Jill. We're talking about three innocent lives here."

When I respond by pushing the phone further into my bra, Samuel shakes his head at me, frustration seeping through his pores. I don't care though. I'm not budging.

"I'll be sending over one of my top investigators this afternoon to question you and get any information that might help us—email correspondence from Isla, information on anyone from your past who may have wanted to hurt your sister—all of it. But right now, I need you to let me listen to that message, then get the hell out of my way so I can catch my flight and find your sister."

I can see that Samuel isn't going to change his mind without a fight. I eye his suit jacket, combing my gaze down the front of his firm chest to his pants pockets. I notice a slight bulge in his left pocket, and that's when I know what I have to do.

Before he can calculate my next move, I grab onto his shoulders and run my fingers up to the back of his hairline, right to the spot at the nape of his neck that used to drive him wild. Then I tip my chin, trying *not* to inhale his intoxicating scent, and press my lips against his.

Snowflakes cover our faces as I brush my lips over Samuel's once, then twice more. I ignore the familiar way he tastes, the heat pulsing through my veins.

By the third kiss, I have what I came in for.

The keys.

I pull away from him, hit the unlock button and run around the front of the car, climbing into the driver's side.

Samuel stands on the sidewalk, his feet planted to the ground, his green eyes glaring at me through the snow. He doesn't run toward me, demanding that I get out of the car. Instead he climbs into the passenger side, runs his hand through his light brown hair, and shakes his head at me as I turn the key in the ignition and press on the gas.

"You haven't changed a bit, Jillian Chambord. Not one bit."

I speed down Constitution Avenue, thankful for the lack of cars on the street and for the Escalade's ability to plow right over the snow.

Samuel's hand suddenly plunges down my shirt.

"Hey!" I say, but he's already retrieved what *he* went in for—my phone.

"Two can play at this game, Jill," he says. His comfortable use of *Jill* momentarily makes me lose focus. He's the only one who's ever called me by that name.

"What's your voicemail password?" he asks.

"1937," I tell him as I speed right through a red light.

"We're not immune to the law. You might want to be a little more careful," he says, punching in my code.

"We don't have time for careful," I quip. "We're going to Dulles Airport I assume?"

Samuel shakes his head. "No, Reagan."

"But, there aren't any international flights out of Reagan."

Samuel holds a finger up to shush me while he listens to Isla's message. He turns the volume up to full blast on the phone, and listens intently. My grip on the steering wheel tightens, my knuckles turning white as I try to block out the sound of her voice traveling through the car.

What was Isla doing on that train?

I gaze over at Samuel as he hangs up the phone. The look in his eyes is determined, strong, hopeful. "This call came in at 6:37 P.M. yesterday, which would've been 12:37 A.M. France time. This confirms that the time of abduction was most likely during the stop they made in the Alps for mechanical problems. This is big, Jillian. This will help us narrow down our ground search."

Samuel pulls out his phone and begins texting while I focus on the snowy road ahead, swallowing the fear that consumes me at the words *abduction* and *ground search*. How can this be happening to my sister? Why haven't I paid more attention to what was going on in her life recently? What if I could've saved her somehow?

I've been so consumed with breaking the Senator Williams story that I...

God, when will I stop lying to myself?

The truth is that most days, it's easier *not* to talk to my twin sister. It's easier not to remember what happened to us and what ultimately tore us apart.

I know Isla feels the same. Which is why I rarely hear from her anymore.

So why did she call me so many times this week? What was she trying to tell me?

A warm hand lands on my shoulder, breaking up my incessant string of worries. "Jillian, your passport. Do you need to stop by your apartment in Rosslyn to pick it up?"

"How do you know I still live in Rosslyn?" I ask.

He sighs. "Jill, just answer the question."

"I have it in my purse. I always carry my passport with me, just in case."

I decide to stop at the next red light, but I don't look at Samuel. I don't want to see the inquisitive, confused expression that I already know has splashed across his handsome face. It's the way he always used to look at me…back when he would ask me questions I couldn't answer. Questions I chose *not* to answer.

The light turns green, and I floor the gas. "Why are we going to Reagan? Are any planes even going to be taking off in this weather?"

"The Morel family—the family your sister was going to marry into—has arranged for a private jet. And yes, that plane will be taking off no matter what. I'll be sure of it."

"A private jet? Are you kidding me? Who *are* these people?"

"The Morels are essentially the French equivalents of the Trumps, except that they come from old money. They own a ton of real estate in Paris and all over France, and they have strong political ties too."

"I see…but I'm still not sure whether I understand why they would go to so much trouble to hire you to find my sister when you're not even going to be in France for the first twenty-four hours of the search. Isn't this a huge waste of time?"

"The agency I work for is the best in the world, Jill. It's made up of people like me—former special agents who've decided to dedicate their lives to finding missing persons. We've given up everything—our homes, personal lives, *everything*—to find these people."

I think about Samuel's wife, Karine, and the coverage my paper did on her abduction and her gruesome murder, and I immediately understand. Samuel is the type of person who wouldn't be able to sleep at night if he knew that what happened to Karine was happening to other women.

"My two partners who are over there right now are both former CIA as well. They've already put a team together to question the other passengers on the train and the Morels. And I just gave the search team a green light, so trust me, no one is wasting any time."

"Fine. But why is this family pulling out all the stops to get *you* over there, Samuel? Why are you one of the leads on this case?" I swerve the car around the traffic circle, the Lincoln Memorial towering to our left, its normally crowded set of stairs completely void of tourists on this harsh winter day.

"In the three years that I've worked for the agency, I've had the highest success rate at finding victims. I've given my life to this career, Jillian. To finding people like your sister. When I got the call this morning about this case and heard the names of the three women who'd disappeared, I knew I had to take this one."

"Because of me," I say softly.

Samuel nods, the silence of our past together weighing us both down.

I charge over the Arlington Memorial Bridge, the icy Potomac River stretching underneath us. I wonder what it would feel like to jump in the water right now. To be swallowed up into the unbearable freeze. I think of Isla freezing in the snow, lost in the mountains, and for the first time since he stormed into Natalie's office only an hour ago, I am glad it's Samuel here by my side. I'm glad it's Samuel who will be leading the search for my sister.

I won't, in a million years, admit this thought to him though.

"So who are the other two girls that have gone missing?" I ask. "Are they connected to Isla in any way?"

"The three girls all boarded the train from different stops, so it *appears* as if they were chosen at random, but there is a connection we're investigating."

"What is it?" I swerve left onto George Washington Parkway as the windshield wipers bat at the heavy sheets of snow falling from the sky.

"Before I tell you this, you have to promise me you aren't going to leak this back to your editor at *The Daily*," Samuel says, his voice cold. "We're trying to keep the story under wraps to buy us more time to find the girls. Press coverage may tip off whoever is behind this and compromise our search." He pauses and looks away from me. "I've seen it happen before."

"I would never do anything to compromise the search," I say. "And in case this is what you're insinuating, I had nothing to do with the coverage of your wife's story. I would never have—"

"She's dead," Samuel's voice booms through the heated car. "It doesn't matter how those fucking vultures got ahold of the story. Karine is gone."

I zoom down the parkway, letting those words resonate in the air between us. Karine is already gone. I can't let that happen to Isla too.

"I *won't* do anything to mess this up, Samuel," I say. "You have to trust me. Now please tell me the names of the two other girls. Maybe Isla's mentioned them at some point. Maybe I can help."

Samuel types something into his phone and holds up the screen for me to see.

A photo of a young woman with curly brown hair and huge baby-blue eyes stares back at me. "Emma Brooks," he says. "Recognize the name?"

I shake my head. "Sounds vaguely familiar, but I don't think I've ever heard that name from Isla."

"She's the nineteen-year-old daughter of the U.S. ambassador to France, George Brooks."

"Holy shit."

"Which means we only have a day or two tops before every news station in France *and* the U.S. is covering the story."

"A day or two if you're lucky," I say. "An ambassador's daughter was abducted from a train in the Alps. I'm sure Brooks and his family will want to go public with this soon."

"We've already advised them to keep quiet at least until the ground search is underway."

"So what's the connection you need to investigate with Brooks's daughter?"

"We're not sure if Isla and Emma ever met, but we do know that the Brooks family is friends with the Morel family."

"Two high-profile families with tons of money," I say, thinking out loud.

"Exactly. We wouldn't be surprised if we receive a message from the kidnappers asking for millions in ransom in exchange for the two girls."

My foot surges against the gas pedal as I power toward the airport exit ramp. "And what about the third girl? Is she from some other powerhouse French family?"

Samuel punches at the keys on his phone again and produces another photo—this one of a girl with long, silky black hair and striking, almond-shaped eyes. "Francesca Rossi. Italian, twenty-six-years-old. From a moderately wealthy family. No obvious connection to either the Brooks family or the Morel family. She boarded the train in Venice and was sleeping in the compartment right next to your sister."

"Maybe she saw something she shouldn't have, and they took her too. She's probably just collateral damage to the sick bastard who did this."

"To get all three of those girls off the train in the middle of the night without a big commotion, we believe there were at least two, if not three, kidnappers involved."

My stomach curls as I fly down the exit ramp for Washington Reagan Airport.

"Head around this way." Samuel points down a service road that circles the airport. "The plane is waiting for us there."

"Is it going to be a huge problem that the Morel family didn't even know I existed until today, and now I'm boarding their private jet with you?"

"Even if it were a problem, would that stop you?"

Rage soars through my chest as I wonder what the men who took my sister are doing to her right now.

"Nothing would stop me from getting on that plane," I say. "*Nothing*."

CHAPTER 4

The small, fancy jet hums loudly as Samuel and I buckle our seatbelts.

"I need my phone back," I tell him. "I have to make an important call before we take off."

Samuel reaches into his pocket and produces my iPhone. "If you're calling work, please tell your editor to keep her mouth shut."

"I'll do my best. But if she breaks this story tomorrow, remember that you're the one who blabbed about my sister's disappearance right in front of her."

"I only did that because you're the most stubborn woman I've ever met, and I knew you wouldn't leave that office with me unless I told you what was really going on."

Samuel is right, but instead of giving him that satisfaction, I roll my eyes and snatch the phone from his hand. Aiming the screen toward the window so he can't see, I ignore the three missed calls from my boss and quickly type a text to my colleague, Liz Martinez.

Plan B is in effect. You know where to find my files. Sister Three is scheduled to give a statement at 3 P.M. I'll tell her to look for you. You are the only other one she trusts. Make sure Officer Reynolds is on standby to take her statement and put her in protection immediately. I'll clue Natalie in on your involvement, and I'll check in with you in eight hours. This is your story now, Liz. Don't let me down.

Then I type a quick message to Natalie.

Taking immediate leave for family emergency. Please keep quiet what you heard in the office today. I've already given you your next huge story, so leave my family alone. I lied about one other thing: Liz Martinez is on the Williams story with me. She'll be taking over in my absence. Liz has my report, and all we need is Sister Number Three's statement on the record. Story must go to press tonight. You won't regret it.

No more than thirty seconds later, my phone buzzes with Natalie's response.

The girl better show or this story is over, Chambord. And so is your career.

I can only attribute Natalie's lack of concern for my family emergency and her quick willingness to fire me to the fact that she hates liars with a passion. But in this moment, as a violent gust of wind rattles our tiny, private jet, I am certain that I hate my lying self enough for the two of us.

Pushing Natalie's threat to the back of my mind, I dial the contact number I have for Sister Number Three, praying I can reach her.

After the fifth ring, a young male voice answers.

"Yeah," he says.

"This is Jillian, Scarlet's friend. She there?" I try my best to sound young and nonthreatening, but there's no telling if he'll buy it.

The kid doesn't respond, but a rustling sound on the other line gives me hope that he's going to put her on the phone.

A few more moments pass, then suddenly I hear that same male voice yelling in the background. I can't make out what he's saying over the loud humming of the plane, but whatever it is, it doesn't sound good.

Finally, the yelling stops and the phone scratches again.

"Jillian?" It's Scarlet. The terror still hasn't left her voice.

"Yes, Scarlet. It's me. I just wanted to let you know that my colleague Liz is going to meet you there today at three o'clock. She's the one you met the other night, the one who is just like me. Who *understands*."

"Will you be there too?" she whispers.

"I have a family emergency. Something with my own sister… the one I told you about. But Liz will have the police waiting to take you into protection, and everything is going to go exactly the way I promised you, Scarlet. You have nothing to worry about, okay?"

Scarlet doesn't respond. Instead, her muffled cries travel through the line.

"Scarlet, listen, I know you're scared. But you can trust me. I wasn't lying when I told you that I completely understand what you've been through. Liz does too. We want to take him down just as much as you do. You have to promise me that you'll be there. Promise me, Scarlet."

The seventeen-year-old girl who I've worked so hard to save whimpers into the phone. "You're lucky you still have a sister, Jillian," she whispers. "You're so lucky."

Then she hangs up. She hangs up the phone.

I close my eyes and rest my forehead in my palm.

Please, God, let her show up today. Please.

I toss my phone into the cushy leather seat that faces me, thinking of Scarlet sitting in that dilapidated house in Anacostia, with that pimp boyfriend controlling her every move.

Of all days for me to be leaving the country.

I smack the side of my fist against the thick airplane window, then close my eyes once more.

"What's going on?" Samuel asks.

Keeping my eyes squeezed shut, I shake my head. Samuel can't fix this, and neither can I. All I can do is hope that Scarlet has the courage to show up today. Otherwise, she doesn't stand a chance. And the disgusting creep who has stolen her innocence will go free. *Again.*

"We have a long plane ride ahead of us, Jill. You're going to have to answer my questions," Samuel says.

Samuel's fingers tapping loudly on his laptop keyboard make me wish I'd thought to grab my computer before jetting out of the office like a madwoman. How would I keep myself from going insane with worry, from drowning in a murky pool of my own guilt, sitting next to my ex-boyfriend while he grills me for eight hours?

"Shouldn't you be putting your computer away? We're about to take off," I snap.

By the way Samuel's jaw tightens as his eyes skim the computer screen, I can tell he isn't in the mood for my bossy tone. He mumbles something under his breath, but the buzzing plane engine drowns out his words.

"What is it? Did you learn something that could help us find Isla?" I'm nearly shouting now as the jet begins its voyage down the snow-covered runway. I'm not even sure how the pilot received authorization to take off in such dreadful weather conditions, but I don't care. A bumpy plane ride is the least of my worries right now.

Samuel narrows his eyes as he continues to comb the computer screen.

"What is it?" I ask. "Did the press already find out?"

He shakes his head, finally lifting his intense green gaze to mine.

"Why did you choose 1937 as your voicemail passcode?"

"What does that have to do with anything?"

"Just answer the question, Jill," Samuel says, his green eyes boring into me.

I fiddle with the hem of my skirt, tearing my gaze from Samuel's. "It's the time of Isla's birth. She was born at 9:37 A.M., exactly thirty-seven minutes after me, on the first of—"

"January," Samuel finishes for me. He shakes his head, returning his gaze to the computer. "The number must be a coincidence then."

"What are you talking about?" I ask as a chill works its way down my spine.

"I just received an email from one of the other investigators at the agency. It looks like we may be dealing with a copycat crime. Seventy-five years ago, in 1937, three young women disappeared from an Orient Express train as it traveled through the Alps en route to Paris. The train stopped just after midnight because of a snow drift on the tracks, and when it pulled into Gare de l'Est in Paris the next morning, all three of the girls were missing from their sleeping compartments, their luggage still left on the train."

Goosebumps prickle the back of my neck as I clutch onto my seat. "But that was seventy-five years ago. It couldn't have anything to do with what's happened to Isla. Could it?"

Samuel doesn't answer as he continues reading the email. Suddenly, the color drains from his face and he snaps the computer shut. "My team is looking into it. It's nothing you need to worry about."

"What happened to the three girls, Samuel? Did they find them?"

Samuel swallows as the plane surges faster down the runway. "I shouldn't have said anything. I only needed to know why you'd chosen 1937. Like I said, my team will follow up on this."

I snatch Samuel's laptop from his hands. "Tell me what happened to the other girls, or I'll look it up myself."

"I thought you would've become less fiery as you neared thirty, but clearly I was wrong," he says. "One of the girls, a young American socialite named Rosie Delaney, was never found. The other two..." Samuel trails off, breaking our eye contact to glance at the flurry of snow swirling outside the tiny plane windows.

"What happened to them? Tell me," I demand through gritted teeth.

Samuel turns back to me, his deadpan stare instantly making me regret my quest for the truth.

"They were murdered in the Alps," he says. "The killer was never found."

The plane lifts off, hurling us through the stark white skies, but all I can see is bloodstained snow and Isla's panicked violet eyes, pleading with me to save her.

EPISODE 2
CHAPTER 5

December 24, 2012

Évian-les-Bains, France

"You didn't tell me the Morel family lives in a castle," I say to Samuel as the black town car we're riding in turns down a long, winding driveway.

An expansive, snow-covered lawn sparkles as beams of early afternoon sunlight peak through the shield of gray clouds overhead. The lawn leads to a three-story mansion complete with imposing, spiral towers and wrought-iron balconies that wrap around each of the second-floor windows.

"This is only their *vacation* estate," Samuel says as he types the hundredth message he's sent on his phone since we stepped off the plane in Geneva an hour ago. "The Morels own small châteaux like this all over France."

The driveway circles a fountain with an eerie sculpture of a naked woman looming at the top. Icicles form a crown around her head, and her cold, emotionless eyes cast a creepy glance right at us.

As we drive closer, it's not the spectacular view of the crystal blue lake just behind the mansion that takes my breath away.

It's the lineup of news vans, TV cameras, and reporter's microphones aimed at the front door.

"What the..." Samuel mumbles, rolling down his window.

A gush of cool, fresh air wafts into the heated car, helping, only momentarily, to calm my nauseated stomach. "How did this happen already?" I ask. "I thought you told all three of the families to keep their mouths shut so the kidnappers wouldn't be tipped off about where you're searching."

"I did," Samuel says as the town car parks behind one of the news vans. "But in my experience with high-profile families like these, they usually decide to take matters into their own hands at one point or another. And frankly, it's a pain in my ass."

I place my hand on the car door, not in any way ready to face the mob of reporters or the family that Isla never told me about, but knowing that I have no other choice than to move forward. To do everything I can to find my sister.

But Samuel's firm hand on my arm stops me.

"My team has already alerted the Morels of your arrival, so they shouldn't be surprised. That doesn't mean they'll be welcoming though. Let's not forget that they didn't even know you existed until yesterday morning, and they've known Isla for over six months."

I glance at his hand, still resting on my arm and push back the memories of those same strong hands that have invaded my dreams every night for the past six years.

"Let's not forget that I've known Isla for twenty-eight years." I pull my arm from his grasp. "I'm not too worried about the Morels' delicate feelings right now. I just want to find my sister."

Samuel reaches inside his breast pocket and hands me his business card. "My number, in case you need anything while you're here. I'm going to ask the Morels a few more questions, then I'll be heading off to the search site. I brought you here like you asked, Jill, but you need to promise me you'll stay put."

I gaze at the snow-dusted pines climbing up the sides of the château and at the icy lake shimmering in the background, and again

I think of Isla. I want to go with Samuel. I don't want to be trapped in this castle with some random family who thinks they know my sister.

Every family she's stormed her way into these past several years has believed, naively, that they know my sweet, beautiful, charming sister.

But they've all been wrong…and the Morels are wrong too.

"Jillian," Samuel says sternly. "I know what you're thinking, and it's not an option. You'll stay here."

He doesn't wait for the protest he surely knows is coming. Instead, he climbs out of the car and walks purposefully toward the mass of cameras and microphones clamoring toward the front door.

Before I follow him, I lean forward and address the driver.

"*Excusez-moi, Monsieur.* Are you a regular driver for the Morel family?" I ask in French.

"No, just an airport car service, Mademoiselle," he responds.

"Do you have a business card?"

"*Mais, bien sûr.*" He plucks a card from the center console and hands it to me.

"*Merci bien, Monsieur.* You may be hearing from me later."

"It would be my pleasure, Mademoiselle."

Just as I'm opening the door, the driver asks me one more question.

"I must ask, Mademoiselle, how did you learn to speak French with such a perfect accent?"

I hesitate, not wanting to acknowledge her existence. But the exhaustion from all the years of lying urges me to let my guard down for one brief second. I don't know this man. It doesn't matter if I tell the truth just this once.

"My mother was French," I tell the driver. I don't give him a chance to ask any more questions as I emerge into the crisp Alpine air. I discreetly tuck his card into the pocket of my suit jacket, smooth down my wrinkled white blouse and gray pencil skirt, then pace toward the mob.

Just as I reach the back of the press lineup, large cameras begin clicking furiously, and microphones thrust higher into the air.

They're not facing me though. They couldn't care less about Isla's only sister who has left her reporting career hanging in the balance to fly across an ocean with a man she'd planned on never seeing again, all in the dire hope to find her other half...her twin sister.

No, it's not me they want. It's the strikingly handsome French man who has just walked out the front door of the château.

"Monsieur Morel, is it true that your girlfriend, Isla Chambord, has been abducted from the Venice Simplon-Orient-Express Train?" a female reporter shouts in French.

"Any clues as to Mademoiselle Chambord's whereabouts?"

"Have you heard from the kidnappers?"

"Are they asking for a large ransom for Mademoiselle Chambord and Mademoiselle Brooks's return?"

"What about the Italian girl?"

"Is there any hope of finding the girls alive?"

Frédéric Morel doesn't seem fazed by the questions being hurled at him. He poses confidently at the top of the steps, his shoulders pushed back and his slick gray suit the sign of a man who is used to standing in the limelight.

He doesn't appear tired or weary or fearful, the way I would expect someone who has lost the love of his life to look. Instead, he holds up a hand to quiet the hungry reporters and gazes calmly and pointedly into one of the cameras.

"On the night of December 22, my fiancée, Isla Chambord, was abducted from the Venice Simplon-Orient-Express train traveling through Lausanne, on the way to Paris," he says in French. "Two other young women were taken from the same train as well. I will allow their families to comment on their disappearance, but I would like to issue a warning to whomever has taken these innocent women."

Suddenly his calm evaporates, and a fierce anger flashes through Frédéric's dark, narrowed eyes.

Even from my vantage point at the edge of the crowd, I can feel his fury.

"We will not stop until we find you," he growls. "You will not get away with this. And if you hurt Isla, I will personally make sure that you suffer for the rest of your miserable life. "

Commotion surges through the crowd as the reporters revel in the drama. More shouts in French emanate from the press.

"Monsieur Morel, what was your fiancée doing on that train alone?"

"Why weren't you with her?"

"Wasn't December 22 the night of the annual Morel Holiday Gala? Why did Isla leave the party?"

"Does Isla have any family? Where are they?"

"*We* are Isla's family," Frédéric answers coolly. "And we'll do anything to make sure she comes home safely. In fact, we're offering a reward of two million euros to anyone who has valid information regarding the whereabouts of Isla Chambord."

I stand, frozen in place, as I watch Samuel push past the reporters and meet Frédéric at the top of the stairs. Samuel whispers something into Frédéric's ear, then scans the crowd. As soon as he sees me, he motions for me to come up.

"Monsieur Morel is finished with his statement now," Samuel announces in French, his thick accent sweet to my ear. "We assure you that a thorough search for the three women is underway, and we ask that you leave the Morel property immediately."

I push through the crowd, clenching my fists as I think about Frédéric's words—*We are Isla's family.*

He may have insane amounts of money to throw around in her name, but that doesn't mean he knows anything about who Isla really is.

"*I* am Isla's family," I whisper under my breath as I climb the ivory-colored château steps.

And *I* will find her.

Inside the Morels' vacation home, Frédéric storms underneath the foyer's high ceilings and into an elegant, museum-like living room, or *le salon,* as my French monster of a mother would've so eloquently called it.

A petite woman with chin-length, dyed-blond hair is standing next to a shiny grand piano, arms crossed. She charges toward Frédéric. "What were you thinking?" she says in French, the fire in her voice matching that of Frédéric's violent warning outside. "The investigators specifically told us *not* to speak to the press yet. Do you want to get your fiancée killed?"

Samuel clears his throat as we enter the fancy living room, and the Morel woman and her son lift their troubled gazes to us.

"Frédéric, Hélène, I'm Investigator Samuel Kelly. We spoke on the phone earlier."

"Of course," Frédéric answers in English, his accent impeccable. "This is her?" he nods toward me.

"Yes, this is Jillian Chambord, Isla's twin sister."

The room goes unnervingly silent as Frédéric and his mother examine me, no doubt wondering where this mysterious girl came from and why Isla neglected to mention me. I stare back at them and wonder the same thing—why my sister omitted the minor detail that she was in a serious relationship with a French real estate mogul *and* that he'd proposed.

Samuel's deep voice cuts through the tension. "I have to get to the search site, but I'd like to go over the timeline of last night with you one more time. Can we have a seat in here?"

"Of course," Madame Morel says with a tired smile, keeping her intense eyes glued to me all the while. "Please, come in."

Frédéric paces impatiently past the spectacular floor-to-ceiling windows, clearly not in the mood to have a seat. "We've already gone over these questions with the other investigators," he spits in French. "And your people haven't told me anything, they haven't found anything, and they're not doing anything!" He slams his fist on the piano, startling his mother to tears. "I hired you because I was told you're the best, and instead of doing your job, you bring this woman here—some estranged sister who Isla clearly chose to cut out of her life."

And you *are clearly assuming that I can't understand your French tantrum, Rich Boy,* I think to myself as I dig my nails into the Morels' pristine white couch. Didn't Isla at least tell her fiancé that she spoke fluent French? Had she hidden that from him too?

Before I can fight back, Samuel stands and faces Frédéric head on. "Isla never cut Jillian out of her life. She *chose* not to tell you she had a sister, but we're not here today to figure out why your own fiancée didn't feel she could be honest with you about her past. We're here to find Isla. And since you've already compromised our investigation by taking this story to the press without our authorization, I suggest you calm down, start cooperating, and let me do my job, so I can go where I'm needed and find your fiancée."

Hope courses through my body as I watch Samuel's broad shoulders, his tight jaw, his dark five o'clock shadow. He is a man on a mission, a man who will stop at nothing to find what he's looking for. And he won't let anyone, even the wealthy Morel family, get in his way.

I realize that in the six years since I'd last seen Samuel, since that wintry day when I left him, I've never met another man quite like him.

And in this moment, as he refuses to break his stance, I am certain I never will.

"I *will not* sit here and do nothing while some monster has taken the woman I love," Frédéric says. "Now ask me your questions, then get the hell out of here and find her."

Frédéric's mother wipes a tear from her eye, then places a shaky hand on her son's shoulder. "Don't make this worse than it already is, *chéri*. We hired Monsieur Kelly to help us, and that's what he's trying to do. Now, sit down."

Samuel and I sit opposite Frédéric and Hélène, where we can see the icy blue waters of Lake Geneva sparkling just outside the massive windows to our left. I can't believe Isla was staying at this unbeliev-able estate. Besides the fact that her French fiancé seems to be a bit of a spoiled brat—handsome, but spoiled all the same—what on earth would've possessed her to leave?

"I'm going to ask the questions in English so that we can all understand," Samuel says before taking out his notepad and pen.

Samuel must be forgetting that I speak French too. I almost correct him, but then I remember that Isla obviously never told the Morels that her mother was of French origin. And I wasn't about to explain the morbid story of our past to these strangers.

"The night of Isla's disappearance, you held the annual Morel Holiday Gala at this property, correct?" Samuel asks Frédéric and his mother, who is looking more distraught by the second.

"That's correct." By the obstinate look on Frédéric's chiseled face, I can tell he isn't used to answering other people's questions… and I can also tell he doesn't like it one bit.

"How long has this party been a tradition in your family?" Samuel asks.

"What does that have to do with anything?" Frédéric snaps.

Hélène places a jewel-studded hand on her son's thigh, then answers the question, her voice quivering all the while. "The Morel family has been holding this holiday celebration for over seventy-five years now, at this exact same residence. Some of the most famous dignitaries, politicians, and businessmen in history have been in attendance. It's quite the event, Detective."

"I see," Samuel notes. "Before the party, did Isla mention to either of you or to any other guests, her plans to take the Orient Express train overnight to Paris?"

Frédéric's face grows somber. "No, she didn't."

"I understand you proposed to Isla during the party," Samuel says. "How did she react?"

"Well, of course she said yes," Frédéric huffs.

"Yes, we know she accepted your proposal, Monsieur Morel, but how did she react? Did she seem genuinely happy?"

"What kind of a question is that?" Frédéric says, scrunching his forehead. "Isla and I were in love. Of course she was happy with my proposal."

Frédéric's flagrant show of confidence is maddening. I want to slap him across his smug face. For the past several years that Isla has been traveling around Europe, she has always gone for those rich, conceited, stuffy types. Unfortunately, I never could cure her of that problem.

"I don't mean any disrespect, Monsieur Morel," Samuel continues, "but it's no secret that Isla was hiding something from you. Something that would make her decide to slip out of this party without telling a soul, take the last ferry all the way across Lake Geneva into Switzerland, and climb on a midnight train to Paris. Do you have any idea, *any idea at all*, what Isla was hiding from you and your family?"

"Why don't you ask *her*?" Frédéric says bitingly, pointing at me.

I try to hold my tongue so Samuel can do his job, but the arrogant, entitled look on this French guy's perfect little face has crawled underneath my skin, and I can't take it anymore. "My *name* is Jillian," I say, louder than I intend to. "And *I* am Isla's family. I understand your shock at finding out about me, but until twenty-four hours ago, I had never heard your name out of her mouth either. Isla was clearly keeping secrets from all of us, so get over your hurt ego and answer the damn question."

Frédéric lifts his angry glare from me and shoots his gaze back at Samuel. "I had no idea Isla was planning to leave the party. I had no idea she was hiding anything. She was happy here with me, with *my* family."

"Something made her leave without telling you, and I'm guessing it wasn't because she was happy here," Samuel pushes.

Frédéric stands, then pounds his fist on the coffee table, a grown man with the temper of a two-year-old. "If you want proof, you can watch the video from the gala. I've never seen a woman who looked happier or more beautiful than Isla did that night."

Hélène stands abruptly and places a hand on her son's shoulder, her diamond bracelet sparkling in the late afternoon sunlight. "I don't believe we've received the video yet," she says coolly. "Are we finished here, Detective? This has been a difficult two days for us all, and my son could use some rest."

"No, Madame Morel, I'm not quite finished." Samuel stands to his feet, his six-foot-two frame towering over both Hélène and her son. "When my colleague requested the video from the party, you specifically told him that you didn't have one made this year."

Hélène flares her nostrils just the slightest bit, then switches into French. "I don't believe so, Detective. That must be a mistake on your colleague's part. You're welcome to see the video when we receive it. It usually takes about a week or two to arrive, but hopefully you will have found Isla by then."

"The name of the videographer?" Samuel asks.

"I don't handle those sorts of details, Detective. We have an event planner, of course."

"The name of the event planner then?" Samuel asks.

"You'll find her name and title on the guest list I've already provided to your agency. Now if you'll excuse me, I have to be on my way. Before you arrived, I found out that my sister is quite ill. I have to take the train up to Paris immediately to be with her."

Then the matriarch of the family turns to me, placing a chilly hand on my arm. "I'm sure you understand how it is with sisters. It's a bond you can't break, no matter what happens. I am curious, though, as to why Isla never mentioned you. We were so close…Isla and me. She was like the daughter I never had. She was really a part of our family, and if something were to happen to her, I…well I just don't know what we'll do."

A stab of jealousy hits me as I watch this frail older woman, whom I'd heard of before today, shed tears over my sister.

The daughter she never had.

Our own mother never even treated us like daughters…had Isla found a new mother in Hélène? Had she really decided to be finished with her traveling lifestyle, her escapades of dating one rich, handsome man after the next, so that she could settle down with this absurdly wealthy family?

It's not like I could blame her. The life Frédéric and his family could give Isla is certainly a far cry from the nightmare of an existence we'd known as children.

But then why didn't she tell me about her new plans?

And more importantly, why did she leave?

"Madame Morel and Frédéric," Samuel speaks up. "I do have one more important question for you both."

Hélène raises one of her pencil-lined eyebrows and purses her full lips. "*Oui?*"

"You said your family has been holding its annual holiday gala at *this* property for over seventy-five years now. Are you aware that a crime of this exact nature occurred in 1937, exactly seventy-five years ago? Three young women were abducted from an Orient Express train passing through Lausanne en route to Paris, right around Christmas."

Hélène shoots her hand up to the shiny pearl necklace adorning her neck as her skin turns from light pink to a sickening shade of gray. "What are you saying? That someone is repeating the same crime seventy-five years later? But that's absurd!"

"We can't rule anything out at this point, Madame Morel. If there's even a slight chance that studying this past crime could lead us to Isla, then it's a lead we must explore."

Frédéric nods his head in agreement. "He's right, Mother. This could tell us something valuable. What more do you know about the 1937 incident?"

"A young woman by the name of Rosie Delaney was never found. Have either of you ever heard that name?"

Both Hélène and Frédéric shake their heads.

"No, I don't believe I have. What happened to the other two women?" Frédéric asks.

Samuel clears his throat and looks from Frédéric to Hélène before speaking. "They didn't survive unfortunately, and the kidnapper was never found."

"How dreadful," Hélène says, letting her teary gaze turn toward the glossy lake outside. "I can't bear to think about it another second. Have we answered all of your questions?"

"I'll need to speak with your husband, Madame Morel. Is he home?" Samuel says.

"He left some time ago, and I'm not sure when he'll be back," Hélène says curtly. "I'm sorry, but I really must leave now."

"I'll have my father call you as soon as he arrives," Frédéric says, gazing aimlessly out the window.

After Hélène leaves the room, Frédéric walks up to Samuel. "I apologize if what I did with the press has messed up the investigation, but what if someone sees her? What if someone out there has information? The public needs to know about this catastrophe, Monsieur Kelly."

Samuel nods. "I understand your urgency, Monsieur Morel. It was mainly due to the high-profile nature of your family and the Brooks family that we wanted to hold off on giving this situation media attention. The kidnappers want to see how desperate you are. They want to hear how much money you're willing to give to get her back."

"It doesn't matter how much money they want. I'll hand it over. As long as she comes home safely." For the first time, there isn't even a hint of arrogance in Frédéric's tone, but as much as I want to sympathize with him, I'm still angry for what he did.

"Even if we *were* in a ransom situation," I interject, "and your family handed over millions to these monsters, how can you be so stupid to think that they would keep Isla and the other girls alive?"

Frédéric glares at me. "Don't talk about Isla like that."

"She's my sister. And if you loved her as much as I do, you wouldn't have blatantly ignored the investigator's instructions to keep your mouth shut."

Samuel takes a step between us, holding his hands up.

"You're both wasting time here. Jillian, I need to speak with you outside before I leave. And Frédéric, we'll be in touch as soon as we know more."

Samuel places a hand on my shoulder and leads me away from the fuming French man, who most definitely hates my existence right now.

CHAPTER 6

An eerie curtain of steam rises from the expansive crystal blue waters of Lake Geneva. I walk along the water's edge, my gaze darting to the snow-capped mountains in the distance.

We need to go to those mountains. We need to find Isla.

Samuel paces beside me, waiting until we are far enough away from the Morel Château to be out of earshot. "You refused to answer any of my questions for the entire plane ride, but you're going to talk now, Jill. You're going to talk whether you want to or not. Your sister's life is on the line here."

I keep walking, picking up my pace. I don't care that my heels are digging into the blankets of snow that cover the lawn. I'd just as well strip them off my feet and walk barefoot.

"Why are you quizzing me?" I ask. "Frédéric is *clearly* hiding something, and you're just going to let him get away with it!" The scents of snow, pine, and cool water fill up my lungs, but no matter how deeply I try to breathe, I can't seem to get enough oxygen.

Samuel grabs my shoulders and swivels me around to face him. His hands are warm through my thin suit jacket, and as I stare into those truth-seeking eyes of his, I feel my resolve melting away. I want to cave. I want to tell him everything.

But I promised Isla I wouldn't tell a soul.

"There's absolutely nothing I can tell you about our past that will lead you to Isla today. Her abduction obviously has to do with the fact that the Morels have insane amounts of money, and someone wants to cash in. Plus there's that whole copycat crime possibility from seventy-five years ago. Why aren't you spending your time researching those possibilities instead of asking me questions that have nothing to do with why Isla's been taken?"

"My team is already out there researching every possible angle, Jill." Samuel keeps his hands wrapped firmly around my shoulders, so I am forced to look him in the eye.

"Do you think it was an accident that I chose to take this assignment?" he says. "My agency knows that we used to be together, that we dated before I married Karine. But only *I* know why we broke up—because you never wanted to open up to me, to tell me the truth. Whatever it is you and your sister have been hiding all these years—that's what I'm here to find out."

"You already know my mother is in prison. What more do you need to know?"

"I know she's serving a life sentence for murdering a man named Russell Hughes, and I know that you and Isla were present when she murdered him. But in the short time we've had to investigate, it's been nearly impossible to find any more details surrounding the murder. The records are sealed, and it could take days or even weeks to find the information that could help us find Isla. By that time, it could be too late." Samuel steps closer to me, his warm breath grazing over my nose, his persistence wearing me thin.

It feels both horrifying and comforting to hear Samuel acknowledge what happened to Isla and me. Horrifying because I'd sworn to Isla that I would never tell a living soul as long as we lived, and comforting because it is the truth. That incident, that day that forever changed the course of our lives, is part of who I am, and it is part of Isla too, despite the years we have spent trying to erase it.

But the story Samuel has just told is only a small piece of our truth, and the rest he will never know.

"I need to hear the story from your mouth, Jill," Samuel says. "I need to know all of the details, names of anyone from your and Isla's past who may want to hurt her now. Names of anyone else who may have been involved in that murder. I know you think it's not relevant, but *every* possibility needs to be explored in a case like this."

I pull away from Samuel's grasp and march farther down the lake. "Isla isn't a *case*," I mutter under my breath.

"I knew you wouldn't open up to anyone else, Jill," Samuel calls after me, his voice earnest, softer now. "I thought that with our history, you'd at least consider talking to me."

I keep walking, ignoring the urge to stop running away, to take Samuel's hand and never let go. "Our history is exactly why you're the *last* person I would open up to."

I may have refused to let him in, refused to tell him the truth about who I really was, about what had happened to Isla and me, but is he forgetting how much hurt he caused me? How quickly he jumped from me to Karine, professing his wedding vows to her only months after we'd split?

Samuel's cell rings out into the empty space, the piercing sound rattling my already frazzled nerves. But before he answers, he grabs my arm.

"You know, Jill, in the years since you left me, I've read all of your articles. Every single one. I find it interesting how you've based an entire career around your search for the truth. But in real life, to the people who matter most, all you do is lie."

I rip my arm away from Samuel and turn my back to him. I can't let him see the tears that are pooling at the corners of my eyes.

I think of jumping in the lake. Of letting the freeze swallow up these rotten lies, this horrid past that Isla and I share. The past we've both spent our entire lives running away from.

Maybe Isla was running away again. Riding the midnight train to a new life when someone took her.

As I wonder what it would feel like to slip my feet into these ice-cold waters, to let it all slip away, another thought invades my mind.

Maybe Isla wanted to be taken.

A hand on my shoulder jolts me from visions of Isla running across snow-covered train tracks in a pitch-dark night.

"Jillian, something has happened."

The stern, sorrowful tone in Samuel's voice demands that I turn to face him. That I listen without talking back for once.

He hesitates, the lines around his eyes scaring me, making me dread whatever he's about to say.

"Emma Brooks was just found in the Alps."

I gulp for air, but my efforts to breathe are to no avail. "Is she... is she...?" I stammer as my shoulders shiver violently from the cold.

"They were too late. She was already gone," he says.

I expect my body to collapse into a heap on the snow-covered grass, but that same invisible portal of strength I've been relying on for my whole life keeps me standing. The lake, the mountains, the trees all spin furiously around me, but I don't cave.

For Isla, I will never give up.

I reach out, gripping Samuel's arm. "Go find her, Samuel. Go find my sister."

Back inside the Morel Château, Frédéric already has the television on.

We stare at the screen in silence as TV crews riding in helicopters swarm over the mountainous forest where Emma Brooks's nineteen-year-old body was just found.

The reporters tell us that police have not yet released information on *how* the ambassador's daughter was killed, but by the way Samuel is clenching his fists at his sides, I can only assume that he already knows the details.

And for once, I don't grill him. I don't want to know.

"I have to go now," Samuel announces to Frédéric and me. "They need me on site."

Frédéric turns from the TV, his face pale and drawn. "Is there any hope of finding her alive?"

"What happened to Emma Brooks is a tragedy, but that doesn't mean we won't find Isla in time. You've hired the best team in the world, Monsieur Morel. And I promise you, we'll do everything we can to bring Isla home safely." Samuel's green eyes are unwavering, strong, determined. I can see that he isn't allowing even an ounce of doubt to invade his consciousness.

In this moment, I'm beyond thankful for Samuel's ability to believe that he and his team will find my sister, bring her home unharmed. Otherwise, the doubt swarming between Frédéric and me would be enough to drown us all in a giant pool of despair.

I leave Frédéric staring hopelessly at the television as I follow Samuel through the dimly lit foyer and out the front door. Night has descended upon this lakefront resort town, but no matter how beautiful my surroundings are, I can't shake the belief that as long as there are monsters out there who get off on harming innocent women, the world will always be an ugly place.

At the top of the stairs, Samuel surprises me by taking my hand.

"I don't want anything to happen to you, Jillian. Promise me you'll stay here."

I realize that I love the way Samuel's hand feels wrapped around mine. And in a moment of irrationality, I suddenly wish that all those years ago, I'd never let him go.

"I promise," I say. "I won't leave."

With each breath, our lips release little white puffs of air. Samuel steps closer to me, the heat emanating off his chest making me remember what it was like to have my entire body wrapped up in his. What it was like to have his hands exploring the skin on my back, my legs, my stomach, my breasts.

No one since has ever made me feel so beautiful, so loved, so whole.

Samuel leans into my ear, the scruff on his cheek brushing against my face. "I want you to pay attention to everything that happens in this house once I leave," he whispers. "And don't let on that you speak French. They have no idea. You have full license to snoop around. And if you find anything—anything at all—call me immediately. There will be a car waiting just around the corner in case you need it."

"I thought you didn't remember that I speak French," I say, closing my eyes as Samuel keeps his face pressed against mine.

He squeezes my hand, his lips brushing ever so slightly against my ear as he whispers one final message. "I remember everything about you, Jillian Chambord. *Everything.*"

And with that, Samuel slips into the silky blue night, leaving me alone to wonder why on earth Isla's disappearance would be the one thing to finally bring us back into each other's lives.

Back inside the château, I walk toward the palace-worthy salon and find Frédéric taking one last look at Emma Brooks's beautiful face flashing across the television screen. He turns off the TV and hurls the remote through the elegant living room, muttering French obscenities under his breath. The remote lands with a thud against the wall before Frédéric turns and sees me watching him.

"I'm sorry," he says, his cheeks flushed.

"It's okay," I say quietly. "I know how you feel."

We stand together in an awkward silence, and I have a million questions I want to ask him. But by the way he acted with Samuel earlier, I decide it's best to leave him alone for now. There's no telling how long I'll be staying in this stranger's home, and I don't want to make the situation worse than it already is.

"Would it be okay if I use your bathroom?" I ask.

"Yes, of course. I'll show you to a guest bedroom in the right wing, and I'll bring you some of Isla's clothes. I'm sure you'll want something to change into tonight, before bed."

Frédéric leads me up a grand staircase in the middle of the château. I run my hand along the smooth ivory banister and gaze up at the crystal chandelier overhead. For as beautiful and regal as this vacation palace is, I can't help but notice that it has a certain chill to it. The property doesn't feel warm or welcoming like a home should feel.

More like a museum—cold and impersonal.

The complete opposite of my sister.

"Isla left some of her clothes here?" I ask as we continue climbing the never-ending set of stairs.

"Yes, she left almost everything here. All of the beautiful pieces I bought for her. The jewels, the high heels—all of it." Frédéric doesn't even try to mask the bitterness in his tone. "All they found of hers on the train was a small suitcase and a purse."

He stops when he reaches the second floor, gazing below at the showy grand piano and the life-sized paintings adorning the ivory-colored walls. "I have so much to give Isla. What girl in her right mind would give up all of this?"

"Maybe she just needed some air, some space. All of this wealth… it can be suffocating to people who aren't used to it, you know."

Frédéric turns to me, pursing his lips as he eyes me up and down.

Here we go again.

"What could you possibly know about how Isla was feeling? She didn't even tell us you existed," he hisses. "What did you do to her to make her hate you so much, Jillian? Tell me, what did you do?"

His words sting me, even though I know this angry little jerk has no clue what he's talking about. In his world of glamour, money, vacation homes, and ski trips, there isn't room for the kind of atrocities Isla and I faced growing up.

"The real question is what did *you* do to make her want to leave you and your precious riches?" I snap back. "If Isla had never met you, this never would've happened. She never would've been taken from me!"

"*Ça suffit—that's enough,*" a stern male voice booms from the bottom of the stairs. "Frédéric, a word please."

The tall man hovering at the foot of the stairs looks like an older version of Frédéric. His dark, piercing eyes hide behind a set of round black glasses as he watches his son storm down the stairs and straight past him, without so much as a second glance.

The bright lights from the chandelier overhead reveal deep wrinkles around the man's eyes and across his forehead. He shakes his head and gazes wearily up at me. "I apologize for my son," he says in English, his accent much stronger than Frédéric's. "You must be Jillian, Isla's twin sister."

I nod at him without smiling. I don't think I could smile if I tried.

"I'm Laurent Morel, Frédéric's father. I've just spoken with Investigator Kelly. He told me you would be here. Please use any of the guest rooms in the wing to the right. Dinner will be served by Florian, our chef, at nine o'clock. Now if you'll excuse me, I need to speak with my son."

Laurent takes off through the château, leaving me alone on the second floor. As I hear Frédéric and his father erupt into shouts downstairs, I remember Samuel's instructions outside.

You have full license to snoop.

I try to understand what the two men are shouting about, but their muffled voices in quick French are incomprehensible to me. As long as they're arguing downstairs, I decide that now is as good a time as any to do *my own* investigation.

I'm not about to sit alone in some palace-sized bedroom and wait for information to come in on Isla. I need to find out what my sister's angry fiancé is hiding and why she chose to leave him and his rich family behind.

Ignoring Laurent's instructions to find a guest room in the right wing, I head left. Dim lamps light up the long hallway, the shiny wooden floors creaking slightly with each step I take.

Three golden-framed portraits line the smooth walls, each of them a life-sized painting of one of the Morel women. Three obvious empty spaces reveal gaps in the Morel lineage where portraits should've been, or perhaps used to be. A shiny gold plaque below each regal canvas reveals the women's names, their husbands' and children's names, their birthdates, and when applicable, dates of death.

First, of course, is Hélène Morel, wife of Laurent, mother of Frédéric. A shiny string of pearls adorns her neck, the sparkling diamond bracelet I noticed her wearing earlier resting loosely on her tiny wrist. I can see by the gleam in her eye that she likes the jewels, the glamour, the riches, the power that this family brings. Most women would.

She seems younger in the painting, happier.

But of course, whenever this portrait was painted, Hélène hadn't been looking for her son's abducted fiancée and rushing off to take care of an ill sister.

Moving on to the next woman in this long line of wealth, I find Thérèse Morel, wife of Alexandre, mother of Laurent and Madeleine. I search the walls for a portrait of Laurent's sister Madeleine, but she's nowhere to be found. I wonder whether she died at a young age or if she is one of the missing portraits. On that note, I wonder if the Morel men—the people who've actually earned the money in this family—get their own personal wall of fame too. Or perhaps while the Morel men are out running the family real estate business, the wives are the ones calling the shots behind the scenes. It certainly seemed that way earlier with Hélène.

The third and final portrait is the creepiest of them all—Agnès Morel, born in 1891. She only had one son, Alexandre. Her grayish black hair is pulled back into a tight bun, and the lines on her face make her appear powerful, domineering, and a little bit evil.

For a moment, I lose myself in her commanding gaze, her eyes like an endless black sea of history, of stories. She died in 1990, which would've made her ninety-nine years old.

At the very end of the dark hallway, I notice a door slightly ajar. I hesitate for a moment, but when I hear Frédéric and Laurent's tense voices still echoing downstairs, I open the door. Flipping on the light, I discover the only cramped space in this massive mansion—an old, dusty storage closet. I run my hands over boxes filled with books and picture frames, but stop when I see a large white sheet covering something up toward the back of the closet.

Peeking underneath the corner of the sheet, I find the three missing gold-framed portraits stacked against the wall.

I whip off the sheet and kneel down to find a painting of the most beautiful, elegant woman of them all, smiling gracefully back at me. She has a full head of glossy white hair, rosy cheeks, and warm, inviting blue eyes with silver specks in them. Something about those silvery sapphire eyes strikes a familiar chord with me, but I'm not sure why.

The plaque lying next to her painting reveals the name I was searching for just moments ago: *Madeleine Morel, daughter of Thérèse and Alexandre, sister of Laurent, born in 1938.*

Interesting. She looks nothing like her brother Laurent. And why did they take her portrait down?

I remember that I don't have much time, so I place Madeleine's portrait to the side and gaze at the second hidden painting.

But I gasp when I find that the canvas has been slashed to pieces, leaving only a glimpse of a woman's dark brown curls, and a dimple pressing into her rosy cheek. The rest of the painting has been destroyed, ripped to shreds.

I search the ground around me to see if there is another name plaque, but Madeleine's is the only one here.

Suppressing the feeling that I should get the hell out of here right now, I push the second frame aside and realize I don't care about the mysterious drama that would've caused someone in the Morel family to destroy a painting of one of their own women or to strip Madeleine's tasteful, elegant portrait off the wall.

Because there, in front of me, is a portrait of my own beautiful twin sister, her violet-specked eyes casting a seductive gaze at the painter, her full pink lips curving upward into a sensual grin.

Ever since we were little girls, Isla was always the prettier twin, the one all of the men stared at, lusted over.

I'd always wished it had been me they had chosen. That those sickening men had taken *my* innocence away and left her alone.

As I stare at the long strands of wavy, chestnut hair that fall effortlessly over her bare shoulders, for the millionth time I wonder how things would've turned out if Isla hadn't been so damn beautiful.

Even our mother was jealous of her beauty.

But then that's why I'm here, searching for my lost sister in some cold French mansion in the middle of winter. That's why Isla escaped to Europe when we were only twenty years old, and why she never came home again.

Because of our demented, jealous mother.

I lay the painting of my sweet, gorgeous sister back down on the chilly hardwood floor and realize that it's been almost two years since we've seen each other. I am instantly jealous of the man who was lucky enough to paint this portrait of Isla, this man who must've stared at her beauty for hours while he crafted the perfect contours of her face, the warmth and the love in those eyes that we share.

The signature at the bottom of the painting reads *C. Mercier.*

Of course, the artist could've been a woman, but I know my sister, and only a handsome man would earn such a provocative gaze, such a bewitching smile.

A rustling noise outside the closet startles me. I flip off the light and peek through the crack in the door, but don't see anyone in the hallway. The men's voices are still muffled downstairs, but they sound a little bit calmer now.

Moving swiftly, I cover the paintings back up with the sheet, slip out of the storage closet, and continue my quest, this time quietly opening up all the bedroom doors in search of Frédéric and Isla's room…of the possessions she left behind.

On the fifth try, I find what I'm looking for: Isla's laptop.

I work quickly, searching through her recently opened files to see if something stands out. When I don't find anything relevant, I begin scanning through her pictures. Photos of Isla posing with Frédéric at glamorous galas and Morel family business functions fill the page. In all of the pictures, my sister is dressed impeccably in long, silky gowns, dangly diamond earrings, and three-inch heels.

A pang of jealousy hits me as I mull over the fact that over the past eight years, Isla has created a life that I know nothing of. A life that she didn't want me to take part in.

Of course she didn't want me here in her new glamorous world. I was a reminder of her dark past. Of the atrocities that had happened to her when she was only a teenager.

Of the fact that she had suffered tremendously more than I had. While all along, I'd been completely oblivious.

I push away the familiar rage that threatens to boil over inside me as I continue scrolling through her photos.

At the bottom of the page, I spot a picture file labeled *Charity Gala*, dated December 21, only a day before Isla disappeared. Opening up the file, I scroll quickly through the slideshow. About halfway in, I find a photograph that makes me feel like I must be going insane. But as I examine it closely, I realize that the scene before me is *not* an optical illusion.

Frédéric is smiling a cheeky grin, looking stuffy and arrogant as hell in his tux, with one arm around his father, and the other around a man with thinning gray hair and a husky, round face that I could never, ever forget.

It's Senator Parker Williams—the sick, perverted man who I've been working tirelessly to expose for running a child prostitution ring and murdering two innocent sisters in D.C..

What in the hell was he doing *here* with the Morel men, only three days ago?

And what was Isla doing taking a photograph of him?

I notice then that Senator Williams is the only man *not* smiling in the photo. In fact, he looks nervous, like he's been caught.

Suddenly my mouth goes dry and my vision blurs. My hands begin trembling so fiercely that I'm unable to scroll through the rest of the photos.

All I can see are Parker Williams's big, rough hands fondling my thirteen-year-old sister, ripping off her clothes, then covering her mouth every time she tried to scream.

He didn't want me. I wasn't the sexy one. He only wanted Isla.

At thirteen, my innocent twin sister had been Williams's first *conquest* with a young girl. It was before he became a senator. He'd started off sleeping with my mother, paying her for sex just like all the other wealthy men who traveled to the other side of the tracks from their rich D.C. neighborhoods, looking for something more exciting than their cookie-cutter wives. After our dad left, there was a different man in our mother's room every night. When we were little, she lied, telling us they were just "playing games," but Isla and I weren't stupid.

Williams was one of my mother's regulars, but when he caught Isla prancing home from school early one day, wearing the short jean skirt that used to drive the junior high boys wild, that sick man dropped my mom so fast, she almost went blind with jealousy.

Our mother hated Isla from that day forward, but she allowed it to go on. And she continued collecting money from Williams every time he slept with her thirteen-year-old daughter.

I was too busy working at the school newspaper every day after school to know what was going on in my own home, to my own sister.

And Isla lied to me too. She was ashamed, horrified, and embarrassed.

We'd been best friends up until that point.

But after her first encounter with Parker Williams, she was never the same, fun-loving twin sister I used to know. She became moody, angry, secretive, and distant.

And I didn't know why until it was too late.

I shake away the memories of the horrific day that stole our innocence forever and promise Isla that I won't be too late this time.

I know who is behind my sister's abduction, who took that young, lovely Italian girl, and who killed the ambassador's innocent daughter, Emma Brooks.

I wonder if Senator Williams knew about the 1937 train abduction. Maybe in his warped mind, he decided it would be fun to reenact the exact same crime with three other young, beautiful women. He always *was* obsessed with Isla.

Whatever his twisted reasons are for doing what he did, I am sure it was him. I am sure it was Senator Williams.

Now I just have to find out if Frédéric and Laurent are working with him too.

Because if they are, I have to get the hell out of here *fast*.

EPISODE 3
CHAPTER 7

December 24, 2012

Évian-les-Bains, France

I dial the number Samuel left me on his business card, but each unanswered ring only serves to make me feel more frantic.

"You've reached the voicemail of Samuel Kelly. Leave a message."

"Samuel, it's me," I whisper into my cell phone, praying Frédéric and his father continue ranting a while longer downstairs to buy me more time. "You need to investigate a U.S. senator by the name of Parker Williams. I am one hundred percent certain he's behind all of this, and I'll explain more when you call me back. I'm emailing you a picture of him with Frédéric and Laurent Morel, taken only one day before Isla's disappearance, at a charity gala. Obviously, this means you need to be investigating the Morels' potential involvement in the abduction as well. Please call me as soon as you get this."

With shaky hands, I hang up the phone, then turn the ringer on vibrate. I don't want the Morels to hear the ring when Samuel calls back. Next, I sign into my email, attach the Williams photo, and send the message off to Samuel.

I'm sure he'll call me back soon.

He has to.

Quickly, I scan through the emails I've missed from the past twenty-four hours.

There are five unread messages from Natalie, my boss, and piles of unread emails from my other colleagues.

Judging by the fact that Senator Williams was photographed in France only three days ago, and most definitely had something to do with my sister's kidnapping, my original plans to expose and bust him back in D.C. have obviously been botched.

Bracing myself for the possible loss of my job, I open Natalie's first email, which she sent last night, while I was en route to France.

> *Jillian,*
>
> *The third sister in your conspiracy theory did in fact show today. We took her statement on record, then set her up with Officer Reynolds for protection, as you requested. Everything with the girl checked out exactly as you said it would. I'm sorry I doubted you.*
>
> *One rather massive hitch: as we were taking Scarlet's statement, Williams appeared in a live press conference from France, announcing his resignation from the Senate. Obviously, he was onto you and wanted to preemptively try to save his sorry ass.*
>
> *I know you did your homework on this story, but how could you have missed the fact that the senator left the country?*
>
> *Now that law enforcement has heard Scarlet's testimony, Williams is wanted for murder. By the time officials made it to his family's vacation home in the French Alps to take him into custody, he was already gone.*
>
> *He's now officially MIA.*
>
> *His chief of staff, however, is already behind bars. They're grilling the shit out of him to find out if he knows where Williams is hiding.*
>
> *Somehow the senator found out you were onto him, Chambord. There's simply no other reason he would've resigned exactly when he did and fled the country. Is there anything you're not telling me?*

On that note, what is going on with the whole "I have a sister I never told you about" debacle? Is she really missing? And who in the hell was that smoking hot man who came in here to deliver the news? I could tell by the way you two looked at each other that there's a sizzling history there. When you get back, I want the full report on what goes down between you and the investigatory sex god.

I'm serious Chambord—either you dish the dirty details, or you're fired.

—Natalie

P.S. When are you coming back?

In Natalie's subsequent emails, she tells me that the search for Williams is still on and that news of the train abduction has traveled back to the States. *The Washington Daily* is, of course, covering Emma Brooks's murder and the abduction of both my sister and Francesca Rossi.

Then in Natalie's most human moment ever, she tells me that she's sorry I'm going through this, to stay safe, and not to worry about the Senator Williams story.

If she only knew.

I don't take the time to email her back and fill her in, though. Instead, I check my phone, but still no word from Samuel.

The tense voices downstairs have subsided, making my heart pound violently inside my chest. Why isn't Samuel calling me back? What if the Morels are working with Williams?

Besides their photo with the senator, I don't have any concrete evidence to believe that Laurent and Frédéric are in any way involved in Isla's abduction, and even though Frédéric's spoiled, rich-boy demeanor drives me insane, he does seem to be genuinely distraught over Isla's disappearance.

I consider walking downstairs, questioning the Morel men about their connection to Williams, and telling them that we need to get in the car immediately and drive to the site of Emma Brooks's murder, where the ground team is searching, so we can sic them on Williams.

But then I click on the photograph again. The way Frédéric has his arm loosely strung around the senator's shoulders, as if they're all old buddies, makes me cringe. If Williams has a vacation home close by in the Alps, that could explain how they know him. And when Samuel first told me about the Morel family, I remember him saying that they had close *political ties.*

I can't risk opening up to the Morels about Williams. I imagine they've already gotten wind of his resignation and potentially of the fact that he's now wanted for murder back in the U.S.

If they had anything to do with the abduction, or even if they know that Williams is behind it, wealthy, powerful businessmen like the Morels would do anything in their power to keep their names clear.

Which would mean shutting me up at all costs.

I glance at my phone again, but Samuel still hasn't called. So I send him a text.

Please check your email and call me. It's urgent.

Closing the computer, I do a quick scan of the luxurious bedroom. The glowing lamplight catches on a silver sequined dress sparkling inside the massive walk-in closet at the back of the room. I walk toward the dress, imagining Isla's shining violet eyes lighting up as she wore it. Running my hand along the rows of silky designer gowns, I remember Frédéric's words on the stairs earlier.

What woman in her right mind would leave all of this behind?

Isla was certainly no stranger to leaving people and things behind, but the way she'd left this time was different. Hopping on a luxury train to Paris in the middle of the night after accepting a marriage proposal was a little extreme, even for my sister.

Given Senator Williams's connection to this whole disaster, I could only guess that she must've been running from him. Had he made it onto the train when she boarded? But like Samuel had said, there had to have been at least two or three kidnappers to get all three girls off the train without the other passengers seeing or hearing anything.

So he must've had at least one accomplice.

I continue thumbing through Isla's ritzy clothes as I try to piece together the mystery of her disappearance. And suddenly I remember something—Isla's voicemail to me on the train.

You're not going to believe what I've done this time, she'd said.

Then she giggled. A devious, silly giggle.

Isla wouldn't have laughed like that if she thought Williams was following her.

Which meant she couldn't have been running from him. She wasn't running *from* anyone.

Perhaps it was what or *whom* she was running *to* that had excited her.

And at the end of her message, before she was taken, she'd said she had something important to tell me.

What could it have been?

I peek my head into the bedroom to make sure Frédéric hasn't come upstairs, then check my phone once more. No missed calls. No text messages.

I can't wait around here much longer. If Samuel isn't going to call me back, I'll just have to go to him. I pull the town car driver's card out of my pocket, dial his number, and feel relief flood through me when he picks up on the first ring.

"Hello, this is Jillian. We met earlier this morning," I tell him in French.

"Of course. Will you be requiring my services?" he asks politely.

"Yes. Immediate service in fact. Please pick me up at the Morel estate."

"I'll be there in fifteen minutes, Mademoiselle. Will that be okay?"

"Yes, of course. Thank you so much."

I'm just about to flick off the light in the obscenely large closet when a long black suitcase shoved into the back corner catches my eye. Isla always liked to travel with colorful suitcases, so this one must be Frédéric's.

Everything else in this entire closet must've been Isla's—the dresses, the heels, the elegant scarves.

Except that plain black suitcase.

My hands shake as I unzip Frédéric's bag, my ears painfully alert for any sound that he might be coming. But to my dismay, the silky black lining inside the suitcase is completely empty. No useful clues here.

Just before I close it up though, I spot a little lump beneath the zippered lining.

Running the zipper down the middle, I peel back the lining to find a small, black velvet ring box. This must've been the box that Isla's engagement ring came in, but why would he hide an empty box in the lining of his suitcase?

When I open the delicate velvet case, I realize why he'd hidden it. A massive round-cut diamond that must be at least three or four carats sparkles up at me.

I can't see Isla's dainty hand with this gaudy ring weighing her down. Not in a million years.

I realize that when Samuel was questioning him earlier, Frédéric conveniently left out the part of the story where Isla gave him the ring back *before* she left the party. Why would he do that? I snap the box closed and slip it back below the lining, but gasp when I feel a piece of paper crinkle underneath my fingers.

Tears sting my eyes as I unfold the paper and see my sister's pretty, delicate handwriting dancing across the page.

> *Frédéric,*
> *These past few months with you have been incredible. You really are an amazing man, and you have so much to give.*
> *But I haven't been honest with you.*
> *The truth is, I've fallen in love with someone else, and it's for this reason that I can't accept your proposal. I know you were just*

trying to do the right thing because of the baby, but you don't have to worry. The baby isn't yours.

I know you'll fall in love with the right woman someday, and she'll adore this beautiful ring and this glamorous lifestyle. I'm sorry, Frédéric, but it's just not for me.

—Isla

The paper shakes in my hand as I try to digest this insane news. Isla left to be with another man. She left because she was pregnant. And it wasn't Frédéric's baby.

That's what she was going to tell me on the phone.

I have something important to tell you, Jillian. Please call me back. I...I'm...

I'm pregnant.

Frédéric knew this. He knew all of this, and yet he chose not to tell the police.

I have to get out of here.

I storm out of the closet with the note clutched tightly against my chest, but just as I round the corner, I smack straight into a hard body.

The dim lamp in the bedroom casts an eerie glow on Frédéric's tight jaw line, on the crazed look in his dark, fixed eyes.

I try to push past him, but he squares his tall frame in front of me.

"Frédéric, get out of my way," I say firmly.

"I loved your sister, Jillian. I wanted to marry her. Not just because of the baby. I loved her!" The high-pitched panic in his voice makes me squirm.

He snatches the note from my hands and tears it to shreds right in front of me, Isla's beautiful handwriting, her words, her truth, now a pile of trash at our feet.

"That baby is *mine*," he growls. "It belongs to this family. But Isla was selfish. A dirty, little selfish liar." Rage flashes in those dark eyes as he clenches his fists. "She lied about having a sister, she lied about the baby, and she lied about him."

Frédéric's fist goes flying past my face and punches the wall behind my head.

I duck to the side and rush for the door, but Frédéric is quicker. His hand wraps tightly around my elbow as he yanks me backward, then grips both of my arms in his trembling hands.

"Why didn't you just tell the truth, Frédéric?" I say as I try to wriggle out of his grasp. "Why didn't you tell Samuel the truth?"

"Your whore of a sister humiliated me. She humiliated my entire family. She deserves what's happening to her. That little bitch deserves it."

The fury that boils over inside me is uncontrollable. Isla's bloodstained tears flash before my eyes as I ram my knee into Frédéric's groin not once, but twice. He doubles over, losing his grip on me.

Grabbing the sides of his face, I smash his forehead hard against my knee. He winces, stumbling to the ground, while I grab my cell phone and purse off the desk and bolt out into the hallway and down the stairs. Loud footsteps echo through the house, and just as I'm skimming over the smooth white tiles in the foyer, I glimpse Laurent running down the hallway toward me.

"Jillian!" he calls.

But I'm not about to wait around here and get myself killed.

I fly through the front door, slamming it at my back as I jog down the ivory steps and out over the snow-covered lawn.

Tall, snow-dusted pines hover over the dark winding road ahead, but there's no sign of the black town car.

Shit.

I run down the never ending driveway, pumping my legs as quickly as I can in these stupid heels, ignoring the bitter wind that shoots right through my thin suit jacket and blouse.

"Jillian, wait!" It's Laurent, crossing the lawn to reach me.

I don't know if Frédéric's father knows about my sister's lies or if he has anything to do with her abduction, but I can't take any chances. His son is clearly a psychopath who used his connection with Williams to take my sister down, all because of his own hurt pride.

I pick up my pace, turning down the empty street, wincing as my ankle rolls. Just as I consider tossing my heels into the bushes, a bright set of headlights comes into focus.

Racing even faster than before, I hear Laurent's footsteps close behind.

"Jillian, I'm not going to harm you! Please, come back. My son, he's—"

But I don't hear the rest of his words because I've already slid into the backseat of the sleek black town car, slammed and locked the door behind me.

"*Allez-y!*" *Go!* I yell to the driver. "*Vite!*"

The car zips right past Laurent, who throws his hands up in frustration as we drive into the dark night and away from that god-forsaken château.

CHAPTER 8

Thick white flakes blanket the windshield and swirl around the car as the driver floors the gas. We skid over the crunchy snow, past another lakeside mansion, until the image of Laurent waving wildly in the rear view mirror vanishes completely.

My fingertips are numb from the cold, my hands trembling as I turn over my phone to dial Samuel's number. But before I can get my shaking fingers to cooperate, my cell vibrates.

"Samuel, thank God," I breathe into the phone.

"Jillian, listen. You have to get out of there."

"I already did. I'm riding away from the château of horrors as we speak."

"Who are you with?"

"I called the driver who picked us up from the airport this morning. I had a feeling I might be needing him."

"Shit, Jillian. I'm so sorry I left you there." Samuel's deep voice is lined with regret, but I'm not angry. This is all happening so fast. How could he have known?

"Where are you headed?" he asks.

"I'm not sure. I just told him to get me away from that house."

"Good. I want you to meet me at the train station in Lausanne," Samuel says.

"The same station where Isla boarded the train?"

"Yes. I just left the crime scene, and I'm pulling into the closest station. With the snowstorm wreaking havoc on these mountain roads, the train will be the quickest, most direct way for me to get to you right now, and Lausanne is only an hour ride from where I am.

Plus I want you on the other side of the lake from the Morels. So I'll need you to follow these exact instructions to get there. You ready?"

"Yes. Just get me the hell away from here," I say, wishing the driver would crank up the heat. My race through the snow in this thin blouse, skinny pencil skirt, and these open-toed heels is beginning to take its toll on me. Not to mention the fact that I just kicked a psycho French boy's ass and learned that my sister, who is still missing, is pregnant.

I could use a little warmth right about now.

"Tell the driver to take you to the ferry that runs across Lake Geneva. It will take you from Évian-les-Bains straight to Lausanne," Samuel says. "The next one should be leaving at 10:00 P.M., so you don't have much time."

"Okay, hold on," I say, before leaning forward to instruct the driver in French. After I do so, I ask him to turn the heat up. He eyes my outfit with a perplexed eyebrow lift, then turns the heat up to full blast.

"What then?" I ask Samuel as I watch my bare knees shake uncontrollably in the darkness of the car.

"It should only take you about a half an hour to cross. When you arrive, I'll have a car waiting for you. My colleague will take you to the train station to meet me; it's only a few minutes away. When you get there, stay in the car until I come out of the station. I don't want you standing and waiting anywhere alone, do you understand?"

"Yes, I understand. Do you—" I start, but the driver's loud voice cuts me off.

"Mademoiselle, were you expecting visitors?" the driver asks in French.

"Hold on, Samuel." I lean forward. "What are you talking about?" I ask the driver.

The older gentleman nods at the rear view mirror. "Two cars are trailing us. There is no one else out driving on a night like this, not to mention that it's Christmas Eve. Is it possible someone would be following you?"

The driver wasn't an idiot. He'd seen the way I lunged into his car, and he'd watched as Laurent had screamed after me. Clearly, I hadn't called him to take me for a scenic ride around Lake Geneva.

"Can you lose them?" I ask.

"I'll do my best, Mademoiselle."

I peek over my shoulder and glimpse two bright pairs of headlights, trailing closely behind. The only thing separating us from them is the blanket of snow falling rapidly from the sky.

"Samuel," I whisper. "Whatever happened to the car you said would be waiting just around the corner from the Morels in case I needed anything? Is it possible that he's following me?"

"No, it's not him. Do you have a tail?"

"Two of them. Where's your guy? Can he come scare them off?"

A long pause travels over the line, and I hear a train whistling loudly in the background.

"Samuel?"

"Right before I called you, I received word that he'd been shot in his car."

"What? But how—"

"Listen to me, Jillian. I have to get on the train now, and I'm going to lose reception for a little while. I need you to lose those tails and get to the ferry by ten o'clock. My guy will be waiting for you when you get to the other side of the lake, and police are on their way to the Morel Château as we speak."

"What if the guy who's waiting for me gets shot like the last one?"

"He'll be there, Jillian. I promise you. Do you think you can do it?"

"We may have to start doing wheelies in the snow to lose these assholes, but I'll be there."

The train whistles once more through the line as my driver makes a sharp turn down another dark, winding road.

"Samuel, did you find out about Isla? That she was pregnant? And that she turned down Frédéric's proposal? Is that why you wanted me to get out of there?"

"Yes, we just tracked down the man Isla was going to be with in Paris. The father of the baby. He told us everything."

"Who is he?"

"I'm not at liberty—"

"Samuel, cut the shit. I'm obviously on your side here."

I can hear the train wheels squeaking as Samuel shouts into the phone. "His name is Christophe Mercier. He's an artist—a painter I believe. He was the one waiting for Isla that morning at the train station when she never showed up."

C. Mercier. The signature of the artist who'd painted Isla's portrait for the Morels.

I *knew* I'd seen something in her eyes in that painting... something deeper and more emotional than the usual breezy flirtation that she tossed around to any handsome man who came her way.

Despite the unbelievably grim circumstances I'm facing, I feel the slightest opening in my chest. *Hope.* Isla had finally found love. And she was going to have a baby.

I know my sister, and when she is passionate about something, she will fight to the death to protect it.

In that way, we are a lot alike, Isla and I.

"Jill, lose that tail, and I'll see you in an hour." The line crackles as Samuel's voice is swallowed up by the loud train.

"I'll be there, Samuel. I'll be there."

The pitch darkness surrounding the car is lightened only by the white glow emanating from the falling snow. I glance back to see both sets of headlights making the same turn my obedient French driver just made. He'd managed to put a little bit of distance between us and them, but not enough.

"Is there any way you can get to a main road so we can lose them faster?" I tap my hands nervously on my freezing thighs.

"Yes, right up ahead, we'll come to an intersection that leads to the main part of town. Trust me, Mademoiselle, I have a plan."

He steps harder on the gas, but the car only increases its speed slightly because of the thick layers of snow already coating the slick roads. We arrive at a stoplight just as it turns red, but to my surprise, the driver blows right through it. I grip the door handle as he makes a sharp left, and the back of the car fishtails. Turning around, I see the first car make it through the intersection, but Tail Number Two squeals to a stop in oncoming traffic.

I lean forward and grab the driver's shoulder. "You lost one of them. Now, just one more. Thank you so much."

"*Pas de soucis.*" *No worries,* he says. "I have seen the news," he calls back. "I am sorry to hear of your sister, Mademoiselle Chambord. I hope they find her."

A strange feeling pierces my gut. How does this guy know Isla is my sister? I'd told him my first name, and of course he'd dropped me off at the Morels' house with that press mob outside earlier, but I hadn't told him how I was related to her.

The driver steps harder on the gas, and the engine revs as we plow faster over the snow.

"I'm sorry, how did you know—?" I begin.

"Her picture was on the news tonight, and the minute I saw her violet eyes, I knew you were her sister. I have never seen eyes like yours, Mademoiselle, and I could never forget them. They are stunning…haunting even."

I cross my arms over my shivering chest and try not to think about the fact that Isla and I have always shared these haunting eyes. They are the one thing about us that doesn't resemble our sick mother or our absent, neglectful father.

They are ours.

But if Isla is taken from me, these eyes will forever be a reminder of her. Of what I'd lost.

I can't let that happen.

We race through another red light, but we still don't lose the first car. I squint to make out the driver's face, but all I can see through the heavy snowfall are two blaring headlights.

"Don't worry, Mademoiselle. I've done this before. I will lose them." The driver's calm voice is the only thing reassuring me in this moment. That and the thought of seeing Samuel in less than an hour at the train station.

Samuel will keep me safe. I know he will.

And of course my kick-ass self-defense moves can serve as a backup if need be. They'd already done the job at fending off my sister's crazy ex-boyfriend.

Suddenly, we swerve into a driveway, and as I focus my eyes against the blinding sheets of snow, I realize that this man really did have a genius plan. He has just pulled into a police station.

Breath finally leaves my lungs as I watch our tail drive straight past. Whoever the bastard is, he's not about to pull into the police station.

Patting the driver on the shoulder, I feel myself smile. It's a cold, shivery smile, but I'll take anything at this point. "Thank you so much," I say. "I'm sorry, I don't think I got your first name."

He glances back at me, the lines around his silvery blue eyes crinkling as he smiles. "My name is Georges."

For just the briefest of moments, I feel a connection to him, like I've met him or seen him before. But I can't place it.

He breaks our gaze, putting the car in park. "I am very good friends with one of the police officers here. He will escort you to the ferry, and he will see you all the way to the train station so that nothing happens."

"Thank you so much, Georges. You're a life saver, you know that?"

He strips off his thick black coat and wool gloves, handing them back to me. "Take these. The ferry ride will be freezing tonight, and you didn't quite dress for the mountain snow, did you?"

I chuckle in spite of myself and take his coat and gloves without protest. If this man has grandchildren, he's probably the best grandpa ever. "Thank you again, Georges. I'll keep your card so that when this is all over I can repay you."

"That won't be necessary, Mademoiselle," he says as I'm slipping on the warm coat.

He escorts me into the station, introduces me to his officer friend, then places a hand on my shoulder before leaving. "Remember, Mademoiselle Chambord, the answer to the mystery is not always as obvious as you may think."

And with that, Georges, my angel chauffeur, leaves my side, a bitter gust of wind rattling the double doors at his back and whipping into the station with a fury.

Before I can process what he's just said to me, the police officer rushes me out to his car, turns on the lights and the siren, and speeds through this winter wonderland resort town to get me to the ten o'clock ferry in time.

CHAPTER 9

The Lausanne train station lights up the dark night sky, its glowing white clock reading 10:47 P.M. Samuel's train should be arriving any minute.

All of Samuel's instructions went according to plan: the thirty-minute ferry ride, the car waiting for me right as I debarked, and a smooth, albeit snowy, ride to the Lausanne train station…the same station where Isla was last seen boarding a train only two nights ago.

I wait silently in the back of the heated car, and despite Georges's massive winter coat that hangs on me, I am still shivering, my dazed head trying to make sense out of everything that has happened so far. The chauffeur's mysterious words repeat again and again in my confused mind.

Did Georges mean to imply that the Morels aren't necessarily behind Isla's disappearance even though it seems blatantly obvious that they are? How does he know anything about them though? And he couldn't possibly know about Senator Williams or his connection to Isla, could he?

Who *is* Georges the driver anyway? And what does he know about the Morels, about my sister, and about me?

Before I can get too lost in thought, my new driver—one of Samuel's fellow investigators—rustles around in the front seat.

"Fuck," he mutters under his breath, checking the rear view mirror.

"What is it? Is something wrong?" I ask.

"It looks like we have company."

"What? But how is that possible?"

"No disrespect Miss Chambord, but you have no idea who you're dealing with here. Stay low, and whatever happens, don't get out of this car." He pulls the car away from the curb and takes off down the road.

"But Samuel will be here any minute. We can't leave him," I say, scrunching down in the backseat.

"We have to move. We don't have a choice. Whoever wants to find you is not going to play nice." The investigator checks his rearview mirror once more, then swerves around an empty traffic circle.

I search around me for a seat belt, but I'm too late. Someone smashes into us from behind, propelling our car forward over an icy patch of snow. We fishtail around until we're facing the opposite direction.

Headlights blast straight for us. I don't even have time to flinch. The second blow is so hard, my head whips back, bouncing violently against the headrest.

Just as I'm blinking my eyes open and registering the pain shooting through my neck, the driver reaches his hand into the back seat, slipping me a black nine-millimeter.

"Do you know how to use one of these?" he asks, pulling another pistol from inside his coat.

I rip off my over-sized gloves and wrap my hands around the gun. "Yes, I do," I say. I've had to use one before, in the most unimaginable of circumstances, but I push those memories aside. I have no problem shooting a gun again if I have to. Especially if it means saving my own life so I can reach Isla *before* she loses hers.

"Good," he says, rolling down his window. Without hesitation, he takes aim and shoots.

The deafening sound of shattering glass pierces my ear drums, and before I realize what has just happened, I see scarlet red drops splattering all over the driver's pale hands, oozing down over the curve of the steering wheel, and rolling down his fallen head.

Samuel's colleague—the man who was supposed to keep me safe until Samuel arrives—isn't moving.

I resist the urge to scream and instead focus on the adrenaline soaring through my veins, drowning out the fear that threatens to paralyze me.

Samuel's colleague has been shot in the head. He's dead, and if I don't get the hell away from this car, I will be too.

Gripping the gun tightly in my hands, I notice that for once, I'm not trembling. I crack open the car door, duck down as low as I can, and slip out into the snowy night. Skidding around to the back of the car, I peek up just slightly to see if I can make out the shooter. I don't see anyone coming for me, which gives me hope that the shot Samuel's colleague fired just before he was killed may have actually hit the bastard who was coming for me.

A bitter gust of wind slams into me as snow sparkles in the blinding headlight war ahead. The street is eerily silent, but I am poised, ready to shoot at the slightest noise.

Suddenly the sound of boots crunching over snow makes the hairs on the back of my neck stand up. I crouch against the back of the car, watching the white puffs of breath that form at my lips as I wait for the steps to get a little closer.

I peek around the car and spot a patch of crimson snow. But it's not Samuel's colleague's blood that's pooling on the ground. It belongs to the man who is stumbling along the side of the car, searching for me as blood drains from the wound in his chest.

I don't recognize the man's cold, hard face, his thin lips twisted in anguish. I imagine this killer, who is dressed in black from head to toe, is just a pawn in the Williams-Morel cover-up of whatever has happened to my sister. A hit man who has been hired to take me down and who will probably earn a nice sum of cash when he delivers.

But that isn't going to happen.

I slide up from my crouched position behind the car, aim for his knee, and just as my perpetrator fumbles to lift his gun, I shoot.

He collapses into the bloodstained snow with a groan, and I take off toward the train station, envisioning Isla's violet eyes as I run.

The inside of the Lausanne train station is mostly deserted on this harsh winter night. I imagine families curled up in front of crackling fireplaces, watching Christmas lights twinkle as they sip warm mugs of *chocolat chaud*, and prepare for Christmas Day festivities.

But this winter wonderland Swiss town is not so charming tonight as I shiver alone in a dark corner of the train station, staring at the arrivals and departures screen. I note that only two trains are passing through Lausanne in this last half an hour before the clock strikes midnight. One of them is a Venice Simplon-Orient-Express train—the same luxury train that Isla boarded from this exact train station only two nights ago. The other must be Samuel's.

I head to the platform where both trains will be crossing through on opposite tracks, keeping one eye over my shoulder the whole time to make sure no one is following me.

Sirens shoot through the night just as I reach the platform. The Swiss police are about to discover the carnage waiting for them in the traffic circle just down the road from the station, but hopefully Samuel will arrive before they discover me too.

The pistol weighs heavily inside the large black coat I'm still wearing, and my frozen fingertips are ready to pull for it should the need arise.

I gaze through the blanket of snow that swirls above my head, dusting the round, glowing clock hanging above the platform. The ticking grates at my nerves, but I try to stay calm and be patient.

Round, fluffy snowflakes flitter down from the black sky, covering the tracks, inch by inch. The distant sound of a train whistle blowing sends hope into this frozen body of mine. But just as I'm peering down the tracks, glimpsing the first sign of light through the sheets of snow, a soft female voice travels through the night.

"Jillian."

My heart pounds as I flip around and find an older woman standing before me, her shoulder-length, silvery white hair glistening in the glowing halo of snow that twirls around her.

"My name is Madeleine Morel. I'm Frédéric's aunt and Laurent's sister." The woman's sapphire eyes smile warmly at me underneath thick black lashes, the graceful lines of age on her soft pink skin revealing experience, knowledge.

Madeleine Morel—the beautiful older woman in the portrait that I'd discovered hiding in the Morels' storage closet.

"I'm sorry if I startled you, but I have something urgent you need to see. Something that will help you find Isla," she says.

"How did you find me here?" I ask.

"Georges, the chauffeur who dropped you off at the police station, is my twin brother."

Suddenly that silvery gleam in her pretty blue eyes rings a bell. Georges boasted those same intriguing eyes. And the same warm demeanor.

Something isn't adding up though.

"I read the plaque on the Morels' wall," I tell her. "It said you only had one brother, Laurent."

"It is a long story, some of which I'm about to tell you right now." She peeks warily over her shoulder. "But we don't have much time."

In her hands, Madeleine's carrying an old, tattered shoe box. She lifts the lid to show me the contents. Inside are stacks of old letters along with a few black-and-white photographs.

The train whistle blows again, but the train is still a ways down the tracks as Madeline plucks the top letter from the stack, opens it up, and hands it to me.

I hold the crinkled paper underneath the dim glow of the lamp overhead. Faded French words line the yellowed page, and before I know it, I am transported to another time.

1 décembre 1937

My dearest Rosie,

The days are long and cold without you. But my love for you will never run cold. It is as warm and alive as the sun beating down on the hot coals on a blazing summer day.

As I sit in the barracks, counting the days until my exit from the army, I envision you on that very first day. The day you swooped into my life without warning, an angel with curly brown hair and a dimple that drives me wild every time I see it.

You were wearing that sky-blue dress, the one that brings out the sapphire color in your eyes. All it took was one sweet smile from you, and I was yours. I always will be.

I'll be waiting for you at the train station in Paris on Christmas morning, mon amour. Nothing in the world could stop me from being there to kiss you when you step off that train. It will be the best day of my life...the day I can finally call you my own.

I love you, Rosie Delaney.

Yours, always and forever,

Jacques

Before I can mutter a single word, Madeleine hands me an old photograph. I aim the picture away from the shadows and squint to make out the face of the young man in the photo.

"Turn it over," Madeleine instructs.

When I do, the words staring back at me suddenly make me realize that my ties to this old love story run so much deeper than I ever could've imagined.

Jacques Chambord, 1937.

"But Jacques Chambord is...*was* my grandfather," I say incredulously. "He was my mother's dad, but I never met him. He died before I was born. And Rosie Delaney—she's the girl that went missing in 1937, abducted from the Orient Express train, just like my sister."

Madeleine nods. "Yes, your grandfather Jacques was at the train station that morning, as promised, but Rosie never stepped off the train."

"Just like Isla and Christophe," I whisper. "How did you get these letters? Did you know my grandfather?"

"When Rosie stepped on the train from this very station just before midnight, she chose to leave everything behind. Her family, her fiancé, her riches, everything. All to be with the one man she truly loved. The man she would've married, the man who was the father of the twins she was carrying."

"Are you saying…?"

"Yes, Jillian. Rosie and Jacques were my and Georges's parents. Only we never got to meet them. We were taken from our mother shortly after we were born. I was raised within the Morel family, told I was one of them, and Georges was given up for adoption. But I always knew I was different. I always knew they were hiding something. And just last year, I met Georges for the first time, and the puzzle pieces started falling into place."

"What are you saying? That the Morels kidnapped you and Georges from Rosie? Do you know what happened to her? Who took her and who killed the other two women from that train?"

The train whistle blows a third time as it nears us, its wheels barreling over the snow-covered tracks. Madeleine shoots a glance at the glossy carriages that are quickly approaching, at the steam billowing into the night sky.

She grabs my wrist, her white gloves warm against my frosty skin, then lowers her voice. "I have to go now. They're watching us, Jillian. You need to get on that Orient Express train tonight. The train will lead you to Isla. And the contents of this box will tell you everything else you need to know."

Madeleine pulls two tickets out of the pocket of her navy-blue pea coat.

"Take these. You'll need them to ride the train. And don't stop until you find them. Do you understand me? Don't give up."

"I don't understand. What are you talking about, Madeleine? Who's watching us? Do you know who took Rosie? Are Frédéric and Senator Williams behind Isla's disappearance?"

The shiny blue Venice Simplon-Orient-Express train pulls into the station beside us as Madeleine lowers her face to my ear. "It's more complicated than that, but there isn't enough time to explain. It is up to you to save them *both*, Jillian. This is in your hands now."

She fits the lid firmly over the shoe box, gives me one last mysterious nod, then walks swiftly down the platform until the snowfall wipes her silhouette from my vision.

"Mademoiselle, are you boarding?" the conductor calls out to me in French as he steps down from the train. His spiffy, royal-blue uniform and pristine white gloves are a welcome sight on this cold, frightening evening.

Just as I'm about to answer him, a second train rolls down the tracks to my right. This one isn't as showy as the Orient Express, but it does have something I need—Samuel.

"The Venice Simplon-Orient-Express will be leaving in three minutes, Mademoiselle." The conductor's deep voice booms through the snowy night, but my eyes are glued to the other train as it squeaks to a stop in front of me.

Only a few passengers disembark at this late hour on Christmas Eve, and I am beginning to lose hope that Samuel is actually coming, when suddenly his dark five o'clock shadow—which is even more rugged than it was this morning—catches my eye.

My ex-boyfriend, my former love, and the man who I realize I cannot wait to see, bounds toward me, his green gaze cutting right through the blizzard of snow falling around us. I notice the relief in his eyes as he approaches me, but I don't say a word. Instead, I take his hand and lead him across the platform to the Orient Express.

Releasing Samuel's hand, I reach for the train tickets Madeleine gave me and hand them to the conductor. Like the snowflakes that whip violently around us with each gust of wind, Madeleine's mysterious words continue to whirl through my head. I wonder how she knew I would need two tickets, and more importantly, I wonder what she meant when she said it is up to me to *save them both*.

"Jillian, what are you doing?" Snow dusts the shoulders of Samuel's black overcoat as he shoots me a curious glance. "And what's that box in your hands?"

The conductor checks the tickets, smiles, then gestures for us to board the train.

Ignoring Samuel's questions, I take his hand in mine once more, and although I couldn't explain it if I tried, I simply know that we must get on this train. I can feel myself getting closer to Isla. It's a bizarre sensation—having this twin, this other half, whom I can be worlds apart from, but still feel her as if she's right next to me.

I've felt this invisible, unbreakable connection to her for our entire lives. It was this connection that led me back home to her on the horrifying day when she almost lost her life at the hands of our own mother.

It was the day that forever changed our lives, the day when this bond we share, this connection, was the *only* thing that saved her.

Our connection hasn't lessened with time. If anything, it is stronger, more powerful.

The train whistle sounds through the night, and I know it's time.

My grip on Samuel's hand tightens as I step onto the luxurious sleeper car. The minute I feel the heat blasting through the train and take in the scents of red wine and leather suitcases, I envision Isla boarding only a few nights ago. I can see the excitement in her violet eyes, her hand resting ever so gently on her tiny belly, protecting the even tinier baby that sleeps inside.

"Jillian," Samuel says, the voice of reason in my ear. "I know what you're thinking. But riding the same train that Isla took won't magically take you to her. We've got a team on the ground searching—"

But the conductor cuts him off by slamming the train door closed behind us.

"Jillian," Samuel says firmly. "Let's go."

"Mademoiselle, I believe you dropped this," the conductor says, bending over to pick something up.

Inside his tightly fitted white glove is a sparkling emerald ring.

"It fell out of the box you were carrying," he says.

But I'm unable to respond because I am totally and completely mesmerized by this ring.

The conductor hands the emerald to Samuel, and I notice that he too seems to be enamored with the beautiful stone. Samuel stops trying to convince me to deboard the train with him, and instead takes the ring from the conductor and slips it onto my ring finger.

"A perfect fit," he says softly.

"Cabin number seven, just down the corridor." The conductor nods politely for us to follow him to our sleeping compartment.

But I barely register his voice. All I can hear is the sound of the train wheels spinning, gaining speed, rolling over the snow, taking us to Isla.

Samuel holds my hands in his, his fingers brushing over the gorgeous emerald ring that shines brilliantly between us.

"Jillian, something strange is happening," he says. "Do you feel that?"

The train whistle blows one last time, and a rush of white-hot energy pours through my body, then pools at my hands where I am connected to Samuel.

I don't feel the train beneath our feet any longer. All I see are swirls of emerald surrounded by blasts of sparkling white snow. Finally, one crimson teardrop stains the flashes of white, and before I can call out to Isla, before I can tell her I'm coming for her, the world around us goes pitch black.

One piercing scream rings through the darkness.

But I'm frozen, paralyzed in space, and I have no idea where this train is headed.

EPISODE 4

CHAPTER 10

Lausanne, Switzerland

An ear-splitting whistle blasts through the night as my feet plant on solid ground. Wheels chug and grind all around me, prompting me to force my eyes open. I struggle to focus my blurred vision on something that isn't moving or swirling. I feel slow and heavy, as if I've been drugged, and I have no clue where I am.

"Jillian, it's me," a deep, familiar voice flows through my ears. "Open your eyes, Jill. Come on."

A pair of strong hands wrapped around mine steadies my wobbly legs momentarily, and finally I can see.

Samuel stands only inches from me, his penetrating green eyes flashing in bewilderment. "Jillian, what in the hell just happened?" he whispers.

I shake my head, knowing instinctively that we have just traveled somewhere. But I have no idea how we got here or even where we are. "I don't know," I tell him.

All I *do* know is that I'm relieved to see the scruff on Samuel's face, the familiarity of his defined jaw line, his full lips, his broad shoulders.

"Madame, Monsieur, suivez-moi, s'il vous plaît." Follow me, please.

A conductor appears at our side wearing a gold-trimmed, royal-blue uniform. The top of his blue hat carries a light dusting of snow, and his cheeks blush pink from the cold. His white-gloved hands are carrying two old-fashioned tan suitcases.

I suddenly remember where we are. We've just boarded the Venice Simplon-Orient-Express train from the snowy Lausanne train station. We're looking for Isla. And we don't have much time.

But something is off.

The conductor's bushy black mustache lifts as he smiles at us.

That mustache. The conductor who took our tickets just moments ago definitely did *not* have a mustache.

And we weren't carrying suitcases when we boarded the train—let alone suitcases that look as if they were made one hundred years ago.

I was carrying an old shoe box that Madeleine Morel thrust into my arms just before she instructed me to climb aboard this train.

Before she told me to "save them *both*."

I scan the space around us, but the shoe box has vanished.

"I'm sorry, Monsieur," I tell the conductor in French. "But there's been a mistake. Those suitcases don't belong to us."

The conductor's dark eyes light up as he chuckles. "I understand your surprise, Madame. Traveling on the Orient Express for the first time is a bit like a dream, is it not?"

The conductor's nonsensical response leaves both Samuel and me standing in a stupor as he takes off down the corridor ahead of us.

"Am I going crazy, or did the conductor suddenly grow a mustache?" Samuel whispers in my ear as we pad over the soft blue carpet behind him.

Before I can respond, a young girl with silky brunette curls approaches the conductor from the other direction, presenting her ticket. The shimmering black and silver hat pinned atop her curls boasts a delicate black netting that fans over her forehead and shadows her long, thick lashes and sapphire eyes. A fancy red velvet coat flows down to her calves, revealing the hem of a sparkling silver evening gown swishing past her ankles.

She looks as if she's just left a glamorous vintage Christmas ball.

As she peeks around the conductor's bright blue uniform, she flashes me a hesitant smile, revealing a small dimple in her rosy cheek. Her knuckles turn white as she clutches the handle of her cherry-red suitcase, her other hand cupped protectively over her abdomen.

I smile back at the young girl, noticing how her fingertips have turned bright pink from the cold. I gaze down at my own hands to see if I'm wearing gloves, but I forget all about my search for gloves as the sparkling emerald on my left ring finger steals my breath.

A memory of the *other* conductor handing this mysterious emerald to Samuel just after we boarded the train comes rushing back to me. I remember the way Samuel gazed down at the striking ring, as if the stone had put him in a trance.

The train jolts forward once more, gaining momentum as the conductor speaks. "You'll be sleeping in compartment number three, Mademoiselle." He points a pristine white glove down the corridor. "I'll be by in just a moment, once I install this couple."

I steady myself against the shiny wooden panels lining the hallway as the young girl, who could be straight out of a 1930s black-and-white film, walks swiftly past us. The scents of lipstick, perfume, and champagne swirl underneath my nose, making me feel dizzy again.

What is going on? Why is she dressed like that?

Samuel places a hand on my lower back, prodding me forward as the conductor installs the luggage that does not belong to us in a fancy sleeping compartment to our right.

"A late dinner is being served in the dining car, should you desire a meal at this hour," says the conductor with a polite nod as he eyes our clothing. "Dinner attire is formal, of course. Also, we will be crossing the Swiss-French border en route to Paris, and so as to not disturb you while you are sleeping, I will require both of your passports at your earliest convenience."

I realize with a start that I've never heard someone speak French in such a formal manner. The conductor sounds strangely old-fashioned, almost as if he's from another time.

"*Excusez-moi, Monsieur,*" Samuel says. "Where did the other conductor go? The gentleman who took our tickets a few minutes ago."

The conductor raises a curious, bushy black eyebrow, and his matching mustache twitches slightly. "Why, it was I who collected your tickets just moments ago."

"That's not possible. What is going on here?" Samuel's accusatory tone startles fear into the conductor's eyes.

"If you'll excuse me, I need to help the young mademoiselle who boarded just after you, Monsieur. I shall return in a few moments for your passports." The conductor begins to close the cabin door, but I reach my hand out and stop it just before it clicks shut.

"Monsieur," I call into the corridor. "Do you happen to have a copy of today's newspaper?"

"*Mais, bien sûr, Madame.* You'll find *Le Figaro* on your night-stand." And with a curt nod, he is off to compartment number three to help the young girl with the bouncy curls, the vintage clothes, and the cherry-red suitcase.

I allow the door to close all the way this time, then push past a confused Samuel and kneel down in front of the nightstand. A folded newspaper sits to the right of the lamp. With shaky fingers, I open its crisp pages and blink at the date staring back at me.

That can't be right.

But no matter how many times I refocus, the date stamped on the front page of France's *Le Figaro* newspaper stays the same.

"Samuel, you need to see this." I stand to my feet and shove the newspaper into his hands. "The date at the top of the page...it...it says..." I can't even bring myself to say the words aloud.

I have spent my entire journalism career searching for facts, for tangible truths, and then exposing those truths. But the date that now mocks Samuel's perplexed gaze is neither factual nor tangible. It is the stuff that fairytales are made of—and after the horror show of a childhood I lived through, I learned very quickly never to believe in fairytales.

The color drains from Samuel's cheeks as he reads aloud, "24 décembre 1937."

Wiping the doubt clean from his eyes, he tosses the newspaper onto the fancy sofa bed behind me. "Jillian, the train that we're on—the Venice Simplon-Orient-Express—is a modern-day throwback to the original Orient Express train that ran all through the 1900s. This train is *supposed* to have a vintage feel. They even restored some of the original carriages from the twenties and thirties to make it that much more authentic. To make you *feel* as if you're traveling on the real Orient Express train."

A haze of white flakes flies past the window as the train picks up momentum. I notice once again the loud chugging, grinding, and whistling sounds that this particular train makes as we roll down the tracks. These are *not* the sounds of a modern-day train, but if what Samuel is saying is true, that we are in fact riding on a refurbished version of a nearly one-hundred-year-old train, then the intense sounds vibrating loudly through our sleeping compartment make sense.

But there are still other bizarre parts of the past ten minutes that do not, in any way, make sense.

"You can't deny the fact that something really strange happened to us when we boarded the train." I wave my left hand in his face. "Right after the conductor handed you this emerald ring, and you placed it on my finger…it felt like time was suspended for a moment. It felt like we traveled somewhere. I know this is beyond insane, but you felt it too. I know you did."

A flicker of doubt passes through Samuel's mossy eyes, but he blinks it away. "I think we're both just exhausted from the past two days. We barely slept on the plane last night, and—"

"But what about the conductor's mustache?" I counter. "And the way he talks? And that girl's old-fashioned clothing? She looked like she could've been a 1930s movie star, for God's sake." I snap the newspaper off the bed and flash the date in front of Samuel's face once again, the pitch of my voice becoming more frantic by the second. "How do you explain all of this?"

He combs the front page once more, shaking his head. "Okay. I did feel something strange happening, but you couldn't possibly believe—"

"Oh, my God," I cut him off with a whisper. "This is what she meant." My knees buckle, and I drop to the sofa bed behind me.

"This is what who meant?" Samuel asks, kneeling down in front of me. "What are you talking about?"

"Madeleine Morel—Laurent Morel's sister, and Frédéric's aunt. She followed me to the train station right before you arrived. She was the one who gave me the train tickets and that shoe box I was carrying. The same box that this emerald ring apparently fell out of—the box that seemed to disappear into thin air when we arrived here, on *this* train."

Samuel places his hands on my shivering knees and lowers his voice. "I know who Madeleine Morel is. But why did she follow you here? And what else was inside that box?"

"She told me that she's not really a Morel. And that her real mother was a woman named Rosie Delaney."

"But Rosie Delaney was one of the young women who was abducted from the Orient Express train in 1937..." Samuel trails off, flashing his eyes at me as if he's seen a ghost. "She was the one who was never found."

I wrap my fingers around Samuel's wrists, if for nothing more than to feel the blood pulsing through his veins, to ground myself to something real and solid, because the world around us seems to be moving at a pace neither of us can keep up with.

"There's more," I say. "Madeleine told me that the night Rosie was abducted from the Orient Express, she boarded the train from the Lausanne station—the exact same station *we* just boarded from."

Samuel's eyes flicker toward the cabin door. I can almost see the wheels spinning inside his head as he mulls this over, and I know he is remembering that young woman we saw in the corridor just moments ago, with her simple, yet glamorous, old-world beauty. But Samuel's practicality, that unending rationality that mirrors my own, is stopping him from admitting what I am certain we are both thinking.

I grab the sides of his face so he can't avoid my gaze. So he can't deny what is happening to us right now. "That young woman who boarded the train right after us, the one in the vintage hat with the sparkly evening gown peeking out from under her coat. That could be her, Samuel. If this is really Christmas Eve, 1937, that woman could be Rosie Delaney."

Samuel shakes his head at me, his jaw tightening. "No, Jillian. This isn't real. There's no way—"

"I don't want to believe it either," I say, shooting up from the bed, pacing back and forth inside the tiny compartment. "I can't even believe I'm saying this out loud. Madeleine's words didn't make any sense at the time, but it's all coming together now. She told me that it was up to me...that it was up to me to *save them both*."

"But that isn't possible, Jillian. Get it together!" Samuel stands to meet my gaze, stopping my pacing with a firm hand on my shoulder.

"Maybe this is our chance to find out what happened to Rosie Delaney and the other two girls the *first* time around. And hopefully, somehow, that will lead us back to Isla."

"Jill, are you hearing yourself? How on earth would *time traveling* back to the train where Rosie Delaney was abducted in 1937 take you to Isla in 2012? I mean, it's clear that we're dealing with a copycat crime, and we know that the Morels and Senator Williams are in some way involved in Isla's abduction. We've established that much. But time travel? So we can solve a mystery that happened *seventy-five years ago*? You're losing your mind here."

"Clearly I don't have all the answers," I snap, shrugging his hands off of me. "But Madeleine told me that when Rosie boarded the train that night, just like Isla she was pregnant and heading to Paris to meet the man she'd fallen in love with, the father of her twins. And the piece of this whole crazy story you *don't* know is that the man Rosie was going to meet in Paris was my grandfather, Jacques Chambord."

"What?" Samuel says.

"You heard me. Rosie was in love with my grandfather. I never met him because he died shortly after my mother was born, but his connection to Rosie has to mean something. There has to be a reason for all of this."

"Listen, the Morel family is not to be trusted right now," Samuel says. "That means Madeleine too. You don't have any proof that the details she told you are true, and we're certainly not going to find proof on this train. We need to get off at the next stop, and—"

"The letters," I interject. "Inside the box Madeleine gave me, there were stacks of old love letters. The one I read was dated December 1, 1937, and it was from my grandfather to Rosie. He said he would be waiting for her on Christmas morning at the train station in Paris. But as you and I both know, Rosie never showed up that morning. And while Rosie was never found, whoever took her obviously let her live long enough to give birth to her twins, one of whom—Madeleine—was raised by the Morels. The Morel family never told Madeleine about her real mother, Rosie. And earlier today, when you asked Hélène and Frédéric Morel if they'd ever heard of a woman named Rosie Delaney, they said no."

"Of course it's possible that they were lying…just like they've been lying about everything else," Samuel admits. "My team did some more digging into the Rosie Delaney mystery and found out that she *was* connected to the Morel family. The night she boarded the Orient Express, she was leaving her fiancé, Alexandre Morel."

Chills slither up the backs of my arms. "Just like Isla. Pregnant, leaving her crazy Morel fiancé to be with the man she truly loved. Don't you see, Samuel? It's the exact same story, repeating itself seventy-five years later. And we've come back to find out what happened to Rosie and the other two girls the first time around. Speaking of which, do you know their names? The two girls who were murdered?"

"One of them was a young British woman named Frances Chapman, and the other woman was never identified."

"Never identified? How is that possible?"

"The third woman didn't have a passport or any other identification on her, and apparently didn't leave any ID on the train either. They were never able to find out who she was or where she was from."

"Even her family didn't step forward to say she was missing, to claim her?"

Samuel shakes his head, impatience lining his tone. "No, but that doesn't matter right now. We need to get off this train so I can get back to the investigation and find your sister."

"But what if saving Rosie, Frances, and the third woman, whoever she was, could change everything? What if saving them will help us save Isla?"

Samuel shakes his head and grasps my hands. "This is ludicrous, Jill. Come with me, and I'll prove to you that we haven't time traveled, that we're still in the year 2012, looking for Isla, and that we never should've climbed aboard this godforsaken train at the direction of some crazy old Morel woman."

Samuel leads me out of our compartment, rushing down the corridor ahead of me until we burst into the dining car.

At least ten passengers are dining and drinking, their laughter, cigarette smoke, and late-night banter swirling through the fancy dining car that looks more like an elegant five-star restaurant than the inside of a moving train.

I pinch Samuel's arm as the woman sitting closest to us takes notice of our bewildered faces and our inappropriate evening attire.

A stunning black evening gown hugs the woman's slim figure, while a sheer layer of black lace covers her collarbone and shoulders, and a long string of shiny pears dangles from her neck. A pair of black satin gloves graces her hands—one of which holds a skinny cigarette, while the other is wrapped around the sparkling stem of her wine glass. Her chin-length black hair glistens in the low lamplight, her perfect waves pinned back by a diamond barrette.

The woman's blood red lips puff on her cigarette as she eyes us curiously, then nudges the man who is sitting opposite her. His dark brown hair is combed and gelled perfectly to the side, his black top hat and spiffy tuxedo jacket hanging on the hook at his back.

I catch Samuel staring back at the glamorous 1930s couple, an incredulous look flashing through his eyes.

"I'll bet you a million bucks they're *not* from the twenty-first century," I whisper in his ear.

Samuel places a hesitant hand on the edge of their table. "*Pardon,*" Samuel begins, but I can see that he's faltering. He's faltering because he already knows the answer to the question he's about to ask.

"Can you tell me today's date?" Samuel finally spits out his question in French, his accent thickened by his nerves.

"Why, it's Christmas Eve of course," the man responds before straightening his black bow tie and pinching his eyebrows together.

"Yes, of course," Samuel says. "But would you be so kind as to tell me the year?"

The man hesitates as his eyes dart back and forth between the frantic looks splashed across our faces. Finally, he says the words I'm waiting to hear. The words that prove I am not imagining the dated clothing and the formal speech flittering past my ears.

The words that prove I haven't actually lost my mind.

"*C'est le 24 décembre, 1937, Monsieur.*"

Samuel grasps my hand and takes a purposeful step back from their table before shooting a panicked glance at all of the other dinner patrons who are also dressed in equally elegant, classic clothing, and who are now whispering and staring at us as if we're from a different planet.

That's about how I feel as we jet out of that dining car and lock ourselves back in sleeping compartment number seven.

Samuel runs his hands through his light brown hair and picks up where I left off with the pacing. "Holy shit," he mumbles under his breath. "How in the hell did this happen?"

The train picks up speed once again, and although I feel just as bewildered as Samuel, I also know that we don't have much time to figure it all out. To save Rosie. And to find out how to get back to Isla.

I clutch onto Samuel's strong shoulders and force him to stop pacing, to look me in the eye and acknowledge that no matter how insane this situation is, *it's real.*

"Sometime in the next hour, Rosie Delaney and two other innocent women are going to be taken from this train," I say, refusing to allow my voice to waver, refusing to reveal the fear that is pumping through me faster than this train is barreling down the snow-covered tracks.

"And we have to stop it from happening," I say.

"Jill—"

"You can either help me save them, or you can sit on this moving train and deny what you *know* is happening to us right now. This is our chance, Samuel. And I'm not going to waste it."

CHAPTER 11

Vintage dresses, hats, and undergarments fly through the air as Samuel and I ransack the two suitcases that the conductor deposited in our sleeping compartment, despite my fervent protests that those antique *valises* did not belong to us.

One of the dated suitcases has clearly been packed for a woman of my size, and the other for a man of Samuel's size, which plants the bizarre notion that *someone* knew we would be riding on this 1937 Orient Express train tonight and that both Samuel and I would need period clothing so as not to draw more unnecessary attention to ourselves than we already had.

As I remove one long, flowing evening gown after the next, I remember Madeleine's words just before she left me alone on the snowy platform.

The train will lead you to Isla. And the contents of this box will tell you everything else you need to know.

From what I could see in the dark train station, the box Madeleine gave me only held stacks of love letters from Jacques to Rosie and a few black-and-white photographs. Apparently, it also held the dazzling emerald ring that fits perfectly on my left ring finger.

Did Madeleine know that this would happen to us? That somehow this train, this ring, these letters would transport Samuel and me back in time to Rosie?

"You're not going to have time to try them all on, Jill." Samuel eyes me as he smoothes the wrinkles out of a black 1930s suit jacket. "Any of those dresses will look stunning on you."

A flush creeps up my neck as Samuel strips off his black suit jacket, then unbuttons his white shirt. I tear my gaze away from the muscles rippling down his torso and try to focus on choosing one of these slim, lacy gowns. But when Samuel turns his back to me and slips off his pants, I can't help but take a peek at the man I gave up over six years ago.

The man I've never stopped thinking about since.

The sight of his broad shoulders and ripped back muscles sends a swirl of excitement to my abdomen, and that swirl continues dipping lower…and still lower as Samuel swivels to the side and reveals the tattoo covering his left bicep.

He cocks a brow at me before I can make out the design, and I immediately divert my gaze and pretend to fiddle with the buttons on the dress I'm holding. As soon as he goes back to getting dressed, I can't stop myself—my eyes are combing every square inch of his body.

Three thick scars line the muscles on his lower back, and another jagged scar slices across the left side of his chest. Following the veins that shoot down his forearms and wrap around his strong hands, I spot another tattoo lining the inside of his right wrist. As I squint in the dim cabin light, I make out seven sets of initials.

I want to ask him whose initials are tattooed on his arm, who gave him the scars on his back and chest, and how in the span of six years he has changed from the young man I once loved to this hot-blooded investigator who hunts the earth for missing women.

I want to know the story behind his scars, behind his pain. I want to know the story of the past six years—the experiences he has lived through that have made his stance so much stronger, so much more determined and confident than I remember, and the training that has added a layer of muscle to his entire body, that has made his movements quicker, more calculated.

I know of course that in the years since our all-consuming love, Samuel has lived through the abduction and ghastly murder of the woman he married after I left him. There is no doubt that the horror of it all molded him into a new man, a rougher, wounded, more strong-minded man. A man who even after all the lies I've told him, would still choose to help me find my sister.

Attempting to focus back on the task at hand—*get dressed, find Rosie Delaney*—I only hope that one day I'll be able to erase the image of Samuel's tattooed arms and his rough-around-the-edges, sexy body from my mind.

There was a reason I never wanted to see him again...a reason I *did not* want to be alone with him.

I shrug off the large black overcoat that Georges, the chauffeur, so generously gave me, then slip off my gray suit jacket. Just as I begin to unbutton my thin white blouse, Samuel's hand wraps around my waist.

I can't ignore the heat that blazes through my core and down in between my thighs as Samuel spins me around to face him, then lifts his hand to my chin, tipping it up toward his face.

He still hasn't put a shirt on, and the scent of his bare skin is beyond intoxicating. I can barely suck in a breath as I look into his eyes.

But Samuel isn't meeting my gaze. Instead he is inspecting the side of my neck and the shoulder of my blouse.

"Why are you covered in blood?" he asks. "What happened before you met me at the train station?"

As I recount the terrifying car chase that ended with the murder of Samuel's colleague and me shooting the perpetrator in the knee before escaping to the train station, Samuel's firm grip on my waist doesn't falter. Neither does his intense gaze.

I want to tell him to back away from me, that I can hardly concentrate or speak when he is this close to me, when I can feel the heat of his breath fanning across my cheek, down my neck, and over my collarbone.

But I stick to telling him the facts of what happened outside the Lausanne train station no more than an hour ago—which in actuality, is really seventy-five years in the future. I can't even begin to wrap my mind around the seventy-five-year time gap we have mysteriously erased by hopping on this train. But even more than that, I am having a hard time wrapping my mind around the fact that it is *Samuel*—the only man I have ever truly loved, the only one I have ever had any desire to open up to—who has made this impossible voyage with me.

And whether it's 2012 or 1937, he *still* has the same effect on me. I don't tell him this though.

Instead I tell him about the pistol, the shots, the snowstorm, the murder.

"Do you still have the gun?" Samuel asks after I finish the gruesome story.

I point at the black coat I've just tossed onto the suitcase. "It should still be in there. That is, if it made the trip with us."

Samuel's hand finally slips from my waist, and I am relieved to feel a release of breath exhaling from my lungs. He searches the large coat and quickly retrieves the black pistol from the inside pocket. Checking to see if there is still ammunition, he narrows his eyes at me. "Only someone who knows how to use a gun would be able to hit and escape a trained assassin. When have you used a gun before, Jill?"

I turn away from Samuel's penetrating gaze and continue unbuttoning my shirt. "We don't have time for all of that right now. That snowdrift could be stopping this train any minute. We need to get dressed and get our asses back to the dining car to find Rosie Delaney."

I strip down to my black lacy bra and matching underwear, silently thanking the heavens that I'd found my last clean pair before jetting out of my messy Rosslyn apartment yesterday morning. Samuel rustles around behind me, and just before I slip on the long violet evening gown I've chosen from my new assortment of 1930s clothing, I feel a warm washcloth dabbing at my neck.

"The blood has to go. But the gun will definitely be coming with us tonight," Samuel says.

I turn to the side as he slides the damp towel over my bare skin. I catch his eyes focusing on the tops of my breasts, then running down the length of my body.

"Are you finished yet?" I ask him. I can't take this half-naked proximity with my outrageously sexy ex-boyfriend any longer.

He nods as he runs the towel further down my chest, where I am certain there aren't any bloodstains. He leans into my ear, the feel of his other hand slipping around my waist startling me, making me lose my resolve to stay strong, to resist the overwhelming urge I have to wrap my arms around his neck and let him take me, let him possess me the way he used to.

Samuel's deep voice resonates in my ear. "I'm finished...for now. But one of these days in the not-so-distant future, you're going to owe me."

Desire ripples through my stomach as I try to calm the rapid breath that has seized my chest. "Owe you what?" I ask.

"The truth about who you really are."

CHAPTER 12

Samuel appears by my side, dressed in an old-fashioned tuxedo complete with a shiny black bow tie and a top hat that makes him look like a buffer version of Fred Astaire. He is dashing and rugged all at the same time, and I can't help but feel a violent stab of regret for leaving him all those years ago. The regret only serves to make my hands shake as I prepare to slip on the final touch to my own 1930s dinner costume—a pair of long, black, silky gloves.

First though, I need to remove the sparkling emerald from my ring finger. I try to slip it off, but the stunning piece of antique jewelry will not budge. I tug harder, and even though the ring doesn't appear to be too tight, it still hugs my finger in exactly the same spot—a permanent fixture on my trembling hand.

"Need help?" Samuel offers.

"I'm trying to get this ring off so I can put my gloves on. All of the women in the dining car were wearing gloves, and we've already humiliated ourselves once tonight. I'd like to fit in so we actually have a chance to talk to Rosie and the other girls."

Samuel takes my hand, wrapping his fingers around the ring and pulling lightly, but even for him the ring won't move. He pulls a little harder, but with each tug the ring actually seems to squeeze tighter onto my finger.

"Do you think this ring had something to do with landing us here?" I whisper, knowing how insane my question sounds. But then again, what about this whole time traveling extravaganza *isn't* insane?

Samuel shakes his head in frustration after one last unsuccessful tug, then reaches for the gloves in my other hand. "I don't know how in the hell we got here, Jill. But if we want any shot at making it back, you need to forget about the damn ring and put these gloves on so we can stop whatever is going to happen on this train in the next hour."

Despite Samuel's usual cool, collected demeanor in the face of a crisis, even *he* seems to be on edge tonight. Then again, traveling back in time seventy-five years to stop a mysterious train abduction and double murder from occurring isn't your everyday crisis.

I slide the elegant gloves onto my hands, fitting them *over* the emerald stone and pushing the smooth material all the way up to my elbows. Then I pluck a shiny silver clutch from the suitcase, squeeze the gun into its silky lining, and sling the delicate purse strap over my shoulder.

Samuel holds his arm out to me. "You remember our story? And the plan?"

Even though I have never felt my heart race quite this fast, I give Samuel a confident nod as I slip my arm through his. "I'm a reporter, and I *never* forget a story."

Samuel doesn't question me any further as we exit our sleeping cabin and stroll down the fancy train corridor, just another wealthy, married 1930s couple on their way to Christmas Eve dinner on the famous Orient Express.

Even though it is dangerously close to midnight, every beautifully set table in the elegant dining car is occupied. As I cast a quick glance through the heated car, I marvel at each of the women's luxurious evening gowns, the shimmering diamonds dangling from their ears, the pearls adorning their necks, and the handsome, tuxedo-clad men who accompany them.

Samuel nods toward the back of the car, where two women are dining solo, each at their own table, with their backs to us. We stroll casually in their direction, and I hope that none of the passengers who witnessed the bewildered looks on our faces and our out-of-place clothing a little while ago will recognize us now.

When I catch a glimpse of my reflection in the steamy train window, I realize that *I* barely recognize myself. My long violet gown swishes as I walk, hugging my figure in places I wish it did not… although I'm certain by the way Samuel—my pretend husband for the night—combed my body earlier with that intense gaze of his, he doesn't mind in the least.

As we approach the backs of the two women, I notice that one is donning a showy fur shawl around her bare shoulders while her smooth blond hair twists up into an intricately designed diamond headpiece. The other young woman has silky brown curls that slide over her shoulders as she lifts her striking sapphire gaze to ours.

Rosie.

I just know it's her.

Samuel doesn't miss a beat as he flashes the girl with the curls a warm smile. *"Bonsoir, Mademoiselle."* The French rolls off his tongue with ease this time, melding perfectly with his impeccable charm. *"Parlez-vous anglais?"*

I notice her left hand instinctively running over her abdomen as she peers at us underneath a set of long, curly lashes. "Oh dear, is it that obvious that I'm the only American on the train tonight?" Her big blue eyes twinkle as she smiles sweetly, revealing that same dimple I noticed earlier in the corridor.

"Well, you're certainly not alone," I say. "My husband and I are from Washington, D.C."

"Oh, how lovely," the young girl replies. She opens her plump lips as if she's about to say something else, but then stops herself.

"The late night dinner on the Orient Express must be exquisite. It appears that all of the other tables have been taken," I say with a lighthearted laugh. "Would it be terribly inconvenient if we joined you for dinner?"

Before she gives me an answer, the blond woman in the fur shawl stands from her table behind us and places a silky black glove on Samuel's shoulder. "I would love company tonight," she says in a sophisticated British accent. "Although the ride on the Orient Express is most extraordinary, dining alone on Christmas Eve is still rather depressing. Perhaps we can all join Miss...?" she raises a brow, waiting for the girl with the curls to say her name.

"Rosemary," the young girl responds. "But you can call me Rosie. And of course you may join me for dinner. It is Christmas, after all."

Clad in a spotless white coat with a long white apron tied around his waist, the server appears at our table, a matching white cloth draped over his arm and a bucket of champagne in hand.

"*Une coupe de champagne?*" he offers with a charming smile.

Rosie's curls bob over her shoulders as she shakes her head, smiling politely back at the waiter. "*Non, merci,*" she says quietly as she rests her hand on her abdomen once more.

She's changed out of the sparkling silver gown I glimpsed underneath her red coat earlier and is now wearing a beautiful, yet modest, black dress. I also notice that she is the only woman seated in this dining car who is *not* wearing gloves. Her fingertips are still bright pink, not yet fully recovered from the bitter cold outside.

I remember the voyage I've just made to escape the Morel Château, traveling across the freezing Lake Geneva by ferry, and I wonder if Rosie has just finished the same trip in her efforts to leave her fiancé, Alexandre Morel, and meet my grandfather in Paris tomorrow morning.

Hopefully, we're about to find out, I think as I take Rosie's lead and decline the champagne. As much as I would love to drown my troubles in a bubby glass, I don't think it's in my best interest to get tipsy before attempting to stop an abduction from taking place. Especially considering the fact that neither Samuel nor I have the faintest clue as to how this is all going to go down.

The server makes the same offer to both Samuel and the striking blond seated across from him, and they both accept.

Moments later, Samuel takes a quick sip from his sparkling crystal flute, then gets right down to business. "I'm sorry, Miss, I didn't get your name," he asks the British woman.

"Frances," she replies, gracefully extending her hand. Samuel clasps her fingers lightly in his before kissing the top of her black glove. "I'm Samuel, and this is my wife, Jillian."

Frances—who I can only assume must be Frances *Chapman*, the second woman listed in the 1937 abduction report—reaches across the table and shakes my hand. "How do you do," she says with a nod. The faint creases that line her eyes tell me she is likely several years older than the young Rosie, who couldn't be more than twenty years old.

Introductions are exchanged with Rosie as well before Samuel continues.

"My wife and I adore traveling Europe by train. In fact that's how we first met," he says, shooting me a romantic wink.

I push the thought of Samuel's rough, tattooed body out of my head and smile back at him. God, that man can really turn on the charm when he wants to.

"Oh, how romantic," Frances purrs before taking a bold sip of her champagne. "I can only hope to meet my future husband on this voyage. He has until London to board, so there's still time."

Rosie giggles, then flashes us all a sweet smile. "I've already met the man I'm going to marry. Well, technically we're not yet engaged, but I'm certain it's only a matter of time before he asks me."

"He must be a wonderful man," I say, thinking of Jacques, the grandfather I never knew. I wonder how things might've turned out differently if Rosie hadn't been taken from him so early in their relationship. Maybe he wouldn't have gone off to World War II, where—according to my mother's vague stories of her parents—he would later lose his life.

But then, if Rosie had never been abducted, Jacques might have never met my grandmother, and then my mother would have never been born.

Although the thought of ending my mother's miserable existence on this earth is comforting in a sickly way, I realize with a start what that would mean for Isla and me.

"Will this love of yours be joining you on the Orient Express tonight?" Frances asks Rosie, the odd chill in her tone snapping me back to the present.

"Oh, not tonight. He'll be waiting for me when we arrive in Paris tomorrow morning. The anticipation of seeing him after all these months will guarantee me not a single moment's rest tonight, I am sure of it!"

Rosie's excitement is so endearing, I cannot stand the thought of anyone harming her. I wish I could tell her what we know is going to happen and take her to safety immediately, but I must stick to the plan. Besides, revealing the fact that Samuel and I have traveled back in time would only serve to alienate us from the women we are trying to save.

"Young love," Frances sighs, before taking two more long sips of champagne. "I remember it well."

"If I may be so bold as to ask, what brings you to make a solo Christmas voyage on the Orient Express?" Samuel addresses Frances.

"Oh, dear. I don't think I've had enough champagne to share the details of *that* story," she says with a shrill laugh. "Let's just say I was visiting an old friend…and it ended on a rather sour note, unfortunately." Frances pats her blond hair with gloved hands as she furiously bats her eyelashes, directing her gaze toward the thick snowflakes flying past the train window. Gaining composure, she turns back to the table and levels her gaze at Rosie. "In fact, I believe this old friend of mine may be a mutual acquaintance of ours, Rosemary."

Rosie's smile wilts instantly at Frances's words.

"Am I correct in assuming that you are Rosemary Delaney, daughter of Ambassador Delaney?" Frances asks.

Rosie sits up taller in her seat, fumbling with the cloth napkin in her hands. "My, what a small world. You are acquainted with my father?"

I squeeze Samuel's hand underneath the table. *Rosie's father was an ambassador too?* Just like the poor, young Emma Brooks, who, with her brown curls and pretty blue eyes, actually bears a striking resemblance to the young Rosie.

As if this entire situation weren't creepy enough.

"Not exactly," Frances says. "But I am *quite* intimate with the Morel family. In fact, I attended the Morel Holiday Gala earlier this evening. I must say, you looked simply stunning in that silver gown you were wearing. Your *fiancé*, Alexandre Morel, seemed quite taken with you." Frances's gaze shoots to Rosie's left hand. "Or should I say your *former* fiancé?"

The color drains from Rosie's cheeks as her eyes dart nervously around the dining car, where a few of the other passengers have begun to retire to their sleeping compartments. She lifts a trembling hand to her chest, then turns to Samuel and me.

"And the two of you as well? Has Alexandre planted you all here? To stop me from leaving him? To save his precious reputation?" Rosie cries.

"No, that's not it at all," Samuel assures her.

"Please, we have no idea what either of you are talking about," I add.

Just as the server appears at our side with a tray full of silver platters, tears pool at the corners of Rosie's eyes. She shoots up from her seat and pushes past a smug Frances.

"I won't be dining this evening after all, Monsieur," she says to the waiter, before taking off through the dining car.

I squeeze Samuel's knee underneath the table, but he returns my silent frantic plea with a stern, unyielding gaze.

Stick to the plan.

I force myself to stay seated, even though I want nothing more than to storm back to Rosie's sleeping compartment and keep her safe. As if he can read my mind, Samuel nods at me reassuringly.

We will. We will save her.

The server removes the lids from the shiny platters, placing three plates of *le canard* and *petits légumes au beurre* in front of us.

"Merci, Monsieur," I say politely, but truth be told, I couldn't be less interested in the gourmet spread before us. I am wondering when this supposed snowdrift is going to stop the train, and *who* will be attempting to take Rosie, Frances, and another unknown woman from its warm carriages.

With a dainty flip of her wrist, Frances opens her cloth napkin and spreads it across her lap, not seeming the least bit ruffled at what's just happened. "My, my," she says dryly. "I didn't mean to upset the poor girl. I was simply going to commiserate with her over what pompous *arses* the Morel men are. *I* should know."

Samuel slices into the moist filet of duck. "What *is* your connection to the Morel family, if you don't mind me asking?" Samuel inquires.

Frances lifts a brow, then stabs at a carrot with her fork. "I do mind, actually."

The sounds of silverware scratching on china and train wheels chugging through the snowy Alpine terrain outside are the only noises that cut through the tense silence we now share with Frances Chapman—another woman whose mysterious connection to the infamous Morel family will prove to be the end of her...*unless*, of course, Samuel and I are successful in our quest to change history.

A gust of wind rattles the dining car, making me shiver despite the insides of my black gloves, now covered in sweat. I peek over my shoulder and spot the last elegant 1930s couple leaving the dining car.

I wait a few moments before breaking the silence. "If it was all a misunderstanding, perhaps I should invite Rosie back to dinner?" The words no more than leave my lips when Frances shoots up from the table.

"The duck isn't quite to my liking. I think I'll retire early." She drops her napkin onto her plate, excusing herself abruptly and without even a hint of politeness.

Frances exits through the door nearest us, in the opposite direction of Rosie. Only seconds after she's closed the door behind her, a violent jolt rocks the train, and the wheels screech to a deafening halt. Silverware and crystal champagne flutes slide off the smooth white tablecloth, landing on the floor in a shattering cacophony that pierces my eardrums.

Samuel clasps my hand tightly as the low lights in the dining car flicker off and on. Finally, as the smell of hot steam drifts into the dining car, drowning out the rich aroma of duck and buttery vegetables, the lights fizzle off, and we are surrounded by a deep, endless black night.

I fumble around in my seat, and as soon as my hands wrap around the silver, gun-toting clutch I carried into the dining car, I sling the strap over my shoulder and pinch Samuel's arm. "This is it. We don't have much time."

"Come on," he says, rising to his feet and taking my hand once more. "You need to change into your warmer clothes, and I'll see to Rosie. Stick to the plan, and everything will be okay. I promise you."

The glow emanating from the snow-covered hills surrounding the train breaks through the darkness as I follow Samuel down the aisle of the dining car, our feet crunching over broken glass.

We are almost to our sleeping compartment when I hear a rustling sound down the corridor. I hold my breath and get ready to grab the gun from my purse, but soon the conductor's hat comes into focus. "Not to worry, Madame, Monsieur," he assures us in French. "We'll be off shortly."

Panic soars through my chest, and I want to shout at him, tell him that an abduction is about to take place on his train and he must lock all the doors!

But I keep my mouth shut. That isn't in the plan, and he'll only think I've lost my mind.

Samuel gives the conductor a polite *"Merci, Monsieur"* before pulling me into our sleeping compartment.

I waste no time stripping down to my underwear and pulling on the pants I'd discovered earlier in the old-fashioned suitcase. I'd laid them out on the sofa bed, ready to go, before we'd exited our sleeping compartment.

"I'll be in the bathroom down the hall," Samuel whispers. In the suffocating darkness that seems to be closing in on us with each passing second, I think I can see him pulling his gun out from underneath his tux jacket.

"Lock the door behind me," he instructs. "I'll knock three times *twice* when I return. No matter what you hear out there, do not open the door for anyone else. Do you understand?"

"I understand," I say.

But just as I am trying to ignore the sudden constriction of my heart, I feel Samuel's heat pressing against the bare skin on my stomach and chest, his free hand sliding around my waist with force.

"Jillian, no matter what happens tonight, you need to know that I've never stopped thinking about you. And I've never stopped loving you."

Samuel's lips have no problem finding mine in this dark train car as he presses me up against the chilly train window, then sets the gun down on the nightstand beside us. His hands roam over the curves of my hips, stopping briefly at the small of my back before sliding up to explore the contours of my breasts. At once I am totally consumed and utterly powerless under the heat of his kiss. Our mouths press together almost violently, the years of longing, of needing, of loving this man that I never truly wanted to leave, pouring into the passion that steams up the bitter cold air around us.

Samuel runs his fingers through my hair as he trails kisses down my neck and over the tops of my breasts. "I have to go," he says, his breathing now labored, hot, blazing across my skin.

I want more of him. *All of him.* And I am certain by the way his lips linger on my collarbone, by the way he holds me so confidently in his arms, that he wants all of me too.

That he always has.

Leaving him was a mistake. A grave, terrible mistake.

Remembering Rosie and Isla, I place my hands on Samuel's shoulders and push him away from me. "Go," I breathe. "You have to go."

One final steamy kiss grazes my lips, making me shudder in anticipation. "I'll keep you safe tonight, Jill. I promise you," Samuel whispers.

And with that, he is off, and I am locking the door behind him and throwing on an itchy wool sweater, already missing the feel of his smooth hands on my skin and, even more, longing for one more rough, passionate kiss from that sinful mouth of his.

God, I've missed him.

My entire body is trembling again, but not from the cold that seeps in through the windows. I manage to slip my feet into the black patent-leather oxford shoes I discovered in the mysterious suitcase, then I double-knot the laces. Next, I throw on Georges's large black coat, stuffing his thick wool gloves into my coat pocket. Finally, I remove the pistol from the silver purse, take my stance at the door, and attempt to calm my rapid, violent breathing.

Suddenly the nightstand lamp flickers back on, and just as I'm squinting to readjust to the light, I hear a loud thud out in the corridor. Next there are footsteps passing by.

Then silence.

I wrap my hands tighter around the gun and force myself to stand still. I promised Samuel I wouldn't leave this room, that I would follow the plan and wait until he returns.

The plan is for Samuel to hide in the washroom at the end of the corridor, situated right next to Rosie's sleeping compartment. He is to wait there until the abductor has taken her—a piece of the plan I can hardly allow myself to go through with—so as to avoid endangering more innocent lives on the train. Then Samuel will come for me, and we'll follow the abductors. Samuel will take them down—with me as a backup if need be—but we'll leave at least one of them alive so we can find out who is behind all of this and where they are planning to take the women.

We hope this will be the same place where Isla has been taken.

If we succeed, the question still remains—how we will travel back to 2012 to save my sister?

Another thud out in the corridor startles me, and I forget about time travel and the plan I am supposed to be following.

Samuel should've been back by now. There must be at least two abductors, if not more. What if they've harmed him?

What if he doesn't return?

If he isn't back in ten seconds...

Ten...nine...eight...seven...

Another rustling sound in the hallway stops my silent counting. The lamp hums loudly before flickering off once more, leaving me breathing alone in the darkness.

That's it.

Holding the gun tightly in one hand, I unlock the door with the other. I inch through the doorway with the gun poised at my chest, ready to aim and shoot.

I peek to the left, blinking to readjust my eyes to the darkness, but I see nothing. I look to the right and am seized in silent terror as a tall shadow looms over me. I thrust my gun toward the large mass, but it, or *he,* is faster.

A gloved set of hands rips the gun from my grasp, covers my mouth, then thrusts the barrel deep into my side.

"If you make one sound, I'll shoot," a male voice whispers in French.

The shadow has now morphed into a freezing, solid body that presses firmly into my back as he forces me to walk down the corridor, directly past the bathroom that Samuel is supposed to be hiding in.

I let out the quietest of whimpers as the man shoves me past the restroom door, the gun now digging so hard into my ribs I wonder if one will crack.

But Samuel doesn't emerge from the washroom. I don't hear a sound as we pass through the next carriage, out to the other side, then slip down the stairs and through the doors to the freezing white blast outside.

I think of Isla with a gun pressing into her side, pointing right at her unborn child. I envision her violet eyes as I am shoved, prodded, pushed to the edge of the train and into the thickly wooded hills. As heavy snowflakes stick to my lashes, I realize that it is only through allowing myself to be taken, just as my twin sister has been, that I will have any chance at finding out where they are hiding her...that I will have any chance at saving her life.

And so I allow the massive, grunting man to shove me into the snowy ground, point my own gun at my head, tie my wrists behind my back, and throw a black sack over my head.

In a sick, twisted way, it all makes sense.

I will be the third woman. The third, unidentifiable woman who was taken on that snowy Christmas Eve night in 1937.

I only hope that unlike the girl who was taken the first time around, I will be able to outsmart my murderer.

EPISODE 5

CHAPTER 13

December 25, 1937

The French Alps

The warmth inside the elegant carriages of the Orient Express is only a distant memory as my abductor yanks me to my feet, thrusts the barrel of the gun into my side, then shoves me deeper into the snowy mountains.

With a heavy sack covering my head, I search for any hint of light in this sea of black that engulfs me, but there is no light. No way to know where this man is taking me. No sign of rescue.

Amid the terror that laces through me like poisonous venom, I remind myself that I don't want to be rescued—not just yet anyway. I need to find out who is behind this and where we are going, and in addition to saving my own life, I need to try to save Rosie's and Frances's lives as well.

That is, if I am even given the chance.

At the moment, the only sounds passing through my ears are my abductor's barbaric, labored grunts and the crunching of our feet over snow and branches as he pushes me up a steep incline and farther into the freezing abyss.

The rope he has tied around my wrists digs mercilessly into my raw skin, and the bitter wind bites at my fingertips, turning them numb with each passing second. The snow—which must be at least four inches deep at this point—seeps into my old-fashioned shoes, soaking through my thin stockings and turning my toes to ice.

I think of Samuel, of his firm instructions to stay in the sleeping compartment until he knocked, and I wonder if I have once again made a horrific mistake in leaving him.

Will he find me? And what about the others?

What if I never see him again?

The panic rising through my chest threatens to steal all of my strength, all of my resolve. But then I remember Isla. I think of her being forced to make this same trek through the woods, pregnant and terrified. Isla is strong, perhaps stronger than I ever was. But *this*—being taken from a train in the middle of the night with no hope of ever finding a way back to safety—this would bring anyone to their knees.

As the man at my back gives me a violent shove and the wind whips and howls through the trees around us, suddenly there is no mistaking it—I can feel my twin sister. The boldness of her presence takes root within me, and I know I am getting closer.

It makes absolutely no sense, seeing as how I am stuck in the year 1937 and Isla is seventy-five years in the future, but this feeling of being connected to my twin is as true and alive as the fear coursing through my veins. I imagine her intense violet eyes shining in the unending darkness before me. And I know this is the way.

No matter what Samuel instructed me to do, no matter how carefully he'd constructed our original plan—he was wrong.

After what Isla endured when we were only young girls, after what *she* did to try to save *me*, I know it is in my fate to make an equal sacrifice for her.

And now, as I am at the mercy of an unknown captor, and of the pistol he thrusts viciously into my ribs, it is *only* this thought that keeps me going.

We walk for what feels like hours—but in reality has probably only been a string of freezing, terror-filled minutes—when the man mumbles a French obscenity under his breath, shoves me in the chest, and knocks me to the ground.

The whimper that escapes my lips is met with a harsh slap to the head.

The sac is suddenly lifted from my face, and just as I am blinking, trying to focus my eyes on the dark shadow of a man that hovers over me, I realize what is about to happen.

In being the third woman in this abduction, I am the *only* one who doesn't have a connection to the Morel family. And I can only assume that the reason this man took me was for being in the wrong place at the wrong time.

This brutal kidnapper isn't going to lead me to Rosie or to where Isla might be in the future. He is going to shoot me right here, right now, in the middle of these godforsaken, snow-covered mountains.

Just as my eyes adjust to the darkness, I focus on the sparkly snowflakes flittering down from the sky, landing on the barrel of the pistol, which is now pointed at my head.

It can't end like this.

I won't let it.

My eyes flicker to the man behind the gun, wondering why he hasn't yet pulled the trigger. I can't make out his face, but I can see that he is straddling me, one foot on either side of my legs. And despite his best efforts, he is fumbling with the gun. He's not sure how to use the pistol that came from the year *2012*. It's clear that he's not expecting a fight from the rich, prissy girl he's taken from the luxurious Orient Express as he tosses the gun to the ground and reaches into his coat pocket for another.

I almost smile to myself at how wrong he is.

My foot flies up without warning, the pointy toe of my Oxford shoe delivering a swift kick to the man's groin. Just as he doubles over, I dig my bound hands into the wet ground behind me, and in one forceful push I lunge to my feet. As soon as I'm up, I kick him once more in the groin for good measure.

He collapses into the snowy ground this time, cursing and moaning, but I barely take notice. I am already tearing through the woods.

With my wrists still bound tightly behind my back, I try not to stumble over the snowy branches and tree stumps in my way— landmines threatening to take me down.

I take a sharp left around a massive pine tree, and the downward slope gives me hope that I am heading back in the direction of the train. As the relentless winds snap at my face, I barrel through the blankets of snow swirling through the air and piling up at my feet.

And suddenly, I hear them.

Voices.

A flicker of light off in the distance calls out to me, shaking the freeze right off my limbs as I pick up my pace.

Could it be the train?

I am about to yell for help when a piercing scream shoots through the snowy night.

Rosie.

I blink away the flakes that stick to my lashes with each quick stride, and that is when I hear a set of footsteps nearing.

I peek back over my shoulder and spot the shadow of my abductor coming after me. He is loud, clumsy, stumbling, grunting—a ravenous monster hunting its prey.

My feet carry me to the light, and finally a small wooden shack comes into focus, its slanted roof covered in inches of thick, white snow.

The next scream that rattles my ears is sharper, stronger than the last.

Frances.

I don't have time to figure out my next move because the beastly body that tackles me from behind is swifter.

One final blow to the back of my head sends a third scream blasting through the cold, eerie night.

This time, it is my own voice that rattles the darkness.

The sound of heavy muffled voices wakes me from a dreamless sleep. I try to focus on the words being spoken off in the distance, but the relentless pounding behind my eyes spreads to my temples, making it impossible for me to hear anything beyond the thumping of my own blood.

I feel myself drifting back to sleep. *It will be easier than enduring this pain*, I think—but the sound of a desperate whimper startles me awake.

I hear that sad, weeping voice again, and this time I'm certain it came from a young woman who must be close by.

My lips tingle and ache, but I force them to say the name burning at the tip of my tongue. "Isla?"

"Who's there?" A female whisper shoots past my ears, but it's different, stronger than the meek cries I just heard.

Before I respond, I coax my eyelids to open. It feels like an eternity before my vision adjusts to the darkness swallowing up every inch of space around me. Finally, by the grace of a flash of light flickering from underneath a door, I am able to make out two figures in this damp, freezing room.

They are both tied to chairs, and lumpy sacks cover their heads. That's when I remember my struggle with the man who dragged me out of the train at gunpoint, and his second attack, which must've landed me here.

"Rosie, Frances, is that you?" I whisper.

"Who's there?" the same female voice calls out again. This time, I identify her proper British accent, and I am certain of her identity.

"Frances, it's Jillian. My husband and I had dinner with you on the train. Are you okay?" Right after I say those words,

I notice how natural—and comforting—it feels to call Samuel my husband.

"Jillian?" A hint of relief lines the terror in Frances's voice. "What's going on? Who's doing this to us?"

"Did you get a look at the man who took you and Rosie?" I ask.

"There were two men," she says. "And how did you know the other woman is Rosie? Didn't they cover up your head too?"

I'm not about to explain the real reason why I am certain Rosie Delaney is the other abducted girl sitting in between us, so instead, I force my dazed head to focus on what I need to find out. "No, I managed to get mine off."

"So you can see?" she says. "Where are we?"

I gaze around the small room, noticing a small window up above Frances's head where the glow from the snow outside is giving me a tiny bit more light to work with. I also notice that just like the other two women, I have been tied to a chair, my wrists still bound together behind my back, a taut rope wrapping around my waist and chest, binding me to the hard wooden pegs, making it increasingly difficult to suck in a breath.

"We're in some sort of shack in the woods. I escaped from the man who took me, but he caught me just as I found this place," I say, being careful to keep my voice low. I can still hear the men's gruff voices on the other side of the door, but their mumbling is impossible to decipher.

"I heard the two of you screaming," I continue. "Are you okay? Did they hurt you badly?"

"Only badly enough to quiet us both down," Frances says, an unmistakable quiver in her voice. Even with only the slightest hint of light, I notice Frances's legs and feet trembling as she talks. Her feet are bare, and—I imagine—freezing.

"I've been trying to listen to what they're saying out there," she says. "But all I've been able to make out is that the blizzard has botched some sort of plan they had to take us somewhere else."

"Do you have any idea who they are or who they're working for?" I ask.

"No, and I don't care. I just want to make it out of here alive."

I ignore the excruciating ache that shoots through my head and neck, and start scraping my wrists against the back of the chair.

"Rosie, are you awake?" I whisper as I attempt to thrash my body around to loosen the rope.

Another distressed whimper comes from Rosie, who is still slumped in her chair.

"Rosie," I say again. "It's me, Jillian. We met earlier on the train. Are you okay?"

"Alexandre," she murmurs. "It has to be Alexandre."

"You think he's behind this?" I ask.

A few seconds pass before she speaks, but this time her voice is a little bit stronger. "I know he is. I'm certain."

"Frances, you said on the train that you're connected to the Morel family too. Do you know Alexandre?" I whisper.

"We've met briefly, yes. But all I know is from what his father, Henri, has told me."

Even with my cloudy, pounding head, I distinctly remember the Morel women's paintings adorning the walls upstairs in their massive vacation château back in Évian-les-Bains. And at the top of the Morel family line were Henri and his wife, Agnès.

"Were you close with Henri?" I ask Frances.

Frances hesitates, but finally I hear her murmur in a bitter tone, "Quite close...well, until tonight that is."

Suddenly Rosie's soft whimper turns into a full-on cry. "I never should have left Alexandre...not like this anyway. Not without properly telling him to his face that I've fallen in love with someone else. That's why he did this to us. I'm so sorry."

"If Alexandre is behind this, then where is the little bastard?" Frances hisses. "And will you keep it down? Do you want them to come back in here?"

"I'm sure Alexandre is rich enough to hire men to do his dirty work for him," I say. "But the question is, what did the Morel family want with you, Frances? It can't be a coincidence that you and Rosie both took the same train tonight after attending the Morel Holiday Gala and that you were both kidnapped."

"What about you, Jillian?" Frances snaps back, her voice strained as she struggles to loosen the ropes that bound her to the chair. "If this really is the handiwork of the great and powerful Morels, why would they take you?"

"That's what I'm trying to figure out," I say. "All I can come up with is that I was in the wrong place at the wrong time."

"What about your husband, Samuel?" Rosie whispers. "Did they take him too?"

I think of the determination in Samuel's green eyes, of the way he kissed me before he left the sleeping compartment, and my entire body aches for him.

"No, they didn't take him. He'll be coming for us, though. I know he will. That's why I need you both to stay strong and try as best you can to loosen the ropes."

Despite the pain that continues to course through me, I follow my own advice, thrashing and rubbing at the ropes, but I am bound so tightly, it feels hopeless. My fatigued body is begging me to fall into a deep sleep where this intense fear and this soaring pain cannot touch me, but the minute I think of Isla, I know that is not an option.

"Frances, what happened with you and Henri tonight?" I whisper through the icy room. "Would he have any reason to want to harm you or Rosie?"

This time, I hear Frances sniffling. "What does it matter at this point who's behind this? There are three armed men out there who've tied us up in the middle of some godforsaken shack in the mountains. They're either going to kill us here or take us somewhere else and kill us." A soft whimper breaks through her cries. "It's hopeless."

A newfound strength sweeps through my beaten-down body as I scratch my wrists against the chair with as much fervor as I can muster. "It's not hopeless," I grit through my chattering teeth. "Samuel will come for us. I know it. Now try to loosen the rope. Both of you!"

Both of their chairs begin to squeak as they attempt to wriggle free of the tight ropes. "Good," I say. "The rope that's around your wrists, scrape it against the back of the chair."

"It's too tight," Rosie says. I can tell she is trying to be strong, but the terror in her voice is overwhelming.

"Keep trying," I order.

The men are still quarreling on the other side of the door, but I know it won't be long before they burst in here.

"Frances, were you having an affair with Henri?" I ask.

A few tense seconds pass before her voice breaks. "He ended it tonight—told me to leave the party and never to come back. He was the one who gave me the ticket for the Orient Express back to London. After five years, that's all I get. A train ticket. Not even a kiss goodbye."

"Wait, *Henri* was the one to give you the ticket?" I say.

"That's what I just said, isn't it?" Frances snaps.

"Rosie, when did you buy your train ticket?"

She hesitates, then finally replies softly, "I didn't buy the ticket."

"Then who did?" I ask. "Was it one of the Morels?"

"No, it was Jacques—the man I was telling you about on the train. Before…before Frances admitted she'd seen me tonight at the gala."

Chills roll down my spine at the mention of my grandfather's name. "When did Jacques give you the ticket, Rosie?"

"A few weeks ago. He sent it in a letter."

I think back to the letter I read in the snowy Lausanne train station at Madeleine's request. It was dated December 1, 1937. Jacques had said he couldn't wait to see Rosie at the train station in Paris on Christmas morning…that he couldn't wait to call her his own.

But when this tragic situation played out the first time around, he never did get to see her again...*or* call her his own.

"Did anyone else know you were planning to leave Alexandre tonight?" I ask.

"No, I haven't told a soul," Rosie says.

"Where did you keep the ticket?" I realize that despite the fact that my brain feels like mush right now, the questions are still shooting from my tongue instinctively...just as they've done for all of my years of reporting.

"I kept it hidden in a shoe box full of Jacques's letters," Rosie says. "My parents and I have been staying at the Morel Château in Évian-les-Bains for the entire month of December. Alexandre must've gone through my suitcase and found it. He must've known all along that I was planning to leave him—*and* his massive diamond ring—behind for Jacques."

Frances's harsh whisper shoots through the dark room. "If it was all Alexandre, then why would Henri purposefully send me away on the exact same train as you?"

I think of Laurent and Frédéric Morel, the wealthy, successful father-son combo who—back in 2012—were downstairs fighting before Frédéric stormed the upstairs bedroom where I was snooping and attacked me. Perhaps the desire to get rid of any woman who might destroy their precious reputation is something that is laced into the Morels' blood, in their genes.

"Maybe Alexandre and Henri are in on this together," I surmise, thinking that it must be the same with Frédéric and Laurent. Of course in the future version of this crime, there is the unmistakable involvement of the sick, demented Senator Williams to consider as well.

"Rosie, on the train, you said something about how Alexandre would be worried about saving his reputation. If he knew you were leaving him for another man and that you were pregnant with that man's child, do you truly believe Alexandre would go so far as to have you abducted from a train? And from what you know of his father, Henri, do you think he could be behind this as well?"

I hear Rosie suck in a labored breath. "How…how did you know I'm pregnant?"

Damn.

"That explains a lot," Frances says. "The Morel men could never stand to be disgraced in such a way. Though of course they have no problem keeping mistresses for years, then kicking them straight to the curb without a second thought…sodding hypocrites."

"How did you know about the baby?" Rosie repeats.

I realize that Rosie probably has no idea she's carrying twins. Or that those twins will be taken from her. Will they do the same to Isla? Take her baby…then make her disappear?

"I saw you patting your stomach on the train, and you refused the champagne, so I made a guess," I respond. "Am I correct?"

Rosie answers me with a muffled cry that breaks into a strangled sob.

Nice job, Jillian.

Young Rosie's sobs only intensify when the creaky door wrenches open and three male silhouettes barge into the tiny room.

None of us have managed to break free from the ropes, and with no sign of Samuel, we are, once again, at the mercy of these nameless captors.

The men—who tower over us like giants—are quick but brutal in their efforts to remove Frances from her chair. I watch helplessly as she kicks and writhes in their strong grip, but one solid smack to the head makes her body go limp, her cries drowning in the darkness.

Rosie whimpers by my side, but when two of the men reach for her, her sobs dry up almost on contact. And to my surprise she doesn't fight back.

But then I remember the baby, or—as only *I* know—the *babies*. She is cooperating to protect her child. Her motherly instinct has already kicked in.

As they force her to her feet, she doesn't make a sound. And with the sack over her head, I can't help but imagine her as Isla—cold, shaking, and pregnant. Isla is feisty, but like Rosie she's smart.

She would do whatever she had to do to protect her unborn child, even if it meant stifling the paralyzing horror that has surely overcome her.

One of the captors throws a ragdoll Frances over his shoulder while the other shoves a gun into Rosie's side, before both women are taken through the doorway and out of my line of sight.

As for me, I am left alone with the man who tried to shoot me in the woods earlier. The same man who I kicked in the groin—*twice*.

And by the way he paces before me—the pounding of his boots on the floor like a hammer to my temples—I am certain he is *not* happy.

CHAPTER 14

His first slap comes hard and fast across my left cheek. I barely have time to register the intense sting before he smacks me a second time, and quickly after, a third.

My head wobbles, my neck too weak to hold its weight. Vaguely, in the distance, I hear the sound of a door slamming, but the next hit rattles my already throbbing head so hard, I lose track of all sounds.

I squeeze my eyes closed, bracing for another blow, but I am not prepared for the violent punch of knuckles that slams into my cheekbone. I feel the raw, cold skin on my face breaking open, the ripping pain making me wish that my body would shut down, go numb. How much more of this can I handle before I pass out?

Warm blood oozes down the cracked skin on my cheek and settles on my lips, but I don't have the energy to spit it out as it trickles into my mouth.

Quick, arduous breaths pass through my lips as I wait for the next hit, but it doesn't come. I want to lift my head up to see what he's doing, but my neck won't cooperate.

I feel myself drifting in and out of consciousness, but suddenly the sound of Isla's teenage scream rushes into my head.

And there I am again. Back to the place, the scene, the moment I loathe most in my miserable childhood. Crisp as day I see the image that has haunted me for years—the image that comes to me in nightmares, the same one that always accompanies Isla's terrified young scream.

Isla is only thirteen years old—a startlingly beautiful young woman—and she is huddled, naked and trembling, on the floor of her childhood bedroom. The dead man's blood is splattered all over her pale, beautiful skin, and his lifeless heap of a body is hunched over her.

The bullet wound to the side of his head drips sickening scarlet blood all over my sister.

The smoking gun in my mother's hands is pointed right at Isla's bare chest.

Those wicked hands already stole our childhood. I will not let them steal my sister.

"Jillian!"

The memory of Isla's pleading cry shoots adrenaline through my veins, and just as my eyes open back up inside the snowy shack, I find that the barrel of the gun is still there, but this time, it is aimed at me.

With every ounce of strength left in this broken body of mine, I scrape my wrists one last time against the chair, and suddenly, I feel the ropes loosening, one of my hands slipping free.

Instinctually, I swing my arm, knocking the gun out of the man's hands. Just as it rattles to the floor, I tug at the ropes around my chest. But before I can break free, the man lunges for the gun, and a shot fires through the night.

I flinch, waiting for the sudden flash of pain that I know is surely coming. But besides the aftereffects of the beating he's just given me, I feel nothing.

When I summon up the courage to open my eyes, the man lies writhing on the floor, howling in pain as blood oozes from his knee. And Samuel—*my* Samuel—is standing over him, gun in hand, pinning his neck and shoulders to the ground.

"Where have the others gone?" Samuel growls in French.

When the man grimaces in response, Samuel's fist swings around in a fast punch to the man's jaw.

"Where have they gone?" Samuel yells into his face, slamming his head against the hard wooden floor of the shack.

My hands shake as I begin to untie the ropes around my body. Out of the corner of my eye, I see the man reaching toward Samuel, trying to fight him, but this former CIA field agent and trained hunter is much, much quicker. Samuel twists the man's neck into a tight chokehold, cutting off his air supply.

"If you want to live, tell me where the others are going, and who you work for," Samuel says through gritted teeth.

Samuel loosens his hold around the man's neck only slightly, but when he still refuses to respond, Samuel tightens his grip once more.

Just as I have almost completely freed myself from the chair, the man's desperate, strangled pleas howl through the night.

Samuel loosens his grip again, letting him speak.

"The castle—," he sputters in French as he sucks in a panicked breath, "—they're taking them to the castle in the mountains."

"Whose castle?" Samuel demands. "And how do we get there?"

"It's happening tomorrow night. When she arrives," he spits. "I have a map. In my coat pocket."

Samuel looks up at me and nods toward the gun on the floor. With shaky legs, I stand from the chair, reach down, and wrap my hands around the man's old-fashioned gun. I point the barrel straight at his head, willing my hands to stay steady as Samuel uses one arm to keep the man in a loosened chokehold, while his other hand shoots down to the man's coat pocket.

But just as Samuel's hand dips and rustles through the captor's coat, the man's huge body jerks abruptly, bucking Samuel off of him in one violent thrust. His other beastly hand swipes at the gun I am holding, and just as he steals it from my grip, another deafening shot fires, knocking me backward onto the ground.

One look at my abductor, at his limp body and the blood pooling on the ground beneath him, and I realize with staggering relief that neither Samuel nor I have been shot.

Samuel holds his gun over the man's body, waiting silently, as if he's taunting him to take one final breath. But there isn't an ounce of life left in that man's body.

Instead it is me who takes a huge gulp of air into my lungs.

Samuel killed him. I can breathe.

Samuel runs to my side, kneels down before me, and with his thumb, he tips my chin up ever so slightly. Our gazes meet in the cool glow of light shimmering through the window just above his head.

I barely feel the tears rushing down my face as Samuel wraps me up in his strong arms.

"I'm here, Jill," he whispers in my ear. "I'm here."

Samuel holds me until I calm down; then he inspects the cuts and bruises on my face.

"I saw a cabin in the mountains nearby," he says. "I'm going to look for that map—hopefully it actually exists—and then I'm going to take you to the cabin to get you cleaned up and warm."

"But we have to follow them," I say, wincing as Samuel uses his sleeve to wipe at one of the cuts on my cheek.

"They're long gone by now, and you're in no state to trek very far through this blizzard, in the middle of the night no less."

"But—"

My protest is silenced by Samuel's lips on mine.

Nothing in my life has ever felt so good, so safe, as the warmth of this kiss.

Our lips brush together a few more times before he pulls away, his heavy breath warming the chilly draft that blows around us. "I know you like to take things into your own hands, Jillian Chambord, but just this once, I need you to trust me, okay?"

Still reveling in the electricity of his bold kiss, I nod. "Okay."

Samuel works swiftly, searching the dead man's coat pockets once again for the map that will lead us to this supposed castle where Rosie, Frances—and possibly in the future, *Isla*—have been taken.

On the cold, bloody floor of this mountain shack, I am trembling now—the panic, the pain, and the relief all settling into this frozen body of mine at once. But it is the relief that seizes me most as I watch Samuel take charge of the situation. I realize that while *I* did not hold true to my promise to stick to our plan, Samuel did.

He came for me. He saved me.

It is in this moment, as Samuel removes a folded piece of paper from the man's pocket, then lifts his concerned gaze to mine once more, that I am faced with the raw, startling truth.

A truth that I have locked away for years.

And a truth that I am certain I will never again be able to ignore.

I have never stopped loving Samuel.

The bitter winds snap at the raw, bruised skin on my face, but even with the worsening conditions in these snow-filled mountains, I feel a new sense of purpose and safety with Samuel by my side.

He wraps his arm tightly around my waist as we shuffle down the snowy hill, back in the direction of the train tracks.

"Are you sure the train is gone?" I ask, but my voice is immediately swallowed up by a violent gust that causes the heavy sheets of snowfall to swirl around us in a frenzy.

"I heard the whistle blow earlier as I was searching for you. I'm sure they wanted to get out of this storm while they still could."

I don't ask any more questions for the duration of our trek. I trust that Samuel knows where he's going, even though the snow-covered branches jutting out all around us, and the black sky hovering above the trees, make every turn look exactly like the last.

Finally, just when my feet are turning numb and my strength is once again wearing thin, Samuel points up ahead. "There it is. There's the cabin I saw earlier. Come on."

White puffs of air hover over our lips as our breathing quickens along with our pace.

The idea of warmth fuels me more than anything in this moment. I can't bear to think about what might be happening to Rosie and Frances right now, or to Isla and Francesca in the future. I can only hope that the map Samuel stole from my abductor's coat pocket will take us to them first thing in the morning, as soon as we have the sun to light our journey.

There are no lights on inside the tiny wood cabin, so Samuel takes the liberty of kicking open the rickety front door when he discovers it's locked. He does a quick sweep of the interior to confirm there's no one inside, before ushering me in out of the cold.

It takes my eyes a few long moments to adjust to the pitch-blackness, but in that time Samuel has already discovered a thick wool blanket, which he is wrapping around my shoulders. He shows me to a couch, then immediately begins throwing logs in the fireplace.

He strikes a match and lights the fire, the sight of the flames giving me hope that soon I will feel warm again. I have never been so cold in all my life.

I wrap the blanket tighter around my shivering body and scoot down on the soft brown rug next to the fire.

"I'm going to go see what I can find in the bathroom for first aid so we can clean up the cuts on your face," Samuel says.

I realize as he rushes through the cabin that I've never had someone take care of me in this way, not even as a child. It feels odd not to be the one taking charge.

But even more so, it is an immense relief.

Just as the fire is bringing feeling back into my fingertips, Samuel returns with a bottle of hydrogen peroxide and a warm cloth. He kneels down beside me, pours a dab onto the towel, and then tilts my face toward his.

"This isn't going to feel good, but we can't risk these cuts getting infected."

My teeth are still chattering violently, so I give him a silent nod to go ahead. As he dabs at the wounds on my face, I focus on the concern in his striking green eyes; on his nose, which has turned pink from the cold; and on his rugged five o'clock shadow, which has grown thicker over the course of this insane day. The sting of the peroxide brings immediate tears to my eyes, but I blink them away, reminding myself that I am safe now. And that I need to be strong for Rosie. For Isla.

When Samuel finishes his delicate treatment of my face, he eyes my trembling body, then runs a hand from my knee down to the hem of my pants. "You're soaked. We need to get you out of these clothes so you don't get hypothermia."

Even amid the grave situation we have found ourselves in, I can't help but let the slightest of grins slide onto my lips. "*Only* so I don't get hypothermia?"

Samuel has already removed one of my pointy Oxford shoes when he lifts his disarming gaze to me. "You think I have another agenda?"

I shrug my shoulders, then give him my other foot. "Well, whatever your agenda may be, just be happy you're getting these old-fashioned shoes off my feet. The last guy who messed with me got two swift kicks to the groin with those pointy toes."

The flicker of orange flames crackling in the fireplace reveals a curious gleam in Samuel's eyes. "I imagine he wasn't too happy with you after that…which explains the cuts and bruises on your face."

"I wasn't going down without a fight," I say.

"I wouldn't expect any less," Samuel says as he pulls the soaking wet stockings off my feet. "I'm just glad you're okay…and alive." The seriousness lining his tone makes me remember how close I was to death. If it weren't for him, I wouldn't be sitting here right now.

I reach for his hand, gripping it in my own. "Thank you, Samuel. Thank you for coming for me."

He smiles softly, the tenderness in his expression saying more than any words could ever say.

My freezing body is finally starting to absorb the warmth of the flames that lick the hearth beside us, but Samuel is right, I need to get the rest of these wet clothes off me—and fast.

I recline my head back against the couch as Samuel leans over me and unbuttons my pants. "Just tell me if I'm hurting you, okay?"

"I'll be all right," I assure him. "Just get these off, please."

He lifts a mischievous brow before wrapping his hands around the waist of my pants and pulling them down over my hips. His hands feel warm and smooth as they run down the frozen skin on my calves, removing each pant leg with care.

Next he slips the blanket off my shoulders and begins to pull the itchy, damp wool sweater up over my bra. I wince as I lift my arms up, but Samuel moves quickly, removing the sweater, then gently laying my arms back down and rubbing his hands over my shoulders to warm me.

The smoke in my head finally begins to clear, and it is only as I am half-naked and vulnerable, lying before my ex-boyfriend, that I realize he is still sporting that handsome 1930s tux from our stint as a wealthy married couple on the Orient Express.

I slip the black tux jacket off his shoulders, then reach for the black bow tie, pulling it out of his collar and tossing it to the floor beside us. The fire casts a glow on the perfect contours of Samuel's face, and as I focus on his full lips, I am suddenly overcome with desire.

For years, I've longed for the completion I'd only ever felt in Samuel's arms. No matter how hard I've tried to push away the memory of his skin, his touch, his love, I've never succeeded.

And now, in this stranger's cabin in the middle of the French Alps, in the wee hours of Christmas morning in the year 1937, we have found each other again.

Despite the impossibility of our situation and of our surroundings, nothing in my life has ever felt more right.

I unhook the top button on his white, collared shirt and nod for him to come closer.

He leans toward me, and just as our noses touch, I whisper, "Did you mean what you said back on the train? That you've never stopped…"

"Loving you?" Samuel finishes as he cups my chin in his hand and gazes pointedly into my eyes. "I've never meant anything more in my life."

Samuel's hands find my waist as he brushes his moist lips down the length of my neck and over my collarbone. He is gentle, soft, careful not to touch any of my cuts or bruises as his lips continue their delicate journey down my body, only stopping once they reach the curves of my breasts. He slips one bra strap over my shoulder, moving the lacy black material farther and farther down my skin, before he cups my breast in his hand and raises his lips to mine.

The kiss that follows is a burst of passion, longing, and desire. All of the feelings that have been pent up inside of me for so long, hidden and locked away, are now exploding at Samuel's touch, at his sensual kiss.

I reach for his shirt, my fingers fumbling with the buttons as he takes both of my breasts in his hands and kisses me. The feel of his lips on mine is so consuming that I immediately forget the horror of what has just happened to me.

I finally reach the last button just as Samuel has unhooked my bra. I slip the shirt off Samuel's firm shoulders, running my hands down the length of his muscular arms, while I marvel at his rough, sexy chest.

Next I go for his pants buttons, my fingers working with more precision now that the fire—and *Samuel*—are warming me up. I help him pull the black tux pants off his long legs, then tug at his black boxers until his entire firm, ripped body glistens before me in the glow of the flames.

A heavy breath escapes his lips as he climbs over me and slips my black lace underwear off in one quick movement. Samuel runs his hands down my back, grabbing my butt and pulling me in closer as I wrap my legs around him.

He dips his lips onto mine once more, devouring me with his kisses, with each stroke of his hands on my bare, naked skin. The cold has completely evaporated and has been replaced by a buildup of desire that has taken over every cell of my body. I am unable to think of anything other than Samuel, his body wrapped around mine, holding me, kissing me, rocking me in his arms.

In this moment, all I know is the need I have for him. It is intense, forceful, primal. And in this seventy-five-year time gap we have mysteriously traveled together, our connection is the only thing that feels real to me, the only thing that feels safe.

The flames sizzle and hiss beside us as Samuel kisses me on the lips, then lifts his hooded gaze to mine. I know it is dangerous, letting myself fall again. Especially for the one I could never forget.

But as our eyes lock and blankets of snow cover the world around us, I realize there is no choice in the matter. And so, just as our hips are fitting together, our bodies yearning to connect in the deepest way, I whisper into his ear, "I've never stopped loving you either, Samuel. Not for one second."

Samuel pulls me tighter into his safe, warm embrace, then breathes heavily into my ear as he thrusts inside of me. I squeeze my legs around his back and cry out in pleasure as he pushes deeper and firmer into my core, filling me up so completely, I know I will never again leave him.

I wrap my hands around the rippling muscles of his biceps as he continues to move over me, in slow, firm strokes. His mouth traces the skin along my collarbone as his hands roam the curves of my breasts. Samuel's breathing becomes deeper and heavier as he thrusts a little harder into me, then dips his hands to the space right in between my thighs. He knows *exactly* what to do with those hands, and soon he coaxes a moan from my lips.

I grip onto his broad shoulders as our bodies move in synch on the soft rug. With each caress, each loving kiss, each emotion-filled gaze, I know in my heart that Samuel's words were true. He is still totally and utterly in love with me.

Just as I feel him growing harder and firmer inside me, he wraps his arms around my back and pulls me up so we are both sitting, our bodies shimmering with a coat of sweat as the flames pop and crack beside us. My legs straddle his as he grinds his hips into mine, holding onto my butt and trailing kisses up my neck, before finally he reaches my lips.

The relief I feel each time his lips meet mine is powerful enough to make all of my defenses melt away. I have never felt more open, more bare, more vulnerable than in these naked moments in Samuel's arms.

Fear tore me away from him once before—fear of exposing my true self.

But now, with our bodies connected, each quickening rock of our hips bringing us closer together, I know there is no going back. I am exposed, vulnerable, bare. I can only be the true me with Samuel. And nothing has ever felt more freeing.

"Jillian, you're the most beautiful woman I've ever known." Samuel's hot breath grazes my neck as his thrusts come even deeper than before. Tingles roll through my body, the desire pooling in my abdomen and between my legs finally bursting in a sweet, intense climax. I cry out as I hang onto Samuel's shoulders and let him take me farther until he lets out a guttural moan, his muscles tightening then releasing in my arms.

Samuel holds me until our breath slows down, then smiles deviously before he kisses me on the cheek, the forehead, and finally on my lips. He tastes sweet, salty, and satisfied.

Moments after our mouths and hips have parted, I run my hand over the tattoo covering his left bicep, then over the jagged scar on his chest, and finally I find the small tattoo which lines the inside of his right wrist.

Just as I noticed before, the tattoo is made up of seven sets of initials. I trace my finger around them before lifting an inquisitive gaze to my lover.

"They're the seven people I haven't been able to find," Samuel says quietly. "Before it was too late, anyway."

I study the initials, noticing that the first set belongs to his late wife, Karine.

"I loved you even when I was with her," Samuel says, answering my question before I can bring myself to ask it. "It's one of the reasons I've never been able to forgive myself for Karine's death. It wasn't fair to her—loving you the way I did the entire time I was married to her." Samuel runs his thumb along my cheek, being careful to avoid the cuts. "I don't regret loving you all these years, though, Jill. The thought of you, of what it was like to be with you—no matter how hard I tried, I never could forget it. And now, here you are, in my arms again."

"I only wish that Isla didn't have to go missing in order for us to find each other again," I say quietly.

Samuel lifts my chin so that our eyes meet. "I will find your sister, Jillian. I promise you."

The certainty in Samuel's eyes is assuring, but as I gaze once more at the initials carved on his wrist, I am reminded that not all of the women who are taken will be rescued as I was earlier tonight.

Samuel lifts my hand to his lips but stops when he notices the vintage emerald ring on my left ring finger, glinting in the firelight.

"I didn't realize I still had it on," I say, marveling at the beauty in the bright green stone, at the way I feel mesmerized, almost in a trance, each time I look at it.

Samuel traces his finger over the shiny jewel. "Do you think the ring has something to do with bringing us back together and with bringing us here?"

I nod as I inch closer to his warm body. "I have no idea *how,* but yes, I think so."

The corners of Samuel's lips turn up into a grin. "Well, in that case, I'm never letting you take this ring off…because I'm not letting you go again, Jillian Chambord. That, you can count on."

I want so badly to believe that Samuel and I will never again be separated. But as he pulls me into his arms and I gaze out at the thick snowflakes piling on the windowsill of this deserted cabin in the middle of the Alps, I can't shake the ominous feeling that has once again settled in my bones.

"Samuel?"

"Yes?"

"Even if we do succeed in saving Rosie and Frances, what if we never make it back to 2012? What if I never see my sister again?"

The wind howling through the trees outside is my only response as these two lost souls of ours—who have found each other under the most unimaginable of circumstances—hang on for the storm.

We have no way of knowing what will come next, if we will find Isla or the other missing girls…or *even* if we will come out of this alive.

EPISODE 6

CHAPTER 15

The French Alps

This endless night before Christmas doesn't provide a single moment's rest for either Samuel or me. We are both too spun up after everything that has happened—Isla's disappearance, our mysterious time travel to 1937, my own abduction, and now, this most recent development—Samuel back in my life...in a way I never expected.

Just when I begin to shiver in his arms, Samuel grabs the thick wool blanket and wraps it tightly around me, before throwing another log on the fire.

"How did you find me tonight?" I ask when Samuel returns to me, his green eyes gleaming in the glow of the fire.

Samuel slips his warm hands underneath the blanket and wraps them around my bare waist before he speaks.

"Earlier on the train, I *assumed* that you would follow the plan and stay in the sleeping compartment until I came back for you." Samuel pauses, lifting a brow. "I should've known you would take things into your own hands. Unfortunately, when I heard you passing through the corridor, I thought they were taking Rosie. But when I found both Rosie's and our sleeping compartments empty,

I realized they must've taken Rosie *earlier*—right after the train was stopped. I knew then that the woman I'd heard just a few moments before, passing by the restroom, was you. By the time I made it outside, though, you and the others were gone. I searched for a while before I found the shack. By the time I got there, the others had already left, but when I looked in the window, I saw him in there—that barbarian—hitting you." Samuel's jaw tightens as he gazes into the flames. "Which is why taking things into your own hands isn't always the best idea."

"I'm sorry. I know I put us both in more danger by doing what I did. But I kept hearing thumping sounds in the hallway, and the lights were flickering off and on, and…well, you know me."

Samuel levels his serious gaze at me. "That I do. And like I said when you hijacked my car two days ago in D.C., you haven't changed one bit."

I smack him in the arm. "I didn't *hijack* your car. I kissed you, and if I remember correctly, you had no problem kissing me back. It's not my fault if you weren't paying attention to the whereabouts of your car keys during the kiss."

Samuel shakes his head at me, his dark five o'clock shadow looking impossibly sexy in the glow of the fire. "Yeah, well. That was the kind of kiss that makes you not give a damn if the woman who's kissing you is about to steal your keys."

"I'm glad to see I still have it after all these years," I tease.

He grins as he pulls me closer to him. "Oh, you still have it, Jill. Trust me."

A rush of heat creeps up my neck as Samuel brushes the hair out of my eyes and kisses me on the forehead.

"I still don't understand how you managed to track us down in these conditions," I say. "It's pitch-black out there and there's snow everywhere. Not to mention, you were only wearing a tuxedo, for God's sake. You must've been freezing."

"I'm trained for these situations. This is how I've spent the last three years of my life."

"Naked by the fire with a different woman in your arms?" I poke.

"Only *you* get this type of special treatment after a rescue," he says, before brushing his lips over mine. "Since the day I started this job, I've been searching. Searching for women just like you. Just like Isla."

The fire crackles beside us as Samuel runs his strong hands up my arms. "Except you're not like all the other girls. You know how to escape trained assassins. You know how to fire weapons."

In Samuel's eyes, I see that same curious bewilderment from years ago. He's still searching for the truth. For *my* truth.

"How, Jill? What happened to you and Isla when you were younger?"

This time I am the one turning my troubled gaze to the fire, recalling a childhood I wish I could burn in those flames. But no matter how much I hate my past, it is always there—waiting to sabotage my latest relationship, steal another night's sleep, destroy any inkling of happiness. And Samuel is the first person in a long time to make me feel hopeful that happiness might not be so far beyond my reach after all.

But hiding the truth from Samuel will only make him think— as it did once before—that I don't love him.

As we sit at the eye of this blazing storm, where the lines between the past and the future are blurring to the point of nonexistent, I know that Samuel is the only person I can count on. And despite the promise I made to Isla all those years ago, when were only innocent girls, I cannot—*I will not*—withhold the truth from him yet again.

And so, I turn back to the man who has found me after all these years, the man who has succeeded in breaking through the impenetrable wall I'd built around my heart, and finally I tell him my story.

"I have to start from the very beginning for you to understand everything," I warn him.

Samuel shoots a glance toward the steamy cabin windows, where a haze of black night and white flakes swirl beyond the glass. "Go back as far as you need to. We're not going anywhere until morning."

After taking in a labored breath, I launch in.

"Isla and I grew up, for the most part, without a father. He left when we were only five, and he took everything with him. The money, the house, our mother's sanity—well, I'm not sure she ever *was* sane—but regardless, he took it all. Apparently, he never wanted children. He was a wealthy D.C. businessman, and kids were never in his plan. From the day my mother told him she was pregnant, he threatened to leave her."

I hesitate before continuing on with the next part of the story, but one glance into Samuel's compassionate gaze tells me I am safe.

"You see, my parents first met while my dad was on a business trip to Paris. He called a prostitute to his hotel room one night…and the woman who showed up was my mother."

Samuel's expression stays neutral, not revealing even an ounce of the disgust I feel at saying those words aloud.

"Your mother told you this story?" he asks quietly.

"There were no boundaries with her. No concept of what was or *was not* appropriate with her children. So, yes, we learned all too young that our mother, Céline, was a prostitute. She'd been raised in a Paris brothel by her own mother, and it was the only life my mom ever knew. As a result of her horrible childhood and her early foray into the art of pleasing men for money, she wasn't the most stable person. But for as crazy as she was, she was also good at what she did. So good that she managed to put my father under her spell. He fell in love with her that first night in Paris and offered to whisk her away from the world of prostitution and give her a new life in the States. I know you're thinking *Pretty Woman*, but unfortunately, this story doesn't have a happy ending. And although she was certainly beautiful in her day, my mother is no Julia Roberts.

"She knew my dad had a lot of money, and she knew she could keep him happy, so she said yes. He paraded her around to galas and political events in D.C. as his gorgeous French trophy wife, with the agreement that she would *never* tell anyone the true story of how they met. But years later, as soon as he left her high and dry with no money and two hyper five-year-old twins on her hands, she turned back to the only thing she knew how to do—prostitution. All of the politicians and D.C. businessmen who'd admired my mother from afar were now paying her for sex during their lunch hours, after work, overnight, and on weekends. The shabby house we moved into after my father left *became* my mother's brothel."

The muscles in his Samuel's jaw tighten as he shakes his head, but he doesn't say a word.

"This began right after my father left, and even though Isla and I were too young to fully understand what my mother was doing with all of these male *houseguests*, we caught on pretty quickly. She was such a tyrant during the day that we learned just as quickly to take care of ourselves. We locked our bedroom door at night and played music so we wouldn't hear what was going on just down the hallway. But we heard it…we always heard it."

Concern lines Samuel's large, sweet eyes. "I'm so sorry, Jillian. I had no idea."

"You couldn't have because I always refused to tell you. There's a reason for that though…a reason I couldn't tell you the truth. And it has to do with a promise I made to Isla."

A chilly draft slithers through the dark cabin, sending a shiver through my body. Samuel wraps the blanket tighter around me, then nods, urging me to go on.

"By the time Isla and I were in junior high, our mother had reached the height of her insanity. She would scream at us for no reason at all; she stopped buying us clothes, food, or medication. She blamed us for our father leaving and for the decline of her *business*. The truth was that she was getting older and she wasn't able to reel in men the way she once could. I was so ashamed of her, of the way we lived. I wanted to be as far away from that house as I could, so I immersed myself in the school newspaper every day after school. I'd hang around until the cleaning crew would literally kick me out. During this time, Isla told me she got a job babysitting for some of the neighbor kids after school. She said she was saving her money to get us out of there. She told me she had a plan...that I should trust her.

"But what I didn't know was that Isla wasn't babysitting. One day she had come home from school early, and Parker Williams—not yet a senator at this time—was just pulling up to our house. He'd come to the other side of town to visit my mother for one of their afternoon *sessions,* but when he spotted Isla in her short skirt, prancing into the house, he forgot all about my mother."

A flare of anger passes through Samuel's eyes as I continue.

"Williams worked a deal with my mom. He would pay her double if he could have Isla two afternoons a week. You have to understand that at this point, my mother *hated* Isla...much more than she hated me. Isla was the beautiful twin, and at thirteen her beauty had far surpassed my mother's. But there was something else about Isla—she was pure, sweet, and innocent. The complete opposite of my jaded, damaged, nasty mother. My mother knew her prospects weren't good, so she agreed to Williams's proposition. That night, when I came home from the school newspaper, Isla didn't speak to me. She didn't speak to me for a whole week. At night, I heard her sobbing in her pillow. I kept asking her what was wrong, but she wouldn't tell me. She just kept saying she was fine, that she had a plan to get us out of there and I needed to trust her and stop asking questions.

"This went on for months without me having any clue. But Isla hadn't been lying to me—she did have a plan. One of the *other* men who came for my mother was younger, more handsome than the others. He noticed Isla, and he wasn't as pushy with her—*unlike* Parker Williams, the bastard. This man's name was Russell Hughes."

Samuel raises a brow, surely recognizing the name from the police reports he looked up on my mother.

"Isla approached Russell once when my mother wasn't in the room. She made him an offer. Pay her twice what he paid my mother, and he could have her as often as he wanted. He agreed. He stopped seeing my mother, and he only came over when Isla knew my mom wouldn't be home. Despite the sickness of the situation, Isla actually liked Russell. She saw him as a ticket out of our hellish home life. But what Isla didn't know was that my mother was in love with Russell...or at least in her deranged head, she *thought* she was in love with him. When he stopped seeing her, she went even more mental. She would leave us for days at a time without food, money, or any clue as to where she'd gone."

"I assume your mom found out about Russell and Isla," Samuel says quietly. "How?"

"It was Parker Williams." I dig my nails into the soft rug beneath me as I try to contain my hatred for that man. "He noticed that Isla had become more comfortable in bed with him. 'More experienced and less afraid' were his words I believe. He told my mother this, and she knew immediately that she'd lost Russell to Isla and that Isla must've been hiding the money from her. So one day, our mother said she was leaving for the afternoon, but she hid in her car around the corner and waited. As expected, Russell pulled up within the hour. I was at school, working on the paper, and for some reason, I just knew to come home. I felt it...I knew Isla was in danger. So I ran home as fast as I could, but I was too late. My mother had already shot Russell in the head, and she was about to shoot Isla when I ran into the room." I pause, feeling my breath leave me as my mind recreates the same vivid, horrific scene I only ever see in nightmares.

"I took a vase from the kitchen and smashed it over the back of her head. She dropped the gun, and I managed to grab it before she got to me. And then, I shot my own mother in the knee to stop her from doing any more damage."

I try not to blink, knowing that the memory of my mother's blood will be waiting for me as soon as I do.

"And you were only thirteen?" Samuel says, the look in his eyes incredulous.

"Yes, but after that day, both Isla and I felt like we were forty. Our innocence was gone forever...and Isla's had been gone for a lot longer. I just didn't know it. As we were waiting for the police to arrive, I kept the gun aimed at my mother while Isla cleaned herself up and put her clothes back on. She begged me never to tell a soul what she'd been doing. She didn't want this sickening past chasing her around her whole life. Keeping her secret was the least I could do considering what had happened to her...when all along I'd been oblivious. Lost in my own little world at the school paper. I've felt guilty for years. I don't know if I'll ever shake this guilt."

Samuel tilts my chin up so our eyes meet. "It wasn't your fault, Jill. You know that, don't you?"

I nod, pretending to know. But that familiar stab of regret—regret over something I cannot change—seizes my chest, making it difficult for me to breathe.

"After our mother was sentenced to life in prison for the murder of Russell Hughes, Isla and I were shuffled from foster home to foster home, but I kept my word. I never told a soul about what she'd done...what she'd been forced to do at the hands of the woman who was supposed to love us more than anyone in the world."

"So in your mother's hearing, you didn't bring up Parker Williams's name?" Samuel asks.

"No, Isla made me swear not to say a word. She couldn't bear the thought of having our future caretakers know what she'd been doing. She was so young. You can only imagine the shame, the embarrassment of having something like this follow you around your whole life. Before the police arrived that day, Isla even took the gun out of my hands, aimed it at my mother, and made her swear never to tell the courts what had gone on between Isla, Williams, and Hughes. She forced my mom to testify that *she'd* been the one having sex with Russell Hughes before she shot him, which explains why he was naked. That's the reason you'll never find the entire truth in any of the court records."

Samuel tucks a strand of hair behind my ear and runs his thumb along my cheek, being careful not to touch any of my cuts and bruises. "Jill, I can't believe you lived through all of this. That you survived. That you're such an amazing, beautiful person. How have you held this in all these years?"

"It was for Isla. Always for Isla. Because for her, it was so much worse."

Samuel kisses me on the forehead, silencing the cry that threatens to escape my lips. "It was unimaginable for Isla. But it was just as bad for you. You're brave, Jillian. The bravest woman I've ever known." He wraps his arms around me and kisses me on the lips before squaring his gaze in front of mine. "I understand why you kept this a secret all those years. You're loyal, and Isla is lucky to have you as a sister."

"Thank you," I say quietly. "I wanted to tell you, but I don't think I was ready to tell anyone until now. Until you. It was a nightmare, all of it. Not exactly the kind of thing you want to relive over and over, you know?"

Samuel nods, the creases around his eyes and the grim expression on his face telling me that he knows more than anyone. Karine's murder was as gruesome as they get. He's lived through a nightmare too.

Yet here we both are—survivors.

A new fire blazes in Samuel's eyes as he squeezes my hand. "I know that before Isla's disappearance, you were working on the story that exposed Senator's Williams's involvement in a child prostitution ring and in the murder of those two sisters." Samuel pauses as he gazes out the snowy window. "And you know what? I don't think you were the only one who was putting it all on the line to watch that bastard burn."

"What are you talking about?"

"My team was already investigating Williams's connection to the Morel family when you sent me the photograph of the three of them at the charity gala. And with what you just told me about his connection to Isla, I think I know what might've happened."

"You do?"

The certainty in Samuel's strong profile and the way he holds himself makes me believe him even before he says a word.

"I don't think it was a coincidence that your sister was dating Frédéric Morel and that his family *happens* to be close with Senator Williams."

"Are you saying that Isla started dating Frédéric *because* of his family's connection to Williams?"

Samuel nods. "From what you just described to me, Isla sounds like a smart woman. Troubled, but smart. Someone who knows how to get what she wants."

"That's my sister."

"I believe Isla singled out Frédéric Morel so that she would cross paths with Williams again."

"Okay, you're losing me here. Why in the hell would she want to cross paths with Williams again?" I say.

"To blackmail him."

Suddenly Isla's voicemail comes rushing back to me. She'd sounded excited...and *devious*. "Before Isla was taken on the train, in her message to me, she said—"

"*You're not going to believe what I've done this time,*" Samuel finishes for me. "And she laughed, which shows that she wasn't afraid. She didn't know she had any reason to be. I believe Isla threatened to go to the police or to the press, or even just to the senator's family, with the story of how he exploited her as a young girl...*unless* he resigned."

"If you're right, then Isla blackmailing Williams was the *real* reason he resigned so suddenly—from a press conference in France no less—*right after* he'd seen Isla at that charity ball with the Morels. The insane part is that the story I'd been working on for the past two weeks came to a head literally on the exact same day, making

Williams wanted for murder in the States. Which is why he's now on the run."

"Just like you, Isla wanted that man to lose everything," Samuel says. "And she couldn't move on with her life until it was done."

I think about the fact that Isla and I share the same blood, the same horrid past, and the same contempt for Parker Williams. If Isla had found out that Williams had a vacation home in France and traveled in the same circles as her, it made sense that she would've wanted him gone. That she would've wanted him to lose everything, to see him unravel—the way we both did when we were only children.

"But that still doesn't explain Senator Williams's involvement in Isla's abduction," I say. "Obviously, he had motive if she was blackmailing him, but if he was planning to shut her up by abducting her, why would he follow through with the resignation?"

Samuel shoots a quick glance at the deserted cabin we are nestled inside. "Judging by our surroundings, we know there's *a lot* more to these abductions than the connection Williams has to your sister. But I do believe he was involved in some way. It's just too much of a coincidence otherwise."

"Based on what I found out from Frances and Rosie earlier, it sounds like Rosie's ex-fiancé, Alexandre Morel, and his father, Henri, could be the culprits in the 1937 version of this crime. Frances told me she was having an affair with Henri, and that *he* was the one who gave her the ticket to the Orient Express."

"After what she said on the train, I figured Frances was sleeping with one of the Morel men," Samuel says.

"And Rosie was certain Alexandre was behind the abduction. Jacques—her true love and *my* grandfather—sent her the Orient Express ticket in early December, and she's been staying at the Morel Château for the entire month with her family, so she hid the ticket inside the box where she keeps Jacques's letters."

"So Alexandre easily could've snooped around and found out that Rosie was planning to leave him for another man," Samuel says.

"Exactly. And if he happened to find out she was pregnant with that man's child—or *children*—he would have even more motive to avenge his hurt pride."

"So you believe that Henri and Alexandre hired men to storm the train and take Rosie and Frances?" Samuel asks.

"Yes. And as for me, I think I was in the wrong place at the wrong time."

Samuel runs his hand along his chin, lost in thought. "You may just be right. And perhaps Frédéric and his father, Laurent, are working together in the same way in Isla's case...with some involvement from Williams. All to save the family's reputation. To take care of any woman who might tarnish the family name or hurt their massive egos."

"Yeah, I don't imagine that the Morels would want it going public that Frédéric's fiancée fell in love with a Parisian artist, got pregnant with his baby, *and* that she was sexually abused as a child by one of their longtime political friends."

"No, I don't imagine they would," Samuel says.

"The question we have to answer now," I say, "is where they're taking the girls, and what they're planning to do with them once they get there."

"We'll take a look at the map in a little bit, but first we need to find you some food and water. You're looking a little pale."

"I'm fine, Samuel."

He raises a brow, then leans into me and brushes his lips over mine. "I know it's not in your nature to let anyone take care of you. But as long as I'm around, you're going to have to get used to it."

After his next spine-tingling kiss, I lean back against the couch and smile at him. "Okay. Food, water, and eventually sleep do sound amazing."

He pulls the blanket tighter around my shoulders. "Stay here. I'll go see what I can dig up in the kitchen."

As I watch Samuel slip back into his black tux pants and walk shirtless through the dark cabin, I am thankful that if I have to go through this insane nightmare to find Isla, at least I have Samuel by my side.

The fire crackling beside me lulls me to sleep. I'm not sure how long I've dozed off before Samuel returns with a glass of water and a box of shortbread. A troubled look passes through his eyes as he sits down next to me. "This was all I could find. The cupboards were pretty bare."

"This is fine, Samuel. Thank you. But is something else the matter?"

Samuel nods slowly, not hiding the grim expression on his face. "Yes, there's something you need to see."

CHAPTER 16

Before Samuel will show me his discovery, he insists that I drink the entire glass of water and eat a few cookies. Then he helps me put on his own shirt and wraps the blanket back around my shoulders.

"I tried all of the lamps, but nothing's working in the storm," Samuel says as he lights a candle, then ushers me out of the living room and down a dark, chilly hallway.

When we reach the door at the end of the long corridor, Samuel pauses. "This may just be a coincidence, but after this insane trip, I don't think I believe in coincidences anymore."

Samuel hands me the candle, then opens the creaky door. The minute I take a step into the small room, I feel the unmistakable presence of my sister. I smell her perfume. But most of all, I feel her desperation.

I swirl around, moving the candle in all directions, positive my gaze will lock on her striking violet eyes and her long, silky chestnut waves.

But what I find in Isla's place sends chills snaking up my arms.

"It's a baby's room," I whisper. "A baby girl."

An antique white crib sits in the corner, a pale pink sheet stretching over its tiny mattress. The candle flickers as I move it around the perimeter of the room, revealing a closet stocked full of frilly baby clothes. There are tiny pink dresses, white lace-trimmed socks, teeny black-and-white booties, and even sets of hand-knitted hats and mittens.

Samuel places a hand on the small of my back and gestures for me to move the candle toward the wall over the crib.

A string of carved wooden letters painted in pastel pink hangs on the nursery wall. I move the flame past each letter, until I can read the entire name.

"*Madeleine*," I whisper. "Rosie's daughter, Madeleine. But I don't understand. They've already named her? They must be planning to bring her here once Rosie gives birth."

"How do the Morels already know Rosie's having a girl though?" Samuel asks. "Rosie wasn't even showing. They couldn't possibly know the sex of the baby."

"Maybe they just really want a baby girl," I say. "But would Henri and Alexandre Morel really decorate a pink room for the baby girl they *hope* Rosie is going to have? If they're planning to take her baby, wouldn't they want a boy to be the heir to their empire and keep their family name alive?"

"This room is *not* the work of a man," Samuel agrees. "Which means that we still don't know the whole story."

Samuel's words make me think of my mysterious meetings with Georges, the chauffeur, and his twin sister, Madeleine Morel.

"I forgot to tell you earlier, I—or *we*—met Madeleine's twin brother, Georges."

"What are you talking about?" Samuel asks.

As I turn to face Samuel, I wonder why I still feel as if my sister is somewhere in this creepy baby room. I know that is impossible... but then again, after our mysterious train voyage back in time to 1937, what do I know?

"The driver who took us from the Geneva airport to the Morel Château, and who I called earlier tonight to drive me to the ferry— *he* was Rosie's other child, Madeleine's twin brother. But from what Madeleine told me at the train station, the twins never met their real mother, and they were separated at birth. Madeleine was raised to believe she was a Morel, and Georges was given up for adoption. They only just found each other a year ago, and they've been trying to put the pieces together. It can't be a coincidence that I met them both right before we landed ourselves here."

Samuel shakes his head, confusion sweeping through those big green eyes of his. "No, it can't be."

"And before Georges left me, he said something strange. He said 'The answer to the mystery is not always as obvious as you may think.' Madeleine seemed to know more than she was letting on as well. She seemed to think we were being watched." I glance around the eerie baby room once more, thinking of those stately paintings I found of the Morel women—the ones that lined the wall—Agnès, Thérèse, and Hélène. Could they have something to do with this?

Most of all, I remember the paintings that were hidden in a storage room, draped underneath a dusty white sheet and banned from the Morel women's wall of fame. Madeleine and Isla were among those that had been cast aside, along with a third painting that had been slashed, torn to shreds. I could still see traces of the images that remained—those dark brown curls and that sweet dimple.

Now I knew it was Rosie's dimple and those were Rosie's curls.

The Morels must have destroyed her painting after she betrayed Alexandre.

A bitter gust of air squeezes in through the cracks in the windowpanes and whips around Samuel and me. "I don't think the Morel men are the only ones behind this. This nursery—this hope for a baby girl—a woman did this," I say.

Before Samuel can respond, another freezing draft wafts into the room, bringing to life the baby mobile dangling above the crib.

A slow, creepy lullaby travels through the cold air in the nursery while the mobile spins, gaining momentum. I vaguely feel Samuel squeeze my hand, but Isla's presence, the memory of her voice, the vision of her pleading violet gaze puts me in a trance. The mobile spins faster, and suddenly I feel the emerald ring tingling, tightening, and squeezing my left ring finger so hard I want to scream from the pain.

But when I open my mouth, there is no sound. No voice. Just like in my nightmares. Before I can figure out what is happening to me, I feel Isla pulling me to her.

"Jillian, please come. You're the only one who can save me."

Isla's thirteen-year-old voice weaves into her adult cries, and I am immediately drawn to her, to my beautiful, innocent twin sister. The one I could never truly save.

I will save her this time, though.

I blink my eyes, and all I see is the baby mobile which twirls in violent, rapid circles before finally, it cracks and falls from the ceiling, crashing into the crib.

The lullaby keeps playing, squeaking out its slow, eerie tune. This is all I hear as I leave Samuel's side and go to my sister.

"I'm coming for you, Isla. I'm coming."

A string of vivid scenes flash before me in full, vibrant color, like a movie reel rolling in slow motion. I have no recollection of what was going on before I arrived here—wherever here is—but I don't care, because there, below me, is Isla posing on a plush red sofa.

Her seductive violet gaze sparkles as she looks into the eyes of the man who sits on a stool opposite her, swiping his brush over a large canvas in short, delicate strokes.

A strapless ivory dress hugs her beautiful curves and her thin waist, and waves of her shimmering chestnut hair fall effortlessly over her bare, dainty shoulders.

With my full, 360-degree view of the room, I see that in between each brush stroke, the painter pauses to study my sister—but his version of "studying" is more of a silent flirtation. He is clearly mesmerized by her. As am I.

In Christophe's sultry dark eyes and in this lustrous painting he is creating, I know that he is the first man to ever truly *see* my sister. The damaged, sweet beauty of Isla is reflected in each bold brush stroke.

And slowly, the painting I found hidden in the Morels' storage closet comes to life.

Isla blinks her long lashes at Christophe, and suddenly, there it is. The moment where she knows she has found him. The one who sees past her stunning, flawless exterior. The one who will love her anyway.

They communicate without words, but I can hear my sister. She is afraid to bare her truth. But the gentleness in Christophe's gaze, the truth in his portrait of her, tells her she will be safe with him.

Better than safe—she can be herself. *Finally.*

In an instant, the vibe in the room changes. Goose bumps prickle my neck. There, hovering in the doorway is Frédéric, his imposing, possessive gaze full of rage and jealousy. He wants Isla all to himself, but he isn't stupid. He knows—he *sees*—that will never happen.

And so it begins. Isla's beauty drives yet another man to total madness. It started when we were only thirteen, and it has never ended.

At once, the scene before me changes in a flash.

Now it is Isla holding something in her hands, tears streaming down her pale cheeks.

I go to her, and even though I can't touch her or even reach for her, I can feel her emotions. I know instantly that the tears she's crying are tears of joy, not sorrow.

The little white stick in her hands reveals two bright pink lines.

"*I'm pregnant,*" she whispers.

The scene flashes yet again, faster this time, and now I see Isla closing the door to a fancy study, a slinky black gown swishing around her ankles. She turns, looking as calm, cool, and collected as ever. But I feel the fear that courses through her entire being, the horror pulsing through her veins.

Her hand shoots instinctively to her abdomen as she takes a step closer to the man staring at her in wide-eyed bewilderment.

Senator Parker Williams.

"I was hoping you'd remember me." Isla's cool tone is laced with hatred.

He approaches her, careful to keep his gaze focused on her eyes, and not on the dipping neckline of her dress. "How much do you want?" he growls.

She lets out a low, sinister laugh, gesturing to her surroundings. "Frédéric is going to propose to me this weekend. I'm going to be a Morel. Do you actually think I want your money?"

The slightest hint of fear passes through his cowardly eyes. "Then what do you want?"

Isla takes another step toward the man who abused her, who used her body when she was too young to take a stand. She takes a stand now, though, her courage unwavering. Only I can feel the terror tying knots in her stomach, the hatred that boils inside her, that makes her want to kill this man.

I want to kill him too.

But I am powerless as I watch the scene unfold. I am here...but not here in the way I want to be.

"You'll resign from the Senate this week, or else I'll tell the Morels what you did to me," Isla threatens.

Now it is his turn to laugh. "Do you think they'll actually believe you? The *whore*?"

Isla's tiny hand comes around fast, slapping the pompous look right off his face. "I've already told the Morels' lawyer—*my* lawyer now—in confidence what you did to me. One phone call, and the story goes to the press, to the police, to all of your slimy politician friends, and straight to your wife. Your life will be over. Unless you resign."

Just as he's about to retort, she pulls a photo out of her shiny silver clutch and shoves it into his chest. "This is only a copy. The lawyer has the original, along with an entire roll of film. I may have been too young to fight back, but I wasn't stupid. I knew I'd find you one day and take you down, you cowardly piece of shit."

The defeat on Senator's Williams greasy old face is priceless as he stares at the photo in his hands, then watches Isla stalk out of the study, slamming the door behind her.

Samuel was right. Just like me, Isla was willing to risk everything to bring this bastard down. She'd infiltrated a high-profile wealthy family and had even pretended to fall in love with their son, all to scare the shit out of Senator Williams and take away his career. Isla had no intention of taking the story of her sordid past to the Morels, to the press, or to the police. I knew her better than that. She would never want the world to know what had happened to her. She simply wanted to take something important away from Parker Williams, the way he had done to her.

Pride and love for my sister overwhelm me as the scene flashes again, now moving quicker than before. It is Isla, in the bedroom I searched at the Morel Château, leaving a note—the note I found in Frédéric's suitcase—and the massive diamond engagement ring on the desk. Next I see her dashing into a black car outside the property, smiling at the driver.

He tips his hat at her, his silvery sapphire eyes twinkling through the darkness. *"Bonsoir, Mademoiselle."*

I know that warm voice, those knowing eyes. It's Georges, the chauffeur.

"I need the ferry to Lausanne," Isla says in French as she shoots one last glance toward the looming castle.

The scenes zip before me, moving faster as I trace Isla's voyage to the train. Next we are on the Orient Express, and she is dialing my number with one hand and touching her belly with the other. Nervous, excited energy surrounds her as she leaves the message I have already heard. I want to scream out to her, warn her, stop what I know is about to happen, but Isla can't see me, and I can't scream. She doesn't know I'm here, and I don't even know *how* I am here.

A brawny man, dressed head to toe in black, storms into the sleeping compartment and takes my sister before she can finish telling me her news.

That she is pregnant. And that she ended the senator's career.

Next, Isla is out in the cold, shivering and surrounded by a flurry of snow pouring down through the trees from the black winter sky above. The man shoves her from behind, pressing a gun into her side. I feel her fear, her pain, her grief, as if it is all my own. This unbreakable bond we have always shared grows stronger than ever as I travel along beside her, willing her to see me, to know that I am here, that I am coming for her.

Every intense emotion that runs through Isla makes an imprint on my heart. She is doing her best to suppress the terror, telling herself she's been through worse. That she will survive. An overwhelming surge of hope and courage fills her up. She does not cry. She will do anything to keep her baby safe. To make it to Christophe, the only man she has ever truly loved.

The wind and the flittering snowflakes disappear abruptly, and now we are inside a tiny, cold room. The lights are off, but I make out the outline of my sister tied up to a chair, a thick piece of duct tape covering her mouth.

The creepy vibe in this space strikes me as familiar, and as I gaze around at Isla's surroundings—at the shiny new crib in the corner, at the teeny baby clothes adorning the closet—I remember the nursery, the cabin, and my voyage with Samuel.

This is why I felt Isla so strongly in that room.

Because seventy-five years in the future, she is being held here against her will. Forced to sit alone in the nursery that will house *her* child if she isn't saved first.

"Jillian!"

Isla's panicked voice cuts through my thoughts. I will myself closer to her until I am inches from her face. One lone teardrop rolls down her cheek as she draws in a labored breath through her nose.

"I'm here, Isla. I'm here." I tell her, even though there are no real words exiting my mouth. Her panicked violet eyes flicker wildly, her brows raising.

And finally, there it is—*recognition*. The invisible connection we've always shared. Somehow, in this frozen, eerie baby nursery in the middle of the Alps, my sister knows I have traveled to her. She sees me.

"I'm coming for you, Isla. Just hang on," I tell her, willing myself not to break. To stay strong. "I'm going to save you and your baby. No matter what they do to you, do not give up hope, do you hear me?"

She nods her head violently.

I want to hug her, to untie her, to rip the goddamned piece of tape off her mouth, but I have no physical abilities, no physical form. Still, she sees me, the tears now pouring down her face.

In an instant, I feel something tugging at me, pulling me away from her.

No. Please, give me more time with her.

But whatever force has landed me here is sucking me back.

"Promise me, Isla. Promise me you won't give up."

One more intense gaze from those panicked violet eyes of hers— the eyes we will forever share—tells me she hears me.

"I promise, Jilly. I promise."

The creepy lullaby swirls through the air, pulling me away from my sister, into a hole of frozen blackness. Sleep comforts me, makes me forget what just happened, making me feel indifferent about where I am going.

But Isla's voice shatters the darkness, breaking the silence that is about to swallow me into its endless depths.

"Wake up, Jillian! They're coming for you."

The piercing sound of shattering glass snaps me awake. My eyes pop open as a panicked breath fills my lungs.

Samuel is inches from my face, his finger on my lips. "Stay quiet and don't move," he whispers before rushing away from my side.

A heavy fatigue plagues me as I realize I am lying on the floor of the old cabin nursery. Before I can analyze the mysterious voyage I have just taken to Isla and back, the sound of knuckles on flesh startles me to a sitting position.

Isla's warning rushes back to me.

They're here. They've come back for us.

Shooting to my feet, I scan the nursery, cursing that sickeningly sweet lullaby that continues to rattle out of the baby mobile which lies in a broken heap inside the crib.

A crashing sound coming from the front of the cabin makes me jump. I grab a rickety wooden chair from the corner of the room and hold it in front of me, creeping slowly out into the pitch-black hallway.

I stop just around the corner from the doorway leading into the living room, where I hear Samuel fighting with some unidentified man—a man who I am certain was sent back through the mountains to kill us.

Finally, I build up the courage to peek around the corner.

In front of the dying fire, Samuel is struggling to seize a shiny blade from the intruder's hands. I recognize the man immediately as the abductor who knocked Frances out and hauled her out of the shack over his shoulder.

Samuel's fist flies back to sock his strong-jawed nemesis in the face, but the man is quicker, blocking Samuel's punch, then attempting to stab Samuel in the side. Samuel jumps, missing the knife by only an inch.

A sudden wave of dizziness threatens to knock me to my knees. I ignore the blood pounding through my ears as I grip the sides of the chair and wait for my moment.

Samuel's back muscles tighten as he blocks another stabbing attempt. Then with a beastly force, Samuel grabs the man's wrist and wrenches the blade from his hands.

I hold my breath, waiting for Samuel to stab the man and end this battle, but instead, the man's fist meets Samuel's abs and he doubles over, stumbling, dropping the knife to the ground.

I feel my feet moving before I am even aware of what I'm about to do. A fierce instinct rushes through me as I swing the chair up over my head and bring it down with a heavy crash over the back of our enemy's thick head just as he is reaching for the knife.

He lets out a strangled cry as his hefty legs fold, and he crumbles to his knees. Samuel delivers a swift kick to the man's face, and I follow up with another bash to the back of his head, giving Samuel just enough time to pluck the knife up off the rug.

The last embers of the fire sizzle beside us as Samuel pins the man to the floor, wrapping his bicep tightly around the man's neck and pressing the point of the blade just underneath his chin.

Samuel nods for me to back away, and for once I follow his instructions. But I don't let go of the wooden chair in my hands. I grip it so tightly that a splinter of wood slices into my palm.

"Who ordered the abduction?" Samuel growls in French into the man's ear.

The man only grunts in response, so Samuel wrenches his neck back to an impossible angle, then presses the pointy blade deeper into his chin, breaking the skin.

"Tell me who is behind this, or I'll kill you right now. I had no problem killing your friend back at the shack," Samuel says, showing not a spec of fear while I stand trembling uncontrollably.

The man struggles underneath Samuel's firm hold, but he still won't talk. This time Samuel pushes the blade deeper, and the man cries out as his blood trickles onto the rug.

Finally, our enemy's strangled voice travels through the dark cabin.

"I don't know her name," he says. "I swear, I don't know her name!"

I think of the pink nursery, of the girly decorations and hand-knitted baby clothes. I see Isla's pleading violet eyes trapped seventy-five years in the future, in the updated version of this same nursery, and Samuel's words from earlier rush back to me.

"*This room is* not *the work of a man.*"

And as Samuel twists the blade deeper into the perpetrator's neck, grilling him for more information, I realize that all along, we've been severely underestimating the power of the Morel *women*.

EPISODE 7

CHAPTER 17

December 25, 1937

The French Alps

The last embers of the fire flicker out just as a haze of early morning sunlight streams through the cabin windows, reflecting off the shiny blade Samuel still holds in his hand. That blade is the *only* thing keeping our tight-lipped attacker in his place. Well—that and Samuel's unparalleled brute strength. I am certainly not helping at this point, as my own putrid fear has me trembling off in the corner, gripping a splintery wooden chair as my only weapon.

"Où sont Rosie et Frances?" Where are Rosie and Frances? Samuel asks for the tenth time as he keeps the burly man pinned to the floor, twisting his neck and arms backward at painful angles.

The man refuses to respond, once again prompting Samuel to nick the skin on his neck, even deeper this time. The trickle of blood dripping onto the dull brown rug turns into a small stream.

The man's bearded face contorts into an ugly grimace, but he keeps his lips sealed.

"Tell me where they are!" Samuel's voice booms through the cabin.

As his face pales to a sickening shade of gray, the man finally caves. "Farther up in the mountains, there's a castle. The girls are there." He sucks in an arduous breath. "But it won't be long."

Samuel flicks me a knowing gaze before digging his knee into the man's back and tightening his hold. "It won't be long until what?"

"Until they're dead," the man replies, gasping for air. "Like *she* was supposed to be." He rolls his haunting black eyes up toward me, but he can't keep them there for long because Samuel slams the man's forehead into the ground, this time pointing the knife into the back of his neck.

The attacker gains a second wind, writhing beneath Samuel and bucking him off his back. Soon the two men are rolling around on the rug, ensnared in another violent battle for the knife that Samuel is holding onto with a death grip.

Panic soars through me as I comb the room, searching for the guns Samuel brought with us to the cabin. Just as I spot a shiny black pistol lying on a side table near the fireplace, the men roll right into one of the legs, knocking the gun to the floor.

The man reaches for the pistol, but Samuel is quicker. He thrusts the knife into the man's side as I lunge forward and grab the gun.

"We're going to ask you one more time," I say in French, forcing my hands to stay steady as I aim the gun at the man who is now doubled over on the floor, clutching his bleeding side.

"Who do you work for?" I command.

He lifts a fiery gaze to mine. "You better enjoy your last Christmas. You and your boyfriend will be dead before sunrise tomorrow."

This time Samuel sends the knife deep into the man's chest, showing no mercy.

The incessant snowfall that lasted through the night has finally let up as Samuel and I are preparing to set off on our voyage to find

Rosie and Frances. A bright beam of sunlight peeks through one of the dusty cabin windows, giving us a clearer picture of the dead man sprawled before us on the living room rug.

Staring at this lifeless, bloody mass, I feel no remorse as the brutal fight Samuel endured to save both of our lives replays through my fatigued head. I am certain that if Samuel hadn't finished the job, *our* bodies would be the ones slumped in a pile on the cabin floor. Which would mean that Rosie and Frances would have no chance of survival…and neither would Isla.

Samuel knew that wasn't an option, so he did what he had to do.

Dressed in the heavy wool sweaters, winter coats, and oversized snow boots we've just discovered in one of the bedroom closets, we give our attacker one last glance before Samuel takes my hand. "We don't have much time before they'll send someone else after us. Are you ready?"

"As ready as I'm going to be," I say, as we turn together and head for the front door.

Besides the guns we are each carrying—one from 1937 and one from 2012—we are armed only with a hand-drawn map to the supposed castle where the other two girls are being held, and with the knowledge that it was a *woman*—a woman who wants Rosie's baby and who is expecting that baby to be a girl—who ordered the abduction.

The grueling finale to our night did not give us a single moment's rest, and so here we are, beaten, bruised, and exhausted, wading through a foot of freshly fallen snow on this freezing Christmas morning seventy-five years in the past.

Even though the winter air is still bitterly cold, I notice that the strong winds that howled through these mountains the night before have died out along with the snowfall. Save for the sound of our boots crunching over snow and broken branches, the forest is eerily silent.

Samuel pulls the crumpled map out of his coat pocket as we attempt to orient ourselves amid the sparkling winter wonderland that surrounds us. His fingertips are already turning pink from the cold, the cuts and bruises splashed across his knuckles looking painfully raw.

"Are you sure you don't want to wear the gloves?" I ask as he studies the map.

"I'll be okay," he replies. We only managed to find one pair during our frantic closet ransacking efforts, and Samuel insisted that I wear them.

Samuel surprises me with a tender kiss on my good cheek. "After the night we've both had, cold hands are the least of my worries. Let's find these women."

Samuel holds the thin piece of paper up between us, flipping it around a few times. There are two crisscrossed lines on the bottom of the map, and above them a confusing maze of swirling lines that connect several small X marks to one larger X that appears to sit between two poorly sketched mountains.

"How are we supposed to decipher this mess?" I ask.

Samuel points to the crisscrossed lines, then traces his finger up to one of the smaller X marks on the right. "The lines are the train tracks, so that would put us here. And this," he says, pausing and pointing to the larger X, "must be the castle both of the men mentioned."

"How can you be sure?"

Samuel studies the map for a few more seconds before lifting his confident gaze to mine. "You're going to have to trust me on this, Jill. Can you do that?"

I nod as he takes my hand. "Lead the way."

As each strenuous step through the piles of snowfall takes us— *hopefully*—closer to the girls we are trying to save, I realize that I do trust Samuel, more than I've ever trusted anyone. But no matter how much I believe in this man who has saved my life not once, but *twice* over the course of the past twelve hours, I can't shake the last words of our most recent attacker.

"You better enjoy your last Christmas. You and your boyfriend will be dead before sunrise tomorrow."

A violent shiver runs up the back of my neck as I push his threat out of my mind and focus on the winding path ahead.

After a few minutes of walking in silence, Samuel glances down at the map once more. "If the man who stormed the cabin was able to take Frances and Rosie to the castle and make it back to us not long after—and in the dark no less, then the castle can't be too far from here."

"How do we know the men were even telling the truth about the castle?" I ask as I step over a fallen branch and sink my clumsy boot into another mound of snow.

"We don't. But the fact that both of the men told us the same thing while I was threatening their lives at least makes our search a little more worthwhile. I'm not surprised they wouldn't give up any names though."

"They did both mention a woman," I point out. "The first guy back in the shack said something about things happening tonight when *she* arrives, and our most recent friend said he didn't know *her* name. Plus after seeing that baby nursery with Madeleine's name already on the wall, we know there has to be a woman involved."

Samuel checks our surroundings before leading me in between two towering, snow-covered pines. "If Henri Morel's wife found out that he was having an affair with the British woman from the train, Frances Chapman, that would give the wife motivation to harm Frances."

"It wouldn't be the first time a woman lost her mind out of jealousy," I say, thinking of my own mother, of what she did to Russell Hughes and of what she was willing to do to Isla...all due to her *own* wretched jealousy. "Henri Morel's wife is named Agnès. I saw her painting hanging on the wall in the Morel Château, next to paintings of the other Morel women, Frédéric's mother, Hélène, included."

"What about Madeleine Morel?" Samuel asks. "Did she have a place on the wall?"

I shake my head. "I did a little snooping around and found Madeleine's painting, along with Isla's and another one that was destroyed—which I now know was Rosie—hidden in a storage closet at the end of the hallway."

Samuel nods, the lines around his green eyes creasing as he mulls all of this over.

"What do you know about the Morel women?" I ask.

"My team was mostly focused on digging up dirt about Isla's fiancé, but they did find a few details about his mother, Hélène. She grew up in one of the worst suburbs of Paris as the only child of a single mother. They didn't have much money, but of course that all changed when she married Laurent Morel, one of the richest men in France. She and Laurent had a baby girl before they had Frédéric. But..." Samuel trails off, a look of clarity streaking through his eyes.

"What is it?" I ask.

"The baby died only three days after Hélène gave birth."

A sickening feeling seizes my gut as I see Isla tied up in the 2012 version of that disturbing cabin nursery. Could Hélène want Isla's baby?

"Jill, what is it?" Samuel asks, stopping to look into my eyes. "You're fading again, just like you did earlier in the nursery after that baby mobile started spinning. What happened to you back there? And what's happening now?"

"This is going to sound crazy..." I trail off, wondering how I'm going to explain the bizarre filmstrip of scenes from my sister's life that played before me, that I was somehow present for...although not in a *physical* sense.

Samuel gestures to the snow-laden trees surrounding us. "Jill, we stepped on a train and traveled back in time to 1937 to solve an abduction that is almost identical to your sister's. Nothing you could possibly say would sound crazier than what is already happening."

"Good point," I admit as we continue on our hike.

"So tell me what is going on," Samuel prods.

"The minute I stepped foot in that nursery back in the cabin, I felt Isla. I've always been able to feel her like this, to know when something is wrong, when she's in danger. It's this intense connection we have—the same connection that led me home that day when our mother…" Just as I am wishing away the horrifying memories, Samuel wraps his arm around my shoulders.

"It's okay," he says. "I'm here."

Relief floods through me as I realize that Samuel is the first person who knows the story of my past…and he loves me anyway. The warmth of his body pressed against mine as we trek side by side through the mountains gives me the courage to keep talking. To tell the truth about the inexplicable voyage I've just experienced.

"When that baby mobile started playing, something happened," I begin. "I felt my body leaving your side…and I went to Isla. It was like a movie. I saw everything that had happened to her in the past few months in the most vivid, colorful clarity…as if I were actually there."

Samuel nods, taking in my outrageous story as if it's totally normal. "What did you see? Maybe it will help us."

"First, I saw Isla posing for Christophe, the painter. But Frédéric was watching them. The look in his eyes…it was possessive, fierce, jealous. He knew he was losing her. That look alone makes me certain he must've had something to do with her abduction, not to mention the way he went nuts on me when he caught me snooping in his bedroom."

"What else?" Samuel asks as we set off up a steep incline.

"Next, I saw Isla holding a positive pregnancy test, crying out of joy because she knew it was Christophe's baby. Then I saw her dressed in a long black dress, walking into a private room…with Senator Williams."

Samuel raises a brow but lets me continue.

"You were right. She blackmailed him into resigning. He wasn't buying it until she shoved a photo into his hands."

"Proof from all those years ago?" Samuel asks.

"Yes. I couldn't see the picture, but the look on his face said it all. She finally got her revenge. Then the scenes began to speed up. I saw her leaving a note and her engagement ring for Frédéric and dashing out of the party to go to the train. I traveled with her on the train...and I watched it all happen, Samuel. I saw her being taken. As much as I wanted to, I couldn't stop it though. I was powerless. I stayed next to her as the man forced her through the mountains at gunpoint, but the scene zipped by so quickly, and suddenly we weren't outside anymore." I stop speaking, remembering the next terrifying part with such clarity, it sends a violent shiver through my entire body.

Samuel's inquisitive gaze is hanging on my last words. "What happened next?"

"We were in a nursery. The same nursery you and I were just in at the cabin, only an updated version seventy-five years in the future."

"Holy shit," he whispers. "Was she okay?"

"She was tied up to a chair, her mouth covered with tape. But that time, she saw me, and she could hear me. I told her I was coming for her, and I made her promise not to give up. Then, as quickly as I'd found her, I felt myself being pulled away. That was when I woke up back in the *old* nursery...in 1937, with you."

Samuel stays silent for a few moments as he helps me climb over a massive tree trunk lying on its side in the snow. Once we both make it over, he looks me straight in the eye. "I do think Frédéric had something to do with Isla's abduction, and of course we can't rule out possible involvement from Senator Williams because he certainly had motive. But if Isla really is being held in that same nursery in the future, Hélène Morel could have something to do with this too. After all, we know now that she had motive."

"She lost her baby girl," I say quietly.

Samuel nods. "The Morels want Isla's baby. They took Madeleine from Rosie, and they're going to do the same to your sister. Unless we can stop them first."

┼══·══┼

The winding path we are following around this colossal mountain seems to be never-ending. A deep-seated exhaustion like nothing I've experienced before settles into my bones, each strenuous step in the snow making my legs scream in pain.

Samuel powers ahead, each stride more determined than the last. If he is as tired and worn down as I feel, he certainly isn't showing it.

"What if that map was just a decoy to lead us deeper into the mountains and ensure that we would *never* find the girls?" I say in between labored breaths.

"I don't think those men were expecting company last night, so I believe the map is real. It can't be far now," Samuel assures me as he leads us confidently through this abyss of trees, snow, and nothingness.

I ignore the grumbling of my empty stomach as we wade through the snow in silence, and Samuel keeps an eye on our surroundings to make sure *we* don't have any company.

Just as we round a bend in the mountain, a splash of red on the trunk of a large oak tree catches my eye. As I blink, more flashes of red appear before my eyes—this time forming a trail of scarlet drops in the snow.

"Samuel, do you see that?" I ask as the flashes come more violently, faster than before.

"What is it, Jill?"

I barely hear Samuel's voice as a vivid, gruesome scene unfolds before me.

A tall, angry looking man is hiking over this same snow-covered path with a woman thrown over his shoulder. Her long, silky black hair swishes over his back as drops of blood trickle from her head, staining the snow crimson. He grunts as he shoves her limp body off his shoulder, slamming her back against the trunk of the towering oak tree.

She slides down the tree, landing on the ground with a thump, leaving a mess of blood on the trunk. Her chin falls to her chest as her long black hair sticks to the blood speckling her olive skin.

The girl's almond-shaped eyes are closed, and there is no sign of life in her beaten, slumped body, but I recognize her immediately. *"Francesca Rossi,"* I whisper. Twenty-six years old. Italian. The third girl taken in Isla's abduction, and the one who had no known connection to the Morels. I can only assume that poor Francesca was taken for the same reason as I was—for being in the wrong place at the wrong time.

The hefty man who was carrying her lifeless body bends over, hands on his knees, sucking in a long, deep breath.

Just as I envision pushing him over and shoving the barrel of my gun into his temple, a piercing cry breaks the silence in these frozen mountains.

Isla.

In an instant, Isla and her abductor appear before me. Her mouth is still covered in a thick piece of duct tape, but she *isn't* being quiet anymore. Fire blazes in her violet eyes as she spots a lifeless Francesca, bloody and fallen against the tree. Isla's captor keeps her moving though, prodding her through the snow at the command of his gun.

"Isla!" I scream into the forest.

My sister's eyes dart frantically in circles until suddenly they lock with mine.

"Isla, show me where they're taking you," I tell her. "Calm down and show me, okay?"

She nods in understanding, silencing her stifled cries and picking up her pace.

She disappears around the next bend in the path, and as I try to follow her, my vision refocuses on the concerned face squared two inches in front of me—Samuel.

"Jill, come back! It's me, Samuel. What's happening to you?"

I grab his shoulders. "They've already killed Francesca Rossi in the future. Isla is the only one left. Follow me. We don't have much time."

I take off running past the looming oak tree and around the same bend that Isla just took. Samuel's footsteps follow close behind as I pump my knees and charge ahead, not allowing the deep snowdrifts to break my pace.

Suddenly the path we were following around the mountain disappears into a sea of pine trees that soar so high into the sky, they block almost all light from breaking through. I stop running, my heavy breath forming puffs of icy white air at my lips as my heart thumps in my ears.

Come on, Isla. Show me where they're taking you.

I comb the wall of pines surrounding us, searching for an opening, for the path that will lead us to my sister and to the young, innocent Rosie Delaney. To the path that will help us stop this vicious crime from going any further.

Samuel's hand lands on my shoulder just as Isla's voice soars into my consciousness.

"Look to the right."

I follow her instructions, flicking my gaze over my right shoulder. At first, all I see are two more massive trees blocking my view. But as I take a few steps closer, a glistening, pointy white spiral off in the distance comes into focus.

Breaking into another wild run, I squeeze in between the thick tree trunks, pushing heavy, snow-covered branches out of my way until finally I reach the top of a clearing.

"Jill, what the—" Samuel starts as he catches up with me. But the spine-chilling view before us swallows up his words.

Nestled at the bottom of the clearing, in between two steep, tree-covered mountains, is an immense castle adorned with four

freaky ice palace hidden in the middle of the Alps in *1937*, I realize *farfetched* doesn't even begin to cover it. "If there is some secret entrance, how are we going to find out without running right into the clearing? We'll be spotted immediately."

"If I'm right, then there has to be a small part of the hill where the snow has been shoveled aside to reach the entrance. I'll go search for it, and I want you to stay here with your gun ready."

"But, Samuel—"

His finger on my lips shushes me. "Jill, I know what I'm doing. I'll be quick. I want you to keep an eye out. And don't be afraid to use the gun if you need it."

"If you find this secret tunnel entrance, what then?"

"I'll get the door open first, then I'll motion for you to come. *Do not* come a moment sooner, no matter what happens. Do you promise?"

"Yes, I promise," I say.

Samuel lifts a brow at me, the look on his rugged face still strikingly handsome despite the stressful circumstances we are facing.

"*I promise*," I say once more. "What's the plan if we make it inside?"

Samuel takes my hands in his, locking his strong gaze on me. "*When* we make it inside, no lives will be spared if they're blocking our way to find Rosie and Frances."

Just as I am nodding in understanding, Samuel brushes his lips against mine, the warmth of his passionate kiss sending tingles through this freezing, tired body of mine.

As our lips part, I press my forehead against his. "Thank you for being such a bad-ass partner in crime," I whisper.

A sly grin spreads over his full lips, and after one more toe-curling kiss, Samuel takes off past the shield of trees and into the open clearing. Fearless and determined, he runs swiftly and quietly, a moving target willing to sacrifice everything to save these women.

My heart thumps inside my chest as I reach for my gun and aim it toward the castle. I comb the endless rows of windows that line its white stone walls, before scanning the snow-covered rooftop and the towering spirals, but there isn't a soul in sight. Samuel is almost to the edge of the river when he crouches down so that he is almost completely out of my line of vision.

I creep a little closer, stepping onto a leveled tree stump to get a better view of what he's doing. Not more than a few seconds pass before he stands, takes a quick look around, then motions for me to follow him.

A paralyzing terror seizes me, but the fear evaporates the minute I remember the brutal man who forced Isla through these same mountains at gunpoint, and the men who did the same to Rosie and Frances.

They won't get away with this.

Seconds later, I'm half-way across the clearing, my legs pumping fiercely toward Samuel.

Just before I reach him, he turns, aiming his gun toward the castle. An ear-splitting gunshot breaks the pillow of silence that had been comforting me up to this point. Samuel is still standing, defending me as he fires more shots. I don't break my stride to see who he is shooting at.

"Behind me!" Samuel shouts just before firing another shot.

More blasts sound through the mountainside as I slide to my knees and land right next to a metal door that Samuel has wrenched open.

"Get inside!" he orders.

The sound of one final gunshot blasts past my ears as I slip into the dark hole and fall several feet below to the cold, wet ground.

Samuel tumbles in after me, collapsing back against the wall.

I reach for him through the murky blackness that envelops us, but when my fingertips meet a patch of soaking wet fabric clinging to his skin, I realize why his breathing is so shallow, why his body is slipping to the ground.

Samuel has been shot.

"Oh my God, Samuel, they got you," I whisper as I kneel down in front of him, reaching blindly for his hands.

"It's just my side. I'm okay," he assures me, but by the way he is sucking in air, I can tell he is anything but okay.

"What can I do?" I ask him, trying to stifle the helplessness that is threatening to take over. "I can't see a damn thing."

"Whoever shot me knows we made it inside," he says. "We have to move. We don't have much time."

"Samuel, you can't—"

"Jill, trust me. I've been through worse. This won't stop me. Just help me up, and we'll do this. Okay?"

I remember the thick scars lining Samuel's back and chest, the tattoos and muscles he has acquired in the years since we broke up. He knows what he can handle. I need to have faith in him too.

"Okay," I say. "Just tell me if I'm hurting you."

I slide my arm around his waist and help him to his feet. With my other hand, I reach through the icy blackness until my fingers brush against a stone wall. The two of us set off together through the tunnel, keeping silent in case our next attacker is hiding somewhere in this spooky underground maze.

I can feel Samuel clutching his side, but he keeps my pace without a single complaint. The dimmest of lights off in the distance sheds an eerie glow down this damp, suffocating pathway, and as we tread a bit farther, we reach the bottom of a winding stone staircase. One lone candle flickers at the top, inviting us to its heat, to its light. With each step we take, Samuel's muscles tense up, and my own chest tightens with fear.

Although I know we have no other choice but to continue on this crazy path, I can't help but wonder if we are we walking ourselves right into a trap.

A tall stone archway looms at the top of the dungeon-like staircase. Before I can get a clear picture of what lies beyond its opening, the candle that lights our way flickers, and a gust of wind steals its flame.

Oh, shit.

"Don't move," Samuel whispers as he leaves my side, pulling his gun and heading toward the doorway.

I blink my eyes, trying to readjust to the darkness, when a whisper of a voice passes through my ears.

"Hurry, Jilly. She's going to kill me."

Chills slither up my arms as I remember hearing these exact words when I was only thirteen years old, on the day I ran home from the school newspaper to save my sister from dying at the hands of our own deranged mother.

Isla's message had reached me then, loud and clear, but this time, as I shiver in this dark, freezing staircase in some godforsaken castle buried in the Alps, I know that Isla *isn't* talking about our mother.

A loud clattering noise snaps me back to the present.

Samuel.

Yanking my gloves off, I shove them in my coat pocket and reach for my gun. The metal feels shockingly cool against my hands as I inch toward the doorway, being careful to keep my back pressed against the wall. The unmistakable sounds of a struggle on the other side send a shot of adrenaline through my veins.

Samuel is strong, but he is also wounded. I can't let him do this alone.

I aim my gun and round the doorway, but a sudden blast knocks me back against the wall.

My heart constricts before I can bring myself to open my eyes.

A hand on my shoulder prompts me to let out the breath I've been holding. It's Samuel, standing before me, gripping a smoking gun in his other hand.

Two feet away from us, a man lies slumped on the ground, silky red blood pooling out from the hole in his chest.

"It was either me or him," Samuel whispers. "Come on, let's go."

But Samuel's voice is cut off by a wretched shriek that soars through the castle and into the candlelit hallway. I flinch as another shrill scream rattles my ears.

"What is it, Jill? Did you see something again?" Samuel says.

"Didn't you hear that? The screaming?"

He shakes his head. "No, I didn't hear anything."

I take a deep breath, hoping I'm not losing my mind.

"Just because I didn't hear it doesn't mean it wasn't real, though," Samuel says. "Everything you've seen so far has led us to the right place. Where did it come from?"

But again, I barely hear Samuel's voice because another panicked cry rings through the castle—this one from a voice I recognize.

Isla.

"Follow me," I tell Samuel as I take off down the dim hallway, chasing the sound of my sister's cries, which grow louder and more desperate with each passing second.

A few moments later, we emerge into a large salon. Pale blue candles line the perimeter of the room, their flames casting eerie shadows on the periwinkle walls while wax drips onto the slippery, white marble floor. Shimmering white drapes billow as gusts of bitter winter air blast in through the open windows.

The wind picks up, relinquishing all of the flames in one unforgiving gust. I grip Samuel's arm as another distressed cry travels through the newly darkened space.

"I heard that one," Samuel whispers. "It's Rosie. Come on." He takes my hand and leads me through the icy salon and down another winding maze of candlelit hallways.

I try to focus on the path ahead, on keeping pace with Samuel, on making it to Rosie and Frances before another life is lost, but intense, terrorizing visions seize me with each step.

I see the gun pointed at my sister's unborn child as her nameless captor forces her along this same path. I see her blood splashing across the smooth marble floor as the man smacks her across the face when she refuses to stop screaming.

And I hear her voice.

Isla is calling for me. She is howling my name.

"Jill, come on!" It's Samuel, calling me back to the present—or the past—or wherever the hell we are. "We're close," he whispers. "Stay with me, Jill. Please, stay with me."

I focus on Samuel's strong stance, on the way he is charging ahead despite the wound in his side that is leaking blood through his shirt, threatening to drain all his strength.

"We are close," I say, trying to blink away the raging flashes that plague my vision.

I have never felt Isla's presence, her fear, her terror, more than I do in this moment.

At the sound of footsteps thumping down the hallway behind us, Samuel grabs my hand and breaks into a run. More screams and cries blast through my ears, and as we round another corner, I realize I don't know anymore whether those panicked voices belong to Rosie, Frances, Isla, or even to myself. It's as if I'm straddling a tightrope between the past and the future, and at any given moment, I could plummet to either side.

Tall white candles flicker alongside us, lighting our way through these icy, stone-arched hallways as the pounding footsteps grow louder.

"See that door up ahead to the left?" Samuel says. "Go hide in there, and have your gun ready."

"But what are you—"

"I'll handle it, Jill. *Go.*"

In an instant, Samuel's strong hand slips from mine. Without turning back, I sprint toward the tall white door down the corridor. Just as I push through and close the door behind me, the booming sounds of bodies slamming against walls out in the hall and fists breaking skin make me flinch.

But when I open my eyes, the scene before me steals my breath.

Three snow-white cribs circle the shadowy room, and dozens of baby mobiles dangle from the ceiling, swirling violently with each gust that blows in through the open windows. Creepy, off-pitch melodies swim through my ears as I run toward the center of the room, to the young woman with the sweet face and the dark brown curls who is beaten, bloody, and tied to a chair.

"Rosie," I whisper, kneeling down before her and tugging frantically at the ropes that bind her limp body. "Rosie, it's me, Jillian. Wake up, Rosie. Wake up!"

"So, Jillian is your name." A bone-chilling female voice calls out to me in French.

I flip around, my gaze landing on a woman dressed in a long, billowing black dress, her matching stone eyes and jet black hair immediately making me recognize her as the *original* matriarch of the powerful Morel family—Agnès Morel. Wife of Henri, mother of Alexandre. The woman who *would've* been Rosie's mother-in-law, had Rosie stayed true to Alexandre.

"So *you* are the third, mysterious woman we plucked from the Orient Express," she says in French as she taps a shiny silver blade against her palm, the blood that covers the tip of the knife smearing all over her pale skin. "We're so glad you could finally join us. Aren't we, Rosie?"

CHAPTER 19

Agnès Morel paces toward me, turning the jagged blade over in her bony hands. Her wicked gaze is void of any kindness, love, or hope she may have once possessed. Instead, all I see in those endless black holes are rage, jealousy, and pure, unadulterated evil.

She doesn't shiver or show even a hint of discomfort as a glacial blast of air swoops through the room, swishing the hem of her long black dress around her ankles and twirling the baby mobiles above her head in ferocious circles.

Their wretched song makes me nauseous.

The fact that I've already witnessed this same brand of crazy in my own sick, imprisoned mother should give me an advantage over the knife-wielding woman before me. But in my experience, women who are this far gone are not capable of feeling any true, virtuous emotions, leaving no point in trying to reason with them.

Still, I have to try.

"Why are you doing this?" I ask her as I crane my neck toward the door, wondering what has happened to Samuel. "What has Rosie ever done to you to deserve *this*?"

A loud, deranged cackle breaks through the incessant melodies that twist and stab like daggers through my eardrums. I turn back to Agnès, wondering why it sounds as if her voice has suddenly changed. But in a flash, her face morphs from the creepy 1930s woman with black hair and haunting eyes to that of a *different* Morel woman—one with chin-length, dyed-blond hair, a pearl necklace, and angry, flaring nostrils.

Hélène Morel?

Hélène's sparkly diamond bracelet dangles loosely on her wrist as she taps the dull side of a clean knife against her palm. She glares past me as if I'm not even here, her vengeful gaze settling on the girl behind me tied to the chair.

But when I turn to find Rosie, I realize exactly what is going on.

It isn't Rosie tied to the chair anymore—it's *Isla*.

I am having another vision of the future, and in 2012, in this same haunting ice castle, it is Hélène Morel who is holding my sister hostage.

Just as I lunge toward my sister, the image flashes once more.

Agnès is now towering over me, her pointy black heel pinning me to the ground as she grips *my* gun in one hand and her bloody knife in the other.

Shit.

"For as brave as you seemed storming in here to save the day, you're certainly not very quick on your feet," Agnès says to me as she removes her foot from my chest and paces toward one of the cribs. "You know, Jillian, it's not *only* Rosie who has wronged me and my family name." Without looking down, she points the dagger toward her feet.

Following her gesture, I have to stifle a scream as I discover a mess of blond hair, stained brown with blood, sprawled on the white marble floor. The victim's face is turned away from me, and the rest of her body is hidden by one of the large cribs, but I recognize her nonetheless.

It's Frances Chapman.

Just like Emma Brooks and Francesca Rossi in the future version of this monstrous crime, Frances has been slayed.

Which means that in this impossible convergence of the past and the future, *only* Rosie and Isla are left.

And with no sign of Samuel, it is up to *me* to save them both. Just as I was told I would have to do.

I sit up slowly, lifting my heated glare back to the heartless, deranged woman who surely has no plans to spare my life either.

"You killed Frances for sleeping with your husband, and now you're going to steal Rosie's baby? What happened to you, Agnès? Why would you take it this far?"

She tosses the gun into one of the cribs before charging toward me with the knife. She thrusts the bloody tip toward my neck, but my instincts are quicker. I reach up and wrap my hand around her weak wrist before she can break my skin.

"Who the hell are you to question me?" she spits in my face, struggling against me. But for as evil as she is, I am stronger. I shove the old hag off me, slamming her back into one of the cribs. She pushes herself away from the railing, smoothing out her dress with the knife, streaking blood all over the heavy black material as she sets her vindictive gaze on me.

"How dare you," she growls. "I am the queen of one of the wealthiest, most powerful families in this entire country. My husband may get all the credit for making our fortune, but he was *nothing* before he met me. *Nothing*! All I asked for in return was his faithfulness and a baby girl to carry on the Morel line of *women*."

"Why isn't your son enough?" I shoot back. "Why do you need to steal someone else's child? You have no right!" I block Rosie's body with my own as I stand to look straight into Agnès's hollow eyes.

"I grew up watching my father and my brothers make horrific, selfish mistakes, and I knew a son could never cut it. A son could never carry on the legacy of a powerful, smart, wealthy woman—and I was right. That idiot son of mine, Alexandre—while I'll do anything to protect his name, *our* name—he's as worthless as they come. Mesmerized by Rosie Delaney, the innocent little *américaine*. Little did he know, she's a heartless floozie who fell in love with a pitiful French soldier and got herself pregnant with his baby."

As Agnès speaks, her disturbing facial features warp into Hélène's and back again several times, making me realize that Hélène is telling almost the exact same story in the future. Like Agnès, she loves the jewels, the money, the power of her position in the infamous Morel family. And like Agnès, she thinks her son, Frédéric, is an idiot for falling for Isla...a woman who would choose the love of a lowly artist over the authority and wealth she could have had by marrying the son of the Morel dynasty.

Which meant that as crazy and jealous as he was, Frédéric *wasn't* involved in Isla's abduction. And Alexandre wasn't involved in Rosie's.

All along, it had been the demented mothers.

I should've known.

Agnès walks around the still unconscious Rosie, smearing fresh blood on her cheek with the dull side of the blade. "It better be a girl, Miss Rosie," she whispers in her ear. "I've already lost three of them, and I won't lose another."

Agnès had lost *three* baby girls? Suddenly the old cabin nursery, the three white cribs surrounding us, and the incessantly twirling baby mobiles make sense.

Agnès's threat makes me remember the story Samuel told me about Hélène Morel—how she once lost a baby girl as well. The similarities between the two mothers and between their equally atrocious crimes is uncanny...making me wonder if before Agnès died, she had the opportunity to *groom* Hélène into the kind of woman who would stop at nothing to hurt anyone who messed with their precious family name. The kind of woman who would go so far as to steal someone else's baby girl just to carry on her sick legacy.

Agnès keeps her gaze pinned to me, pacing in frantic circles around Rosie and me, as if she is trying to keep time with the baby mobiles that continue to spin wildly over our heads.

"You want to know why I would take it this far?" she shrieks. "Why I would orchestrate such an elaborate abduction? Hiring a team of trained men to obstruct the train tracks, storm the Orient Express, take Rosie, Frances, and *you*—a third woman simply to make the entire incident look random. Because I won't stand for the kind of betrayal my husband has made me suffer through. I've known for years that he was seeing that whore, Frances! After everything I've done for him, after the man I've made him into, how dare he go behind my back with *her*. I was not going to allow him to make a fool out of me any longer."

A devious grin spreads over Agnès's thin lips. "*I* gave Henri the Orient Express ticket to give to his precious little mistress, and I even pretended to fall ill the day before our Morel Holiday Gala, so he could break up with her in *private*."

"But you weren't ill," I say, finally putting all the puzzle pieces together. "You were on your way here, waiting for the girls to arrive at your secret castle. So *you* could have your way with them." A sudden, vivid memory of Hélène Morel dashing out of the Morels' lakefront château to be with her supposed *ill sister* flashes through my mind.

Hélène's sister was never ill.

She was heading *here* to this exact castle, to reenact the crime Agnès had committed seventy-five years prior.

I don't have time to analyze the similarities any further, though, because Agnès's hysterical voice breaks my concentration. "I chose that exact train because I already knew that Rosie, my son's disloyal fiancée, was planning to leave him and take the midnight Orient Express to meet her lover in Paris. Rosie may be beautiful, but she was stupid. So, so stupid. Keeping that box of sickening letters and the train ticket her lover sent her in a suitcase in *my* vacation château? Did she actually think I would never find out?" Another disturbing laugh breaks through her dry, cracked lips, making my stomach curl. "So I figured, why not kill two birds with one stone?"

I steady myself against the railing of one of the cribs, waiting for the moment when Agnès becomes careless in her ranting and looks away so that I can charge her and steal the knife from her death grip. But for as crazy as she is, Agnès *isn't* an idiot. She knows if I had the audacity to storm this freaky ice castle, I won't hesitate to take her down at my first opportunity.

"It wasn't easy, building this empire," she rambles. "It wasn't easy creating something from nothing, especially during this vile depression. I was raised in the slums of Paris, eating crumbs for breakfast, working the streets as a child. But I was determined; I wasn't going to allow anyone to stand in my way. And now, look at me," she says, gesturing to the high ceilings and creepy paintings adorning the nursery walls. "I have the richest husband in the country, I have jewels, castles, *power*. Do you actually think I would allow these young, promiscuous harlots to storm in and ruin everything I've worked so hard to create? I need an equally strong woman to mold, to carry on my legacy."

I already knew that the sweet daughter Agnès would kidnap from Rosie wouldn't grow up to be the heartless, power-hungry woman Agnès was hoping she'd be. I'd only met the elegant Madeleine Morel briefly, but from what I'd seen in that snowy Lausanne train station, she was much too warm and entirely too kind to be Agnès's pawn. Which explained why Madeleine's portrait had been removed from the Morel women hall of fame.

And so, before Agnès died at the ripe old age of ninety-nine, it must've been *Hélène* who she chose to mold into her likeness.

"I should've known Rosie would never cut it," Agnès continues as I eye the gun lying behind her in the crib. "It's a shame, though, because her father is in such a strong political position, and her mother was always so loyal to our family. Stupid like her daughter, but loyal. If Rosie had any eye for power, for wealth, it could've been a perfect match. She could've been the daughter I never had. But you see, Jillian, when Rosie turned on my son, she turned on my whole family. She threatened to disgrace the family name *I've* worked so hard to build. I am only taking what is rightfully mine—the baby girl I was always supposed to have."

The story Madeleine had told me was true. She'd been taken from Rosie at birth and raised as if she were a Morel. She'd always known she was different, though—nothing like this monster of a woman who stole her from her rightful mother. And Madeleine's twin—Georges, the generous chauffeur—was given up for adoption because Agnès clearly had no interest in raising another son.

"I suppose this was always our destiny, sweet Rosie," Agnès says as she walks past me and whispers in Rosie's ear. "Too bad you won't live long enough to watch your little girl grow up. Don't worry, though. She'll be in good hands."

Just as I take advantage of the slip in Agnès's gaze to lunge toward her, the image in this ice-cold nursery flashes abruptly. Now, instead of defeating the crazed Agnès, I am standing beside my bound up sister, whose violet eyes are darting frantically toward the door.

I follow her gaze, my insides revolting in disgust at the scene before me.

Dagger still in hand, Hélène Morel leans forward and plants a long, sickening kiss on the lips of the man both Isla and I hate most in this world—Senator Parker Williams.

EPISODE 8

CHAPTER 20

December 25…

The French Alps

The sight of Senator Williams's lips on *anyone*—let alone on Hélène Morel—is enough to make both my twin sister and me physically ill…not to mention physically violent.

The problem is that Isla is still tied to a chair, her mouth covered with tape, and I have only traveled to the future as a helpless spectator—a fly on the wall with no physical abilities, no way to save my sister from the sick, unlikely couple who have worked together to plan and execute her abduction *and* the murders of two other innocent women.

And there is no telling when this revolting scene will flash and I will find myself back in 1937, very much physically present, and most likely at the mercy of the evil Agnès Morel.

Hélène pulls her lips from Williams's round face, then nods to the center of the room, where Isla is squirming beneath the taut ropes that bind her.

I am invisible to our enemies, but as Isla lifts her fiery gaze to mine, I am certain she knows I'm here. Now I just have to find a way to save her life before Williams finishes what he surely came here to do.

Williams's bushy gray eyebrows pinch together as he meets eyes with Isla. "I thought you were going to take care of her," he quips, turning his gaze toward the clean knife in Hélène's hands. "What are you waiting for?"

Hélène paces coolly toward Isla, pointing the dagger at Isla's stomach. "How far along are you, Isla?" she says in English, her thick accent jarring to my ears. "Two months? Three months?"

"She's pregnant?" Williams says, not hiding the shock on his greasy face.

Hélène gives a slow, calculated nod. "Which is why we'll be waiting until *after* she has the baby to take care of her, as you say."

Williams storms toward Hélène, digging his fingers into her shoulder. "This wasn't in the plan," he growls. "And the *only* way this will work is if we stick to the plan, Hélène."

She flips around, shrugging him off of her. "And I suppose kidnapping the Ambassador's nineteen-year-old daughter and murdering her was in the plan too?" she shrieks, pointing the knife at her lover's chest. "How could your men have made such a grave error? *Both* of our families are friends with the Brooks family! And why in God's name would you resign from office while all of this is going on? Was that all a part of your brilliant plan too?"

Williams wraps a strong hand around Hélène's wrist, stopping her from coming any closer with the sharp edge of the knife.

"My men followed the instructions you gave me to a tee. Just like you asked, they kidnapped Isla and two other women at random so that there wouldn't be a connection made between the three women, and consequently no connection would be made to you *or* to me. The fact that Emma Brooks *happened* to be on the same train as Isla was a complete coincidence. And there's nothing we can do about it now."

Isla lets out a muffled scream as she thrashes underneath the ropes. Her frantic movements tell me she knows something about why Emma Brooks was taken…and that it *wasn't* a coincidence.

I need to figure out a way to get that damn tape off her lips so we can all find out *exactly* what she knows.

The lovers' quarrel continues to erupt behind me as I will myself closer to my sister.

Suddenly I am engulfed by the stench of evil.

It is Senator Williams, approaching my sister, staring her down with his menacing glare.

"Need I remind you, Hélène, that this woman who made a fool out of your son, out of your whole family, is a whore. Do you really want a whore's baby?"

A thousand men could not hold me back from the rage that plows through me at Parker Williams's revolting words.

My sister is not a whore!

I lunge at the monster who stole everything from Isla, and to my complete surprise, his tall, blundering body actually stumbles backward, knocking right into Hélène.

Annoyed at his clumsiness, Hélène pushes past him, dagger pointed at Isla. "Whore or not, that baby belongs to *my* family!"

Hélène switches into her native tongue of French as she slithers up to my sister. "I always knew there was something off about you, Isla... from the first time Frédéric brought you home. It's funny because my husband's dear grandmother Agnès warned me about you on her death bed. She told me to be on the look-out for a woman just like you. And to do *everything* in my power to protect this family from the money-grubbing whore who would defame my family name, who would try to take away everything I—and she—worked so hard to build."

Hélène gestures above to the tall, arched ceilings, and around to the same creepy paintings that still adorn these walls seventy-five years after Agnès spilled blood in this exact room. "On the day Agnès predicted your arrival, she gave me the keys to this very castle as she told me the story of a woman just like you, a young girl by the name of Rosie Delaney, who stole Agnès's son's heart and *tried* to steal her son's baby. But the story didn't end so well for Rosie, and it won't end so well for you either, Isla Chambord."

Hélène's voice cracks with desperation as she continues on her diatribe. "I lost a child once. A little girl. It should never have happened. *Never.* And I just know that baby you're carrying is a little girl. But after the way you lied to me and to my entire family, you don't deserve her." Hélène crosses her arms tightly over her chest, tapping the dull side of the knife furiously against her arm. "That's right, Isla. I know *all* about your dirty little past. I had my close friend here, Monsieur Williams, perform a background check on you. Lo and behold, my instincts were correct, as usual. He told me all about your days as a prostitute. Do you actually think I would allow a woman like you to marry my only son? Did you think I would stand idly by while you ran off with that pitiful artist and tried to steal my son's baby?"

Without warning, Hélène smacks Isla hard across the cheek. "Before she died, Agnès also gave me the keys to the nice little cabin where you'll be staying until you have the baby. I believe you made a quick stop there on your way to the castle, no?"

Isla struggles beneath the ropes as Hélène moves in closer. "The only reason I've kept you alive is so I can claim what's rightfully mine. Once I have that baby in my hands, you're finished, Isla Chambord. And I'll personally see to it that no one ever finds your disgusting, used-up body."

This time I go for Hélène. I'm not sure how this invisible presence of mine is able to turn physical, but it doesn't matter how because *it works.*

Hélène plummets back into Williams with a thud, a startled look splashing across her heavily made-up face.

"Who did that?" The diamonds dangling from Hélène's ears swish around as she scans the chilly room.

But I'm not paying any attention to her or to her equally slimy partner-in-crime any longer. I've turned all of my focus, every ounce of my energy, onto Isla.

As I envision peeling the tape off of my sister's mouth, I watch in disbelief as the silver tape actually unravels and falls into her lap.

She sucks in a loud breath while I go to work on the ropes that bind her wrists together.

"The story your *friend*, Parker Williams, told you isn't true," Isla says coolly in French as both Hélène and Williams stare with mouths agape at her newly freed lips. Williams storms toward Isla, but I redirect my force right at his groin this time, and I almost laugh as he crumbles in half, clutching himself and moaning like the pathetic weasel of a man he is.

Isla winks at me, then continues on her rampage as a petrified Hélène cowers on the ground. "I was never a prostitute," Isla says. "My *mother* was the prostitute. And when I was only thirteen, before your knight in shining armor here became a senator, he used to stop by our house for weekly *visits* with my mother. The first day he saw me though, he cut a deal with my mom. He paid her twice the normal rate to have me instead."

Hélène's pencil-lined brows lift in horror as she glances at the man still writhing on the cool marble floor before her.

"That's right Hélène, your lover is a sick pervert who sleeps with young, innocent girls like me...and Emma Brooks," Isla says.

While Hélène climbs slowly to her feet, her vindictive gaze turning now to Williams, I lean closer to my sister and quickly tell her the story on Senator Williams that went to press the day after the train abduction.

I have no clue how, but Isla can hear me, and she doesn't miss a beat. "And you want to know why the senator resigned so suddenly, putting your abduction plans in jeopardy?" Isla quips. "Because he's wanted for the murder of two young sisters who were sold into the child prostitution ring that *he* was running back in D.C. Oh, and he was funneling money from that prostitution ring directly into his campaign."

With each word of truth that is spoken in this godforsaken castle, both my twin and I feel a surge of empowerment. I focus with all my might on the ropes that bind her wrists, and like magic, they slip from her hands and fall into a pile on the floor.

Luckily, the knife-wielding woman in the room isn't paying any attention to my sister. Instead Hélène Morel towers over her lover, pointing the knife at his chest.

"Is this true?" she shrieks in French. "Is it all true?"

Isla works furiously to untie the ropes around her waist and legs while Hélène—with her back to us—continues grilling the speechless, despicable man at her feet.

She stomps a pointy boot into his groin, making him cry out in anguish. "Is it true?" she demands one more time.

Hélène doesn't need to ask him again because the defeated look in his hollow eyes says it all. The knife that was meant to scare Isla and that would've eventually served to end her life now finds its rightful home in Parker Williams's chest.

Just as my sister is untying the last rope from her bloody ankle, Hélène wrenches the knife from the senator's lifeless body and turns to Isla.

"I don't care about that baby anymore. This has to end," Hélène says flatly. "*Now.*"

As Hélène charges Isla with the bloody weapon in hand, her eyes turn the color of an inky black sky. Pooling every ounce of energy I have in this incorporeal body of mine, I throw myself in front of my sister.

But in an instant, the wicked face before me flashes and morphs into one with those same dead black eyes—*Agnès*.

She is coming at me with the dagger, poised and ready to kill.

I glare at Agnès, knowing *she* is the vile seed who started it all. It was the inherent evil, sickness, and desperation of *this* woman that set off the entire chain of ill-fated events that will ultimately lead to my sister's abduction seventy-five years in the future.

Even though I am aware that changing the course of history could have irreversible consequences, I know without a doubt that *this* is the reason Samuel and I have been sent back in time. I must end the evil that has plagued my sister and me since the day we were born.

Agnès's long black dress swishes around her ankles as she charges me. I should be scared as she presses the tip of the knife into my neck. I should be shaking with terror at the wickedness that pours out of her like a gushing black river.

But I grew up with a woman just like Agnès—a mother with no motherly instincts.

A mother who I wasn't afraid to fire a gun at when I was only thirteen.

I am older now. Stronger. And I'm still not afraid.

I look Agnès straight in the eye and shoot my hand up to hers, stopping her from pushing the knife any farther into my already broken skin.

A visceral cry sounds from my lips as I wrench the blade from her cold, decrepit hands, lift the dagger and thrust it deep into her nonexistent heart.

She crumples to the ground, her thick black dress swallowing up her frail, limp body.

Breath and adrenaline course through me as one final gust of wind swoops through the frosty nursery, slamming the windows closed at my back. The baby mobiles finally cease spinning, their dreadful tune dying out with the wind. I turn toward Rosie, who is awake and—*thankfully*—alive, but my eyes lock instead on a man who is collapsed and bleeding in the doorway.

Samuel.

The dagger spills from my hands, landing on the marble floor with a clatter as I run to Samuel's side. He is slumped against the door frame, lying in a pool of his own crimson blood.

Air is no longer passing through his lips, and his chest is still.

"Samuel! Samuel, come back," I beg, shaking his shoulders and checking his neck for a pulse. My hands are shaking too much though, my fingers smeared with blood, tears clouding my vision.

"Samuel!" I scream into the icy nursery. "Don't leave me. Please, don't leave me."

Sobs rack my body as I collapse against the man I have always loved, the man I will never stop loving.

The man who saved me from my own wretched lies.

"Please, no. Samuel, please." In the slippery blood, through my frantic tears, I fumble, searching for his strong hands. I weave my fingers into his and pull him to me. "I'm so sorry, Samuel. I'm so sorry."

The slightest hint of warm air brushes past my ear as a spark ignites on my left ring finger. I barely feel any of it though. I just want him back. I would do anything to have him back.

"I love you, Samuel," I whisper. "Since the day we first met, I've never stopped loving you."

The spark grows in intensity, until it feels as if our hands are melding together, becoming one. And as another puff of warm air blows against my cheek, I lift my head to find Samuel's striking emerald eyes blinking back at me.

"Samuel? Oh my God, Samuel, you're back!" I shower his gorgeous face with kisses, pulling him to me. He squeezes my hands even tighter, sucking deep breaths into his lungs.

The electricity swirling around our hands dies down, but the spark blazing in Samuel's eyes is as alive as ever.

"I will never leave you, Jill," he says. "Never."

CHAPTER 21

December 31, 1937

Lausanne, Switzerland

A loud train whistle blasts off in the distance, and within minutes, the glossy blue carriages of the Orient Express come into focus. As the vintage train barrels over the snow and chugs to a stop in the bustling Swiss train station, a gloved hand squeezes my forearm.

"I can't believe I'm actually going to see Jacques in only a few hours." Rosie Delaney's sapphire eyes twinkle in the early morning sunlight as her other dainty white glove runs over her tiny belly. "Jillian, you saved my life...and my baby's. You're an angel from heaven. How will I ever repay you and your husband?"

I take Rosie's hand in mine and smile warmly at this young, sweet girl who has been given a second chance...and who has no idea that she is about to change the course of history.

"My only wish for you, Rosie, is that you live a life filled with love and happiness," I tell her.

She pulls me into a tight embrace, and just as I am wiping my own tear from my eye, Samuel's deep voice sounds behind us.

"Paris is waiting, ladies."

"And so is the love of your life," I say to Rosie with a wink.

Dressed in a spiffy, gold-trimmed, royal-blue uniform, the conductor steps onto the platform and tips his hat to us.

"*Mademoiselle Delaney*," he says, taking Rosie's white-gloved hand.

Then he smiles at Samuel and me. "*Monsieur et Madame Kelly*, the entire Orient Express staff would like to convey our sincerest apologies for what has happened to all of you," he says in French. "We have arranged a special, private carriage for you today, including a gourmet lunch prepared by our most famous chef. And before you deboard in Paris this afternoon, I will be providing all three of you with a lifetime pass to ride the Orient Express anytime, to any destination you wish."

His offer is generous, but if it's up to me, this will be the *last* Orient Express ride I ever take. Still, we all smile kindly at the conductor as he motions for us to follow him aboard.

Inside the elegant, warm carriages of the Orient Express train that will *finally* transport the three of us to Paris, the conductor leads us down the corridor, then stops to gesture inside the sleeping compartment to his left. "*Mademoiselle Delaney*, I believe this red *valise* belongs to you," he says.

Rosie cannot contain her excitement as she shoots up on her tip-toes and pecks the conductor on the cheek. "*Merci, Monsieur. Merci!*" she squeals, rushing past him and popping open the old-fashioned suitcase.

As the conductor leads Samuel farther down the hall to our own private compartment, I linger outside Rosie's doorway, watching as she removes a tattered shoe box from her luggage. Inside are stacks of letters—love letters from Jacques, my grandfather.

Tears stream down Rosie's cheeks as she clutches his words tightly to her chest. I watch her joy, her hope, her love spill onto Jacques' letters, and I too am gripped with a mixture of overwhelming emotions as I recall the events of the past week.

After our horrifying Alpine castle ordeal, Agnès's body was taken away, and sadly, so was Frances Chapman's. The thought of Frances's blood-stained blond hair dangling from the stretcher as the paramedics walked her body out of that freezing, wretched nursery still makes me shudder. I am consumed with guilt that we didn't arrive in time to save her from Agnès's rage. At the same time, I am beyond grateful that we *did* arrive in time to save Rosie and her unborn children.

Rosie and Samuel each spent four days in the Lausanne hospital, recovering from their wounds—which, according to the doctors, healed miraculously fast. *Especially* Samuel's. The physicians on staff told me that between the gunshot wound Samuel suffered outside the castle and the knife wound he took from the giant guard who chased us down the candlelit hallway, he'd lost enough blood to have died twice. There was no medical explanation as to how he had survived.

Gazing down at the sparkling emerald that is still molded tightly to my left ring finger, I remember the sparks that ignited when I laced my hand with Samuel's right at the moment that I believed I'd lost him. I remember the breath that filled his lungs seconds after this ring touched his skin.

There isn't a medical explanation for Samuel's survival, but I know that somehow this ring—or the power behind it—played a part in saving his life.

I only wish I knew if I had saved Isla's.

After leaving my sister's side to travel back to the past one final time and kill Agnès Morel, the flashes and visions that had taken me to Isla came to a dead halt. And now, that invisible connection we've shared since the day we were born feels weaker than ever.

Dread pools in my stomach as I wonder where she is and why I cannot feel her presence any longer.

As I stand in Rosie's doorway and watch her pour over Jacques's sweet love letters, my only comfort lies in the fact that in driving that dagger through Agnès's heart, I have ended the original seed of evil that began this entire mess. And now, in this mysterious loophole of time and space we have jumped through, we are on our way to right a wrong that happened so long ago.

I have no idea what will happen in the future or what will become of Samuel and me, who are still trapped in 1937…or what will happen to my lovely, sweet sister.

All I *do* know is that the new version of the past is happening *right now*, right in front of my eyes…and this is what I must focus on if I don't want to drive myself insane with worry.

I give Rosie privacy with Jacques's letters, knowing she will probably spend the train ride to Paris reading through each and every one of them, preparing to see the man she thought she would never live to see again…and preparing to tell him that she is carrying his child—or as only Samuel and I know, his *children*.

I reach our private compartment and find Samuel gazing out at the charming Swiss town that passes by the steamy train window. As I rest my head on his shoulder, I know that no matter what happens in the future, we are doing the right thing. Rosie deserves to live; her children deserve to know their mother; and my Grandpa Jacques, who I am about to meet for the very first time, deserves to spend his life with the woman he loves.

"That two hour gourmet lunch we just had may have changed my mind about refusing the lifetime Orient Express pass," I say to Samuel as we settle into our private compartment for the remainder of our voyage to Paris.

He laughs as he pulls me onto the plush sofa bed beside him. "That was the best meal of my life," he says. "But not because of the food."

I raise a curious brow. "What do you mean?"

"It was the best meal of my life because I got to share it with you." Samuel leans in, brushing his lips over my forehead. "I'm just so glad you're okay, Jill. That *we're* okay. Only a week ago, I nearly lost you."

I run my finger along his strong jaw line and gaze into those gorgeous green eyes of his. "And I nearly lost you."

Taking my hand in his, Samuel peers down at the sparkling emerald ring still fitted tightly on my ring finger. As he runs his thumb over the finely cut stone, a spark ignites underneath my skin.

By the shocked expression that passes over his face, I know he feels it too. We both know that this ring had something to do with landing us in the past *and* with saving Samuel's life.

And the even crazier part is that every time I've tried to take it off, it *still* won't budge.

"Have you had any more of your visions?" Samuel asks. "Of Isla?"

I shake my head, not wanting to admit how helpless I feel, not knowing where she is or what has happened to her.

"No, nothing," I say finally. "I keep replaying the last time I saw her over and over in my head, hoping it will help me see what happened after I left her there with that crazy woman charging at her with the knife...but there's nothing. And what's even scarier is that the stories of our past, of our childhood...when I try to remember them, they're fuzzy."

"What do you mean?" he asks.

"Fuzzy as in I can't remember everything, not clearly anyway. The stories I told you about my mom, about the senator, and about Isla...they feel like they're fading. My entire childhood with Isla, it feels like it's slipping through my fingers."

Samuel runs his hands up my arms and gives my shoulders a squeeze. "I'm sure it's just all the stress we've been under. And besides, most of those memories are traumatizing, Jill. It's not a bad thing to stop thinking about them...or to let them go altogether."

"No, you don't understand. It's beginning to feel as if none of it ever happened. Which, if we're honest about what's going on here, could actually be the case. Think about it, Samuel. We're in 1937, literally *rewriting* the past. I killed Agnès Morel *before* Hélène was even born, which means that even if Hélène *does* marry into the Morel family in the future, Agnès will never have the chance to pass on her sick jewels of wisdom or the keys to that vile castle. So while I'm sure Hélène will still be a power-hungry, baby-crazed lunatic, it's not at all likely that she'll commit the same abduction crime in 2012."

"True," Samuel says. "And with what we're about to do—reuniting Rosie and Jacques—Isla may never cross paths with Hélène Morel anyway."

"Isla may never cross paths with Hélène or *any* of the Morels because Isla may never even exist," I reply, swallowing the knot in my throat. "In giving Jacques the chance he never had the *first* time around to pick Rosie up at this Paris train station and to be the father he was always meant to be to their children, we're changing everything. Because he'll be with Rosie now, it's not likely that he'll wander into that Parisian brothel, which is where he met—and impregnated—my grandmother. Which means that my mother, Céline, would never be born. Considering the atrocious person she was, that isn't such a bad thing…except when you think about what that means for both Isla and me." I glance past Samuel out at the wintry French countryside passing slowly by the window and feel an immeasurable sorrow take hold in me.

"I know we accomplished what we were sent back here to do," I say through the stream of tears that have begun pouring down my cheeks. "But what if none of it mattered? What if I've lost Isla anyway?"

Samuel pulls me into his chest, running his strong hands down my hair and over my back. "You can't think like that, Jill. We have to believe that the *new* way things will play out from here will somehow mean a better future for all of us. Saving Rosie's life and taking her to Jacques *is* the right thing to do. We don't know what will happen beyond today…or really, what will happen beyond this moment." Samuel places a finger under my chin and lifts my face to his, wiping the tears from my cheeks. "All I do know is that through this crazy experience, you came back into my life. And whether we're in 1937 or 2012, I don't want to live another day without you."

Blinking my tear-stained lashes, I feel my heart simultaneously overflow with love for Samuel and break with sorrow over the possible loss of my sister.

"I don't want to live another moment without you either," I say to him.

Samuel cups my chin in his hands and presses his lips to mine. Losing myself in the comfort of his safe embrace, in the passion of his warm, sweet kiss, I place my left hand over his heart. Within seconds, a heated spark ignites underneath the emerald. Warmth builds around my hand, spreading over Samuel's chest, but we don't break our kiss.

And if it were up to me, I would stay here, wrapped in his arms forever.

CHAPTER 22

Paris, France

The view of the passing scenery from inside our toasty Orient Express cabin has changed from the frost-covered countryside to the unbelievable, enchanting sights of 1930s Paris.

Elegant French apartment buildings line the streets, and sophisticated French women stroll down the narrow cobblestone sidewalks. Their slim figures are adorned with dark-colored vintage coats that stretch to their calves, and their short, wavy haircuts are covered with dainty, old-fashioned hats.

But as we near the train station, some of the narrow *rues* we pass are not so enchanting. A cluster of shivering families lined up outside a shabby old building catches my eye. My heart breaks for them as I realize they must be waiting in line for bread. And then I remember, we are in the thirties, in the middle of the depression that has plagued France for most of the decade…and which will ultimately take France and its people straight into World War II, and into the Nazi occupation of France.

Before I have time to ponder the tragic events of history—which for Samuel and me are now the *future*—Rosie's excited voice travels into our sleeping compartment.

"We'll be there in two minutes," she says, and I can tell by the way she is squeezing that cherry-red suitcase of hers and bopping from side to side that Rosie Delaney has never been more excited in all her life.

The wounds on her face have faded to mere scratches, and despite the horror she lived through only one week ago, her stunning sapphire eyes are still sparkling brightly with hope. Rosie is a vision of 1930s elegance and style, but even more so, she is a brave survivor with a kind heart and an incredible will to live.

I am honored to have gotten the chance to know her...and even more so, to have helped in saving her life.

My feet carry me to her, and we hug one last time. We don't speak, but the way we hang onto each other after this wild storm has swept through and taken so much from us, says it all.

Before I'm ready to let go, this luxurious old train slows to a stop.

Rosie pulls away from me, squeezing my hands one final time before she skips down the corridor, down the stairs, and out onto the platform, searching for her man.

Hand in hand, Samuel and I follow closely behind. Just as we step onto the platform, a light snow begins to flutter down from the wintry Paris sky...and there, through the sparkling white flakes, stands my grandfather.

Dressed impeccably in his crisp navy-blue uniform, Jacques shoots Rosie a smile so warm, it could melt the thick layer of snow collecting beside us on the tracks. The two lovers break into a sprint, meeting underneath the big round clock, which at this exact moment reads thirty-seven minutes past the hour.

Jacques pulls Rosie into his arms, spinning her around and showering her sweet face with kisses. Tears stream down Rosie's cheeks as Jacques brushes the hair out of her eyes, holds her face in his hands, and pulls her into another long, adoring kiss.

As Samuel and I stand underneath the flurry of snow in the middle of this bustling Parisian train station, the tender, emotional moment playing out before us leaves no question in my mind that *this* was how it was always supposed to happen.

Rosie and Jacques were meant to be together, and whatever is to happen after this moment *will* lead to a better future…hopefully, for all of us.

Finally, the two lovebirds surface for air, and Rosie turns, motioning for us to come meet Jacques.

As I come face to face with my *young* grandfather, I am immediately struck by how much he resembles Isla—the violet specks in his eyes, the chestnut color of his hair, the boldness of his smile.

"Jacques, meet Jillian and Samuel Kelly, the couple who saved my life," Rosie says in French.

Jacques takes not one but both of my hands in his. As he gazes down at me, his eyes fill with tears of gratitude, and so do mine.

"Thank you, Jillian. Thank you for saving my Rosie," Jacques says, squeezing my hands. Then he turns to Samuel. "And Samuel, thank you. You have no idea…" His voice cracks as he brings his gaze back to mine, continuing to squeeze my hands.

Suddenly, beneath the emerald that still shines brightly on my left ring finger, I feel a spark of energy. It pools around my hand, around *our* hands, growing stronger and more powerful until all I can see is Jacques, blinking back at me with love, pride, and appreciation.

He nods at me, letting me know that he feels it too.

And as quickly as it swooped in, the heat surrounding our hands flies away, and Jacques lets go.

Then, grinning his charming grin, my young, dapper grandfather turns to Rosie and gets down on one knee.

Rosie lifts her hand to her heart, furiously blinking back the fresh tears springing to her eyes.

Jacques pulls a tiny red velvet box from his uniform pocket, then raises it to Rosie.

"Rosie, my sweet, my angel. I never want to spend another day on this earth without you by my side. Will you marry me?"

Jacques flips the box open, and tucked inside, all shiny and new, is the gorgeous emerald ring that Samuel placed on my finger when we first stepped onto the Venice Simplon-Orient-Express train in 2012.

My gaze shoots down to my left hand, only to find—as I expected—that the ring is gone.

Rosie accepts Jacques' proposal, and as he takes off her dainty white glove and slips the emerald onto her ring finger, I turn to Samuel, knowing in my heart that this is it.

This is our moment.

Samuel grasps my hands, pulling me closer to him. He knows too.

The sounds of the crowds bustling past us on this snowy platform, of Rosie and Jacques kissing and laughing beside us, of the giant clock ticking overhead, fade to only a whisper of chilly air brushing past my cheeks.

The final noise that breaks through this quiet pillow of air is the blast of the train whistle as the Orient Express chugs faster and faster at our backs.

Swirls of shimmering snowflakes mix with the emerald in Samuel's loving gaze as we hold onto each other.

Come with me, I plead with my eyes. *Please, Samuel. Stay with me.*

Suddenly a force of energy surges beneath our feet, and the snow, the emerald, the train, Samuel—all of it disappears in a flash of blinding darkness.

I don't feel Samuel's hands any longer. I don't feel his presence by my side.

It is Isla who is here with me now, her shining violet eyes radiating through the blackness.

"Jilly! Come on!" Isla calls impatiently, her voice young and naïve, like a little girl who hasn't a care in the world. "Grandpa Jacques and Grandma Rosie are here. Hurry up!"

CHAPTER 23

January 1...

Paris, France

A loud whistle shoots through my ears, startling me from a deep, dreamless sleep. I blink my eyes open, but it's difficult to focus on the passing scenery because everything is moving so quickly.

A slow glance around my surroundings reveals a luxurious train cabin, a little black carry-on bag, and a folded newspaper tucked in my lap. Confused as to what I am doing alone on this fancy train, I lift my gaze back to the rolling images outside the steamy train window.

At first, the glare of the morning sun blocks my vision, but soon, the unmistakable—and *breathtaking*—sights of Paris come into focus. Rows upon rows of lovely French apartment buildings pass by, their black iron balconies filled with frosty, empty flower boxes, waiting for spring to arrive. A woman dressed in a black pea coat and a beautiful lavender scarf strolls down the chilly Parisian boulevard, smoking a cigarette and talking on her cell phone. Miniature cars and fast scooters buzz through stoplights; charming cafés and *boulangeries* dot the sidewalks. Even in the winter, this gorgeous city is bursting with life.

A sudden and distinct feeling of relief washes over me. I made it to Paris. *Finally.*

But where did I travel from? And why do I feel as if the voyage I've just taken was the longest of my life?

Stifling the pressing questions that are popping up every second, I realize that the modern sights whizzing past the train window seem oddly out of place to me…but I'm not quite sure why. Wondering why I feel so utterly confused, I lift up the newspaper hoping that it will give me a little more clarity as to what I am doing in the magnificent City of Light.

The date at the top of *Le Figaro* catches my eye immediately: *January 1, 2013.*

It's my twenty-ninth birthday…and *Isla's.*

Just as a picture is forming in my mind—a picture of Isla and me, blowing out the candles on our thirteenth birthday cake, surrounded by family and friends who look only vaguely familiar—the train rolls to a stop, and the conductor announces our arrival.

"Paris, Gare de l'Est."

Tucking the newspaper under my arm, I grab my little rolling suitcase and follow the line of passengers down the elegant corridor. Just as I am about to step off the train, a gloved hand lands on my arm.

"Mademoiselle Chambord?" It's the conductor, dressed in a royal-blue uniform trimmed in gold. He smiles warmly at me as he hands me an envelope. "You left your lifetime pass to the Orient Express in your sleeping compartment," he says in French. "Please don't *ever* lose this, Mademoiselle. It is irreplaceable."

A vague memory of a *different* Orient Express conductor handing me this same lifetime pass flashes through my mind. But as quickly as the vision shoots through my brain, it is gone.

"Merci, Monsieur," I tell the kind conductor before I tuck the pass and the newspaper into the front pocket of my suitcase and step off the train.

The crisp winter air brushes past my cheeks as my feet hit the platform. Travelers bustle around me, but I stand still, taking it all in. The rolling suitcases, the modern clothing, the cell phones. I glance to my left and catch the time on the giant ticking clock overhead.

It is 9:37 A.M.

Isla's time of birth.

Just as I am thinking about how bizarre that is, a whiff of familiar perfume drifts past my nose.

I turn, knowing exactly who that perfume belongs to.

"*Isla.*"

The minute her name passes through my lips, the minute I see her shining violet eyes, her silky chestnut hair, her high cheekbones and long, curvy lashes, I remember.

I remember *everything.*

Dropping my suitcase, I run to my beautiful twin sister, wrapping her up in my arms.

"Jilly," she says. "I missed you so much."

"I missed you too, Isla. You have no idea."

I pull back to get a better look at the sister I thought I'd lost forever, the sister I traveled so far to save, and am surprised to see that she doesn't have a single bruise or scratch on that beautiful pale skin of hers.

And something else is different about her. She is still just as stunningly beautiful as she always was, but the shape of her face has changed slightly—it is more of a heart shape, friendlier, sweeter. She is wearing less make-up than she usually does—with only a pale pink lip gloss lining her lips and a light coat of mascara brushing her lashes.

I run a hand down her long, wavy hair and look deep into her striking violet eyes—*those* haven't changed a bit.

"Isla, you're here. You're *alive*," I whisper. "How?"

A knowing expression passes over her delicate features as tears rim her eyelids. "You changed everything, Jilly. *Everything.*"

Isla takes my hand and places it over her abdomen, and my tears match hers the minute I feel the growing baby bump and the tiny kick beneath my hand.

"You saved us, Jilly. Me—*and* the baby," Isla says. "I knew you were there with me the whole time. I felt you—the way we've always been able to feel each other. I knew you would figure out a way to save me. And a few times—in the nursery, in the woods, and in the castle—I actually saw you. But that last time, just as you were going for Hélène, something happened—a strange flash, then everything went dark. When I woke up, I was in this beautiful Parisian apartment, pregnant, and engaged to Christophe." Isla gestures to three people chatting over by the escalator.

A handsome man with prominent dark eyes and wavy dark brown hair turns and smiles warmly at Isla, then at me. I recognize him as the man who painted that seductive portrait of Isla—*Christophe Mercier.*

A cute, older couple stands next to Christophe, waving and grinning at me. I focus in on them, noticing how the woman's heart-shaped face looks *exactly* like Isla's. She even has specks of violet in her bright blue eyes. The man's smile is kind, fun-loving, and sweet, and as he gazes at Isla and me, pride fills his eyes.

I squeeze Isla's hand, wondering if I should trust the gut instinct that is telling me—beyond all reason—*those* are my parents.

I wave and smile back at them, and just as I am preparing to ask my twin a million and one questions, a burst of new, vivid memories flood into my consciousness. The mother who plagued our original childhood with nothing but trauma and heartbreak is now barely even a distant recollection. The father who left us when we were only little girls has vanished.

In their place are the two loving, wonderful people who are now walking in my direction.

Leaning into my ear, Isla whispers, "No one else remembers the way it happened the *first* time around. I can barely even remember myself. It's all new now, Jilly. You changed our entire past." Then, just before they reach us, she nudges me in the side. "Just go with the flow, okay? The *new* memories will come to you, just like they did for me."

I smile at my beautiful, vibrant sister, overcome with gratitude that we have all been given a second chance at life…and most of all, that I didn't lose her.

"Jillian, sweetie, happy birthday!" my mom says as she pulls me into her petite frame. Wrapped in her loving, motherly embrace, I breathe in my mom's sweet, flowery scent, and just like Isla said they would, a flood of new memories comes rushing in.

I remember my mom—who I know now is named *Marion*—strolling down the Seine while Isla and I skipped along at her side, two little girls having a ball growing up in Paris with their kind, elegant French mother.

More happy images speckle my mind as my mom kisses me lightly on the forehead. "Thanks, Mom," I tell her, realizing how amazing it feels to say those words.

Next comes my dad—the tall, burly American who fell in love with the petite, sophisticated French woman so many years ago and has never looked back. He leans in, giving me a peck on the cheek. "Only one more year until the big 3-0, Jilly Bean," he says with a chuckle.

"Don't remind me, Andrew!" our mom says, slapping him on the arm. "That only means *we're* getting old!"

"See what you're in for, Christophe?" Dad says, giving Christophe a friendly nudge. "A lifetime of making your wife feel better about her age. I've found it's best to just nod and smile most of the time."

Christophe laughs before pulling me in for a hug. "It's nice to have you back in Paris, Jillian," he says in a thick accent. "Isla really missed you."

Isla shoots me a wink as she rubs her firm belly.

"I missed her too," I say.

Feeling immeasurably blessed as I gaze around at this new, loving family of mine, I realize that I am still missing the most important person—*Samuel.*

The last time I saw him was at this very train station, when snowflakes were falling from the sky and Rosie and Jacques were in the middle of their emotional, heart-warming reunion…in *1937.*

But where is Samuel now?

A stab of panic soars through my chest as I comb the bustling platform, searching for the rugged, handsome face and the penetrating emerald eyes of the man I *cannot* and *will not* live without.

Isla's hand wraps around mine. "Jilly, what is it?"

"Samuel," I whisper, praying Isla won't tell me that in this new version of our past, where we grew up in Paris, and *not* in Washington, D.C., that Samuel and I never even crossed paths.

The corners of Isla's glossy pink lips turn up into a grin as she nods toward the large ticking clock just behind my head.

And when I flip around, there he is.

Samuel's dark five o'clock shadow and his full, sexy grin lure me straight to him.

When we meet underneath the clock in this modern day version of the train station we stood in only seventy-five years and a few moments ago, Samuel swoops me into his arms and pummels me with kisses.

"Don't you ever scare me like that again," I whisper in Samuel's ear as I revel in the feeling of his strong hands wrapped tightly around my waist, his warm breath on my cheek, his lips finding mine over and over again.

"I promised you I would never leave you, Jill," he says. "Do you actually think a time-traveling train would stop me?"

A relieved giggle passes through my lips as Samuel weaves his fingers into mine and turns to face my family.

"Now if that wasn't the kiss to end all train station kisses, I don't know what was!" my dad says with a hearty laugh.

Mom slaps him again on the arm, then raises a flirty brow. "I think we've had our fair share of passionate train station kisses over the years, haven't we, honey?"

Dad wraps his arm around Mom's teeny waist and kisses her on the cheek. "Of course we have. I just don't want to make the kids jealous, you know?"

"I don't think *any* of you can top Grandma Rosie and Grandpa Jacques," Isla says. "Even at ninety-five years old, those two can really put on a show."

My mom's pretty blue-violet eyes crinkle as she laughs. "Speaking of Grandma Rosie and Grandpa Jacques, they're waiting for us with breakfast back at our apartment. You know how Grandpa likes his *pain au chocolat*. He won't be able to wait much longer, so we better get going."

As we take off through the train station together, Isla leans over my shoulder once more.

"Grandma Rosie and Grandpa Jacques are mom's parents. First they had the twins, our Aunt Madeleine and Uncle Georges. Ten years later, they had mom."

"And they're ninety-five years old now?" I whisper back. "Meaning Grandpa Jacques never went off to World War II?"

Isla shakes her head. "No, after Grandpa proposed to Rosie, he left the army. They traveled to America and stayed there for the entire duration of the war. But by the time they had mom, the war was over, and they were ready to come back to Paris."

"And Madeleine and Georges?" I ask. "They're doing well?"

"They're off traveling right now…but I have a feeling you may be hearing from them soon."

"What do you mean?"

"You know how we have that special ability to sense the other one, being twins and all? Well, Madeleine and Georges have the same connection we share…only much, much stronger. And I think they had something to do with helping you save me," Isla says with a serious eyebrow lift.

Christophe pops his head over Isla's shoulder. "What are you two girls whispering about?"

Isla kisses him on the cheek. *"Rien, mon amour." Nothing, my love,* she says before turning back to me. "We'll talk more later, sis," she mouths quietly.

Samuel slips his arm around my waist and keeps me close as we follow Isla, Christophe, and my parents down through the busy station and out onto the sidewalk.

My dad nods toward two black town cars parked at the corner. "That's us," he says. "Samuel and Jillian, you two can take the second car by yourselves. I'm sure you want some alone time after Jillian's reporting trip down in the Alps." Then my dad walks up to me, placing a hand on my shoulder. "We saw your article on the front page today, Jilly Bean. I couldn't be more proud to call you my daughter. You're amazing."

"Thanks, Dad," I say, trying not to show how puzzled I am as I try to put together the missing pieces of my new, improved life.

My dad climbs into the other car with the rest of the group while Samuel lifts my suitcase into the trunk. "Wait," I tell him. "The newspaper in the front pocket."

Samuel hands me the crisp paper, and as I unfold it and skim the front page, the headline toward the bottom catches my eye.

"United States Senator stabbed to death in a lover's quarrel in the Alps," I translate aloud. "Reported by International Correspondent...Jillian Chambord."

I wrote this?

By the look on Samuel's face, I can tell he is just as clueless as I am about how the Morel–Williams scandal wrapped up after our most recent seventy-five-year time hop on the Orient Express. I fan out the paper between us so we can scan the article.

"So, in this new version of events, Hélène still *did* have an affair with Senator Williams," I say. "And she still stabbed him to death in that freaky white palace hidden in the middle of the French Alps." My memories of our terrifying voyage through the snow-covered mountains are fading, but they haven't faded enough to take away the shiver that turns my blood cold as I think about the crazed Morel women and their affinity for daggers.

"And Williams was still a perverted creep," Samuel adds after reading the part about Williams's involvement in the murder of two teenage sisters and a child prostitution ring back in D.C.—a story I am still *quite* familiar with, and as this article proves, a story that I still worked hard to expose, even in this new version of my life.

"But Williams never harmed Isla," I say, letting out a relieved breath. "She never even crossed paths with him because we have a new family now. This also means the abduction never even happened, and the other two innocent girls—Emma Brooks and Francesca Rossi—are alive."

Samuel turns to me, grinning. "And *you,* Jillian Chambord, are a kick-ass international correspondent who just traveled back from the Alps after covering a gruesome murder. I imagine right about now, you could probably use some delicious French pastries for breakfast followed by a little Paris birthday lovin'…Am I right?" He surprises me with another sweet, passionate kiss, making me so incredibly happy that if we had to make this journey…at least we made it together.

"That sounds perfect," I tell him as he closes the trunk, then opens the car door, gesturing for me to get in.

As we slide into the back seat together, a silver-haired couple sitting in the front of the car turns around to face us.

There, in the driver's seat is Georges, the chauffeur, and next to him, his twin sister, Madeleine.

Georges tips his black hat as Madeleine flashes us a bold smile.

"Jillian, Samuel," Madeleine says with a nod. "We're so happy you made it…back to *2013* that is." The French that rolls effortlessly off her tongue is just as impeccable and elegant as she is.

Samuel shoots me a worried glance, but I place an assuring hand on his knee. "Samuel, I'd like you to meet Madeleine, my *aunt,* and her twin brother Georges, my *uncle.*" I turn back to the mysterious pair of twins, remembering the clues and the help they provided along my journey to rescue Isla.

"So you two had something to do with all of this—sending us back in time to save Rosie, and ultimately to set the past straight?"

Madeleine nods as Georges puts the car into drive and takes off down a tree-lined Parisian boulevard.

"Yes, we did," she says. "And while I'm sure both of you have many questions about how exactly all of this works, unfortunately we don't have much time." Madeleine reaches over the seat, handing us each a small, folded piece of paper.

"You see," she continues, "it was not a coincidence that the two of you were chosen to complete this mission together. You are both exceedingly strong and resilient, and your love for one another is unique...and powerful. Because of your fearless quest to right the wrongs of the past, you have changed so many lives for the better, including mine and Georges. On behalf of everyone you've helped, we would like to thank you. And, if you're up to the task, we would like to offer you another opportunity to travel back..." Madeleine nods at the tiny papers in our hands.

"Go ahead, open them," Georges pipes up from the driver's seat.

I gaze over at Samuel, and we nod at each other in unison before unfolding the papers.

"You will have forty-eight hours to make a decision," Madeleine says as we read the description of our next possible *mission*.

The words on the page run laps around my dazed head as I fold up the paper and grasp Samuel's hand.

"Paris in the 1920s could be quite an adventure you know," Georges says.

Madeleine nods in agreement. "And you two certainly have the class to pull it off."

A sly grin slides over Samuel's lips as his gaze locks on mine. "What do you think, Jill? You and me solving a mystery in 1920s Paris? It could be fun..."

Just as I am about to answer him, Madeleine interrupts.

"The real question is, did each of you keep your lifetime passes to the Orient Express? I hope so, because you will *definitely* need them."

THE END

ACKNOWLEDGEMENTS

A huge, heartfelt *merci* goes to my fabulous editor, Kelli Martin, and to the entire team at Amazon Publishing and Montlake Romance for working so hard to bring my Paris stories to readers. If only I could take each of you to Paris to celebrate over champagne and Nutella crêpes…maybe one day!

To my amazing agent, Kevan Lyon, for your loyalty, expertise, and support. I couldn't have come this far without you, and I am truly grateful for everything you've done to get me here. A Paris trip is definitely in order one of these days.

I would like to thank my close friend, Sophie Moss, for reading early drafts of this novel, for our weekly writing pep-talks, and for your constant encouragement and support. I appreciate it more than you know. And to Marion Croslydon and Tracy Hewitt Meyer, I am so grateful we met and became instant friends.

To Alana Albertson, thank you for "getting" my writing and for your help with this novel. I'm so happy to have found such a wonderful writing pal in San Diego!

I'd like to send a warm thank you to my D.C. critique group: Karen, Sharon, and Mary. Over lattes and pastries, you taught me how to write, and I am forever grateful. I miss you all every day.

To my husband, my friends, and my family: Thank you for understanding why I have gone off the map these past several months. Writing a novel—or, in my case, writing two novels simultaneously—is an all-consuming passion, and I'm thankful that you've stuck by me even when I disappear into my writing cave for weeks at a time and forget to change out of my pajamas.

And finally, to my incredible readers. I dedicated this book to you because *you* are the reason I get to wake up every day, stay in those pajamas, and write love stories based in the most romantic city in the world: *Paris.* The next time I'm in France, I will eat a buttery chocolate croissant in your honor.

ABOUT THE AUTHOR

 Juliette Sobanet earned a B.A. from Georgetown University and an M.A. from New York University in France, living and studying in both Lyon and Paris. She worked as a French professor before turning a new page in her career, penning romantic women's fiction with a French twist. She is the author of *Sleeping with Paris, Kissed in Paris, Midnight Train to Paris,* and the upcoming *Dancing with Paris.* Today she lives with her husband and two cats in San Diego, where she devotes her time to writing and dreaming about her next trip to France.

Kindle *Serials*

This book was originally released in Episodes as a Kindle Serial. Kindle Serials launched in 2012 as a new way to experience serialized books. Kindle Serials allow readers to enjoy the story as the author creates it, purchasing once and receiving all existing Episodes immediately, followed by future Episodes as they are published. To find out more about Kindle Serials and to see the current selection of Serials titles, visit www.amazon.com/ kindleserials.

Made in the USA
Charleston, SC
12 December 2013